MW00987959

CLAIMED BY THE BRATVA BROTHERS

A CONTEMPORARY REVERSE HAREM ROMANCE

KAI LESY

DESCRIPTION

It started with a simple mistake.
A knock on the wrong door.

If we were better men, we'd have turned her away.
But we're not.

As Russian Bratva brothers, we had no business pursuing
a naive librarian like Lyric.
She's innocent. Pure. Gentle.

We're ruthless bastards who take what we want.
And we took her innocence.
Watched her tremble. Heard her beg for more.

But once wasn't enough.
We're obsessed with her sweetness, her purity.

She doesn't belong in our world, but it's too late.
She's ours now, and we're not letting go.

Not her. Not the baby growing inside her.

This is a sexy, stand-alone reverse harem romance filled with
humor, danger, and generous amounts of love. It also contains
blistering hot MFMM, ménage fun times, in single and multiple
partner scenes so HOT they're bound to melt your kindle! HEA
guaranteed.

1

LYRIC

"Mr. Bowman is ready for you. The elevator is right down this hallway," the receptionist gestures casually.

I shoot her a quick nod and stride confidently towards the sleek, minimalist elevator doors. The echo of my heels clicks in sync with the soft, electronic beats pulsing through the lobby's sound system.

As I step inside, the elevator doors slide shut smoothly, the gentle hum of machinery enveloping me. Surrounded by a chic, mirrored interior that reflects a cool, ambient light, I'm whisked upwards, ready to ace a meeting I've been waiting months for.

When the doors open, I stride confidently down the hall, eyeing the signs that guide me. Nearing Executive Suite 2008, I slow down a bit, taking a deep breath to master the cool, collected vibe I'm going for.

"You've got this, bitch," I whisper under my breath.

I knock once.

After what feels like forever, the door finally eases open, but the man standing there is not Mr. Jack Bowman.

Nope, this man is most *definitely* someone else.

He's younger than the sixty-something entrepreneur—though not by much—and he's impossibly handsome.

His short brown hair is streaked with just the right amount of gray, the kind that makes it look effortless and undeniably attractive.

His beard is perfectly groomed, accentuating a jawline that could cut glass.

But it's his eyes that stop me in my tracks—sharp, piercing blue, with fine lines that hint at a life full of experience.

And tall.

Very tall.

His presence fills the space, and I feel a strange tension building in the air between us. I swallow hard, the sound embarrassingly loud in the silence. My gaze instinctively traces the broad lines of his shoulders, the way his custom-tailored suit clings to his frame, revealing strength beneath the fabric.

"Can I help you?" he asks, with a hint of an accent I can't quite put my finger on. His voice low and gravelly, dripping with a dangerous kind of allure. The deep timbre sends a shiver down my spine, and the hairs on the back of my neck prickle in response.

"Um, hi. I'm here for the 11 o'clock appointment with Mr. Jack Bowman. I'm interviewing him for my thesis," I stammer. My brain feels scrambled under his intense gaze, and I hate how exposed I feel, like he's seeing right through me.

Pull it together, woman.

His eyes move over me, slow and deliberate, leaving a trail of warmth in their wake. There's a faint smirk on his lips, one that's almost predatory.

Fuck, he's sexy.

"We were expecting someone a little less... demure," he muses, his smile deepening, sending a flare of confusion through me. "But this virginal student thing you've got going —well, we can work with it."

"Excuse me?" I blink, my brain scrambling to catch up with his words. Did he just say that out loud? Who the hell is this guy?

"Come in," he says, stepping back to let me pass.

Run bitch.

Instinct screams at me to scram, but I catch sight of a portrait of Mr. Bowman on the wall and hesitate. Clearly, there's been a mix-up. I have to get to the bottom of this. My thesis—and my career—depends on it.

"Where is Mr. Bowman?" I demand, stepping into the luxurious suite.

The door clicks shut behind me, and I notice two other men emerging from the terrace. My pulse quickens as they approach—both tall, dark, and equally intimidating as the first.

Intimating and *painfully* attractive.

"Max, is this the girl?" one of them asks, predatory eyes narrowing at me.

He's more casually dressed than the first, but his sharp jawline and commanding presence are anything but relaxed. His frame reminds me of an exotic professional tennis player. His black hair falls in messy waves, and his gray eyes hold a mix of curiosity and confusion.

"I know," the first man replies with a smirk. "But I think we can make this work."

"Make what work?" I cut in, my nerves fraying. "I'm here for an interview. With Jack Bowman."

Max chuckles dryly. "Artur, I think there's been a bit of a misunderstanding here."

"I'm so confused right now," I whisper, mostly to myself.

A sly smirk forms on Artur's lips. "What's your name?"

"Lyric," I say. "I'm a PhD candidate, and Mr. Bowman graciously agreed to have an interview with me regarding my doctorate thesis. This meeting has been scheduled months ago. I need it to happen."

"Lyric," Ivan mutters. "That's an interesting name."

"Gee thanks. And who exactly are you?"

"You should take a seat," Max says. "We need to talk."

I continue standing. If I need to run I'm better off on my feet. All of my senses are overwhelmed as I continue to try and wrap my head around what's going on.

"I'm Max," Max says. "This is my brother, Ivan. And this is our best friend and business partner, Artur."

"Okay," I mumble, suspiciously eyeing each of them. "That gives me your names but it still doesn't explain who you are, why you're here and why Mr. Bowman isn't."

I spot the hint of a smile dancing across Ivan's lips through his trimmed lumberjack beard. "This one's a spitfire," he tells his brother. "It's kinda hot."

"Excuse me?" I croak.

"Here's the thing," Max laughs lightly. "Mr. Bowman left the building. He has some issues that he needs to deal with. Had we known that you were coming, Lyric, we would've let the interview happen before sending Jack on his way. Alas, we did not know, so here we are."

"You sent him on his way? What the hell is going on here?"

"Oh, for fuck's sake, Max, you're confusing our guest," Artur groans and rolls his eyes. "Don't mind him, Lyric. Let's just say Mr. Bowman won't be available for any interviews, or anything else, for that matter, at least for the next few days."

"What? Why?"

"Mhm. Mhmmmm. Curiosity killed the cat," I hear Ivan mumble.

What is that supposed to mean? I can feel my heart start to race. Artur picks up on my anxiety and takes a seat on the sofa next to me, keeping a warm smile on his face, like a gracious host. "Forgive Ivan, he doesn't like it when people ask a lot of questions."

"Or when they talk at all," Max grumbles, prompting a light laugh out of Artur.

Ivan, however, doesn't budge or show any type of emotion, for that matter.

5

"Okay, I'd like to leave now."

Max comes closer and my breath falters. I feel tiny as he gets bigger in my field of vision. "Lyric, here's the thing. We were just about to celebrate something, and we ordered an escort. Then you showed up at our door."

"Whoa..."

"I know, right? Pretty confusing," he shoots back with a wry smile. "That doesn't mean we can't still make the most of this conundrum, right?"

"I'm not your girl. I'm a librarian, PhD candidate and I came here for an interview," I state, sounding like an idiot to my own ears.

"Yes, and we've already explained the interview isn't going to happen," he replies. "Do you want to walk out of here feeling like this time was wasted?"

I stare at them, not knowing how to react.

I feel like I've walked into a warped reality.

"I'm sorry, what exactly happened to Mr. Bowman?" I ask.

Max and Artur glance back at Ivan, who replies with a shrug. "She's going to hear about it by tomorrow, anyway," Ivan says. "You might as well tell her."

"Tell me what?"

"Mr. Bowman will be in our custody until he yields to our demands," Max replies.

I gasp. "You kidnapped him?"

"Kidnap is such an ugly word."

"Sequestered him," Max gives me a wink. "That's more like it."

Dear God, who the hell are these people?

And why can't I just find the nerve to get up and run screaming?

"What are you going to do to me?"

"No harm will come to you," Artur assures me. "A few orgasms, maybe, but I'm pretty sure you'll enjoy those."

"I've made it pretty clear. I want out."

Ivan chuckles. "Great. We ordered an escort, and instead we got this hot little prude with a moral code. Now what?"

"At least, let me offer a more thorough introduction. I'm Max Sokolov. This is Ivan Sokolov. Perhaps the surname rings a bell?"

I stare at him in sheer disbelief. Of course, it rings a bell. My father's entire political campaign over the past three months has been centered on the Sokolov Bratva, whom he has repeatedly named "the bane of our great city of Chicago."

Bowman and my father partnered up a while back on a policy proposal designed to rid Chicago of its mobster families—if my father gets the state senate seat in the fall.

"I think she knows who we are," Artur mumbles.

"Russian mobsters," I breathe, my eyes growing bigger, my breaths coming quicker.

"Technically speaking, Russian-American," Max states nonchalantly. "Ivan and I were born and raised here. Artur came over from Moscow when he was a wee little boy, though he's naturalized. Therefore, also Russian-American."

"Fine, Russian-American mobsters," I reply.

"Like I said, why consider all of this time wasted?" Max shoots back.

They seem so matter-of-fact and chill about the whole thing.

These men are basically asking me if I want to hook up.

And here I am, a virginal librarian for crying out loud.

Talk about a complete mind fuck.

"This isn't the kind of thing I do. Seriously, I'm a librarian who spends her spare time on algorithmic equations," I say.

I'm not sure why I don't sound or feel as outraged and scared as I should be.

Either my brain cells are completely fried from this charade, or I've suddenly developed a soft spot for mobsters with big shoulders, hard, strong bodies, and gorgeous chiseled faces.

One thing is *damn* certain.

The way I feel around these men is unlike anything I've ever felt before.

And I'm not sure how I feel about that.

"Look, I'd be lying if I said I wasn't attracted to you. Each of you. Clearly you've got this bratva badass thing going on, but you guys are strangers and I'm not exactly interested in being kidnapped so…."

"Did you hear that, boys? She finds us attractive," Max says with a mischievous grin.

Artur chuckles and heads over to the mini bar. "You're free to walk away. The three of us may be gangsters but we're gangsters with a code. A part of that code is only being with women consensually," he says as he pours himself a drink. "Have we atleast sparked your curiosity?"

I keep my mouth shut, not knowing what to say.

My legs feel frozen, refusing to obey my logical mind.

Max comes closer, glancing down at me with hooded eyes. "May I?" he asks, and I nod, though I don't know what I'm agreeing to.

Slowly, he reaches out his hand and tucks a lock of hair behind my ear.

His touch is subtle, much like the brush of a butterfly's wings, but it's enough to send fires coursing through my veins, and I'm unable to look away from him.

His cologne is heady and laced with pepper, filling my lungs, and my mind, with all kinds of sinful thoughts. "You know what they say about redheads?"

"No."

"That they were kissed by fire," he replies. "I'm willing to bet there's a fire burning inside of you, Lyric. I can see it in those baby blues of yours."

I'm speechless. Breathless. Shocked by my own reaction—or lack thereof.

Artur chimes in. "You have nothing to worry about, we've got all the privacy we need, and we'll make sure you get home safe when you're ready to leave."

"I... can leave?"

"Ofcourse," he says, raising an eyebrow. There's a playful flicker in his gaze and it's making my knees turn to jelly.

Max's fingers linger over my ear, slowly but surely making their way down the side of my neck. "You're free to leave whenever you wish," he tells me. "We wouldn't dream of holding you against your will."

"I can leave, like right now?"

The men exchange brief glances and smiles. "Our business was with Bowman, not you," Max replies. "So, yes. You can leave. Or you can stay and see what it would be like to let go of your inhibitions." His hand finds the back of my neck, squeezing slightly. "You could use a proper unwinding, that much I can tell. Why don't you let us take care of you, help you relax and forget everything, just for a while?"

Fuck, every time one of them touches me I melt all over.

"I…"

"But here's the thing," Artur cuts in, "You stay, you get the three of us. We share you, fair and square."

"Hold on a minute," I say, trying to shake myself back into some semblance of clarity, but before I can, Max bends down to meet me at my level. His grip on the back of my neck tightens, causing me to tilt my head, my lips suddenly less than an inch away from his as he looks right into my soul.

"You are one of the most beautiful women we've ever come across," Max whispers, his lips touching mine. "Indulge yourself. See what it's like to be shared by the three of us. And when it's over, you only need to walk out that door, and that'll be the end of it."

They're serious.

They want to share me?

I should be outraged.

Appalled.

But instead, there's an ache growing in my core. I can feel myself clenching tightly between my legs, liquid heat pooling between my thighs.

My blood's boiling, my breath uneven.

I remain quiet. Not saying a word.

My gaze travels to each of them.

One by one.

They wait patiently.

They seem to sense my need to think this through, not rushing me into my decision.

My choice should be crystal clear. They've admitted to kidnapping one of America's most powerful and influential entrepreneurs.

Like it's nothing.

Just a checkbox in their agenda.

Then again, they gave me an out.

Permission to leave.

It feels strange to admit, but I actually feel safe in their presence.

I can't believe I'm actually considering this.

"How do we go about this?" I ask, surprised by my own words.

Max smiles as he steps towards me. His lips are so close, all I can think about is tasting him.

He kisses me, and everything turns white for a moment.

I melt on the inside, my lips parting as I welcome him.

His tongue is eager and playful, exploring and tasting me.

I respond in equal measure, and the kiss deepens into something that quickly renounces all forms of control.

"First, you need to look at me," Max says as he pulls his mouth from mine.

I open my eyes from the kiss. I can still taste him. The air in the room feels thick and heavy. Slowly, I return to the present and look around. Max, Ivan, and Artur stand close together, barely a foot away. They're all so big, towering over me.

I tremble with anticipation.

Carnal desire burns inside of me.

"Okay," I say.

"That's not the right answer," Max replies. "What do you say when you're given an order that you're desperate to obey, Lyric? Because I can tell from the look in your eyes that you're desperate to obey."

"Yes, sir," I say.

He smiles, unbuttoning his suit jacket.

Ivan does the same, while Artur's fingers deftly work the buttons of his shirt. They're all looking at me, their gazes dark and ravenous with desire.

I've started something I seem to have no control over, but perhaps that's the whole appeal. To give up control.

Let loose for once.

They're not pressuring me in any way. They'll let me leave if I wish.

This is all me. I have the power to stop this if I want.

But, right now, the last thing on my mind is stopping.

"That's a nice suit you've got on," Artur says. "Very 'Future President of the United States' but with a dash of naughty hiding underneath."

"Thanks for noticing" I reply, unable to stop myself from smiling.

He laughs lightly. "It needs to come off."

With shaky fingers, I begin to take my jacket off first.

"Go slow," Ivan cuts in. "We're not in any hurry."

"We're not?"

"You've never been with three men before, that much is obvious," Max chuckles. "Why hasten the experience when it's best enjoyed slowly?"

I haven't even been with one, I think to myself.

"Go slow, okay," I reply, taking a deep breath. I'm worried that if I tell them that I'm a virgin, they might pull the plug, and frankly, I'm way too hot and bothered to step away from this now.

"Like this?"

Ivan is out of his shirt first, and oh boy, does this man look hot enough to give a lady an orgasm without even trying. Sculpted in marble. Ropes of muscle and rippling pecs covered in dark tattoos that spread across his chest and down his massive arms. I spot faint scars here and there. I reckon each tells a story, but I can only lick my lips as I watch his hands reach for his belt buckle next, his wild green eyes continuously searching my face.

Artur's pants come off. This man is pure athletic muscle. Every inch of him is toned to perfection, with black and green tattoos dancing over his shoulders and down his back. He moves closer as I work to unbutton my satin shirt. I'm so flustered and I'm having trouble, my fingers can't seem to cooperate properly. "Let me help you, otherwise we'll be here until tomorrow," he says.

"I thought you said we weren't in a rush," I quip.

"We're not, but here," he replies and gently takes my hand, bringing it down to cup his manhood through his pants. I gasp as I feel the hardness and generous size of his erection. "Get what I'm saying?"

"And then some," I mutter.

He finishes unbuttoning and peels the shirt off my shoulders, while I unbuckle his belt and fumble with the zipper before his pants finally hit the floor. These men are rock-hard for me, and I am soaking wet for them.

How did this happen?

So quick, so spontaneous.

I came here for an interview for fuck's sake.

"Kiss me," I tell Artur, desperate to get out of my own head.

He smiles and obliges, capturing my mouth in a hungry kiss while Ivan and Max lose the rest of their clothes and gather around me. Artur keeps my lips and tongue busy while Max runs his knuckles down my right arm. Ivan kneels and helps me out of my pumps, gently massaging my feet while Artur's fingers swiftly remove my pants and panties in a single swoop. Max unhooks my bra, and just like that, I stand naked between these giant men.

Naked and wet as hell.

"This is insane," I gasp, looking at each of them for a hot second.

"It's how we live," Max says. "We share everything. For as long as we've known each other, we've shared everything. How does it feel, Lyric?"

"Strange."

"Do you want to continue?"

"Oh, yes."

"Yes, what?"

I feel a devilish smile slitting across my face. "Yes, sir."

"Good. Come."

I follow Max into the master bedroom. It's huge—its walls covered in navy-blue wallpaper, the carpet a fluffy cream that soothes my feet with every step that I take. The midday sun pours through the tall windows, and I bask in it for a while before Artur and Ivan join me.

"Don't move," Artur says, trailing kisses down the side of my neck. His lips, his tongue, were made for teasing me. I struggle to breathe properly as I feel Ivan's kisses tumbling down my spine, one inch at a time.

Max comes around to stand in front of me and slips his hand between my legs. "Fucking hell, you're ready, aren't you?"

I moan and hold on to his shoulders as his fingers slide through and tease my slick folds, my swollen clit. "Oh, God."

I look down, dazzled by his erection. His cock is huge and deliciously thick, veins throbbing along the shaft. I feel Ivan come closer, hard between my buttocks, grinding and teasing while my fingers dig into Max's shoulders.

"You taste fantastic," Artur whispers in my ear.

Max lowers his head and takes my right nipple in his mouth, while Ivan's hand reaches around to fondle my left breast. His fingers close around the nipple and pinch, tighter and tighter until I whimper against Artur's lips. They are remarkably well coordinated. This foreplay is a feast for all of my senses. I lose my self-control when Max's fingers penetrate me.

"Oh, God," I groan and tilt my head back, letting it rest on Ivan's shoulder. "Oh, don't stop."

"I have no intention of stopping," Max says then kisses me.

I'm theirs for the taking and I have no intention of stopping this. Tension builds up inside of me like a ball of electricity about to explode. One more stroke of Max's fingers, one more lap of Artur's tongue, one more nipple pinch from Ivan, and I might lose my ability to stand upright.

Then Max gets down on his knees.

Ivan wraps his arms around my torso to keep me in place.

Artur spreads my legs.

"Be a good girl and come for me," Max says, looking up at me.

A second later, he dives right in and proceeds to devour my pussy. I moan harshly as Ivan squeezes and kneads my full breasts, as Artur runs his fingers through my hair and watches me as I'm brought closer to the edge. He strokes himself, insanely aroused. But it's Max's tongue that delivers the ultimate damage, while he finger-fucks me into oblivion.

I come hard and unexpectedly all over his face, my juices glistening in his beard. Max keeps lapping me up, drinking me. I cry out, shaking like a leaf, Ivan holding me as he breathes me in, his strength filling me with a sense of safety, a freedom of exploration.

By the time I come down from the heavens, Max is standing up and peering down at me. I look at him through hazy eyes, still twitching in the afterglow as my pussy aches for more.

"You are dangerously addictive, Lyric," he says.

"So are you," I reply.

Ivan sighs and pushes me against the bed. I fall on my back, giggling naughtily as I allow myself to be admired by these massive men with their huge erections. They watch me for a while, hands on their cocks, stroking slowly, as I instinctively raise my knees and part my legs for them.

I can't believe I'm doing this, but when Max takes the lead and climbs on top of me, I figure I'm definitely doing something right.

"We're going to take turns," Max says, his voice low and sultry while steely fires burn in his eyes.

"Okay. Just... go easy," I manage, unable to think straight.

I feel his tip testing my entrance. A few seconds later, he's thrusting into me, each time deeper than the last. I pull in a sharp breath, letting it out slowly. The searing pain only lasts for a few moments, easing up the more he moves, but then Max freezes deep inside of me. "Holy shit," he says.

"What is it?" Ivan asks as he joins us on the bed.

"She's a virgin," Max says.

I shake my head and lock my legs around his waist. "Please, don't stop. I want this. I need this."

"Fucking hell," Max groans, unable to pull out as I tighten my legs, pinning him against me.

I don't want him to pull away. He's stretching me so good, filling me to the brim. So this is what I've been missing out on. Damn, it's incredible. I cup his face and pull him in for a kiss, while Artur lays on the side of us, planting soft kisses on my breast.

Finally, Max begins to move again.

Back and forth, slowly at first.

"I'll go easy," he whispers against my lips, then raises his head to look at me.

Ivan takes a hold of my mouth while Artur keeps teasing my nipples. Max thrusts himself deeper and harder, building a rhythm between us. The discomfort eventually dissolves into pure, raw pleasure, as I raise my hips to meet him.

"How does it feel?" Max asks, while Ivan runs his fingers through my hair.

"So fucking good," I reply, my breasts bouncing as he pounds into me.

Harder, faster, deeper. The pressure builds up again, my pussy clenching for another release. It comes fast. A devastating wave, a climax that rumbles through me like an unhinged lightning storm.

I scream in sweet ecstasy as Max fucks me harder and harder, losing himself inside of me. I feel him come. I feel his cock pulsating as he shoots his seed into me, filling me with his essence.

But I'm not given a moment's respite.

I moan and attempt to catch my breath as Max lays next to me, offering sweet, tender caresses while Ivan takes his place. Ivan is fucking huge. Even bigger, thicker than his brother. I'm stretched beyond belief.

Artur's fingers find their way down my belly and start stroking my clit. My already swollen nub reacts immediately, and I feel another orgasm approaching.

"Harder!" I scream, my legs locked around Ivan's waist as he rams into me.

Harder. Faster. Deeper, still. I listen to the sound of skin slapping skin, my juices glazing his enormous cock with every brutal thrust. Artur works my clit in a ferocious string of circles until finally I come once more. A third climax has me unraveling as Ivan lets loose and fucks me into oblivion.

By the time Artur gets to me, I'm on all fours, my knees weak and my pussy hungry for more. Ivan and Max watch, smiling like lazy devils as they relax on the edge of the bed in the afterglow, enjoying the view.

"Oh, God, oh, God!" I cry out when he reaches around and plays with my clit while drilling deep inside of me.

I don't know how it's possible, but a fourth orgasm shakes me. Everything turns white as Artur's hand comes down, smacking my ass. Instantly, I clench myself around him. It's all he needs to explode inside of me, each thrust more insistent until we're both spent and sated.

By the time it's over, I'm weak. Boneless. Breathless.

And so fucking happy that I could cry.

2

LYRIC

I t goes on for hours and I lose track of time.

I had no idea that sex could be so enthralling.

It is otherworldly.

And I fear it's setting a dangerous precedent.

My encounter with these three men is a one-time only deal, and I realize that the next man I meet might feel like a disappointment. I lay naked, staring at the pristine white ceiling. Artur is in the lounge area, pouring us more drinks. Ivan is in the shower. Max sits on the edge of the bed, watching me in silence.

I'm exhausted, but it is the sweetest kind of exhaustion. I'm also sore, but in a good way. Moaning softly, I turn over to look at Max. His profile is illuminated in the light of dusk, reminding me of a sculpture from the Renaissance era. A stoic man, or so he seems.

He takes a deep breath and lets it out slowly. "This is where it ends," he says to me.

I blink a few times. "Already?"

"You're a good girl, Lyric. And we are bad men. You shouldn't be anywhere near us."

"Here," Artur says as he comes back into the room. He hands me a drink and an envelope.

Frowning slightly, I take the drink and stare at the envelope. "What's that?" I ask, but I already have an idea, an uneasy feeling working its way through my chest.

"Payment," Artur replies.

"Excuse me?"

And just like that, we switch gears, tumbling into unfamiliar and unpleasant territory as I try to process what's happening. Artur leaves the envelope on the bed, next to my thigh. "It's for you and your missed interview," he says. "You deserve it."

"Oh, wow," I snap, instantly scrambling off the bed and onto my feet.

Fire rages through me. Outrage. And so much shame.

"I'm not some fucking prostitute," I state.

"Don't take it the wrong way," Max says. "We just want to make sure you walk away with the best experience. Especially given that you were incredibly brave to do this, to trust us the way you did."

Ivan comes out of the shower, gloriously naked and wet, steam rising from his smooth, tattooed skin. He overheard everything. "We would never view you as such. But you did miss an interview and you might experience some inconveniences after this meeting of ours. We just want to make sure you're compensated for any discomfort that might come your way."

"I don't understand. Make it make sense," I reply, hands balled into fists at my side.

"Artur here will do his best to scrub you from the hotel's CCTV system, but we can't guarantee a miracle, especially since I presume you went through reception before coming up here, telling them you were meeting with Jack Bowman."

"Oh, God." I had almost forgotten. "Shit, the police will surely want to ask me questions if and when someone reports him missing."

"Take the money," Ivan insists. "Consider it an incentive to keep your mouth shut. We certainly won't be mentioning your name. As far as we're concerned, you were never here."

"I can't believe this is happening."

"Take the money," Ivan says again, more sternly this time. "Play your part. Nothing happened. Bowman wasn't here. You left. You don't know anything."

"But that's only *if* the cops come asking," Max calmly states. "Otherwise, please go on with your life. It has been a veritable and unexpected pleasure getting to know you, Lyric."

I scoff and stomp out of the room, leaving the money behind. In mere seconds, I manage to put my clothes back on and slip into my shoes before grabbing my purse and leaving Executive Suite 208.

The men didn't try to stop me. They didn't say another word nor did they move from their positions in the bedroom as I stormed through the suite and into the hallway.

When I get to the elevator, I find myself looking up. There are cameras in the corners on both sides. My face burns red hot. Bile gathers in my throat. We had such a good thing going on in there, and yet...

How the hell did I get myself roped into this? I wasn't thinking clearly. I must have been under the influence of something.

"Of what, Lyric?" I mutter to myself.

I already know the answer to that and it's beyond shameful given the circumstances. As much as I enjoyed it, tinges of regret test my resolve as I decide to take the stairs instead. I don't know what's going to happen next, but I do know I need to get the hell out of here.

I sneak out of the hotel and head back to my car as fast as I can, flooring it all the way to my apartment, praying the cops don't show up.

* * *

AS MUCH AS I'd like to forget about what happened, the way I feel in the morning prevents me from doing so.

My muscles ache. My pussy aches. My body longs for them and I hate it. I'm angry and restless, yet I can't stop thinking about it. I walked into that situation expecting something entirely different. They gave me an out yet I chose to stay. I can't blame them for anything that happened.

I was in charge the entire time. All I needed to do was say stop and it would have ended. I need to accept responsibility and be honest with myself about it.

It's been quiet, so far.

I guess that's a good thing.

My thesis might need a few changes. I don't know what's going to happen to Jack Bowman, and I'm wondering whether I should just keep his chapter without an interview.

Instead of panicking over what happened or over what might happen next, I decide to brew myself a cup of coffee and begin my day. I have a few things to do before I start my afternoon shift at the school library so I might as well get on with it.

Get on with my life, like Artur suggested. Pretend that nothing happened.

"Everything's all hunky-dory," I grumble as I slip into the shower.

Half an hour later, after dressing and downing one double espresso, I'm ready to tackle my task list. The first item is a coffee date with Shelby. Great. I love my best friend, I just don't love the fact that she's working for my father. It makes it awkward whenever I pop by to take her out for lunch or go shopping. Dad always wants to catch up, to talk. All I want to do is avoid yet another instance of saying, "No, Dad, I'm still not going to come work for you."

Shelby waits for me at her desk, a few feet away from the secretary's workstation. Linda has been with my father for a long time, *too* long, and one can tell just by looking at her desk. And by looking at Linda. The woman is clearly the queen over this domain.

"Good morning, Linda," I say with a pleasant tone, praying she won't tell my father I'm here.

"Good morning, Lyric. Matthew knows you're here. He'll be right out," she replies.

"Great," I mutter with a strained smile, just as Shelby gathers her phone and wallet and slips them into her green snake-skin purse. "Ready?" I ask.

"Almost," she says. "Gotta make sure I set the out of office for my email."

"Geez, Shelby, we'll only be gone an hour."

"Yeah, but the first round of debates is this Sunday," she sighs. "I need to stay on top of everything."

I give her a long look. She's noticeably different from the girl I met in high school. She's taller and slimmer, her pale blonde hair combed into a tight bun, her brown eyes hidden behind a pair of black-rimmed glasses. She looks killer in pencil-skirts and silk shirts. Oh, God, she's turning into Linda. I see it clearly now as they stand side by side.

"Wow, you've gotten really involved," I tell Shelby.

"Of course. You either do something right, or you don't do it at all," she replies as she slings her purse over her shoulder.

I nod toward the elevator doors on the other side of the bullpen. "Come on, let's go."

"Wait, your dad wanted to talk to you."

"I'd rather—"

Too late. My father comes out of his office, instantly putting on his signature, placid, poster-boy smile. "Lyric, honey, glad to see you!"

"Hey, Dad."

Linda watches our exchange with renewed interest. Deep down, she knows I'd probably take his campaign to the next level, but I swore off politics a long time ago. She also knows

26

that since I'm the apple of my daddy's eye, so to speak, she wouldn't get as much attention as she's used to if I were around all the time.

I can tell that she has mixed feelings about me being here in any capacity. Which just goes to prove how dangerously charming my father can be.

"Have you reconsidered my offer?" he asks, getting straight to the point as usual.

"It's still a no for me, but thanks, Dad," I reply. "Not sure if you remember, but I'm currently working on my doctorate thesis. As is Shelby, by the way." I pause and give my best friend a sideways glance.

"In case you forgot why you're working here," I tell her.

Shelby chuckles softly. "I know that silly. It just so happens that I enjoy this internship and I'm learning way more than I had originally anticipated."

"That's right," Dad says. "In fact, I'm prepared to give Shelby an official full-time offer once she's submitted her thesis. You know, you're missing out on an incredible opportunity, Lyric. And just as I'm about to make history."

"Thank you again, Dad, but my algorithm doesn't belong in politics."

"Right, right. You're just going to sell it to the highest bidder in corporate America," he scoffs. And there it is, the muted bitterness of rejection. The one thing my father cannot handle well. And Shelby's biggest issue is that she can never say no. No wonder they get along. "Anyway, you girls have a good lunch. Don't keep Shelby too long, I need her to draft a press response by three o'clock regarding the debate."

"Sure thing," I say, about to roll my eyes when Linda gasps upon checking her phone.

"Oh, my God!"

"What is it?" my father asks.

One by one, phones start chirping and ringing all over the bullpen. His entire campaign is ablaze all of a sudden, with what I can only guess is unsettling news—at least, judging by the worried looks on their faces.

"Jack Bowman," Linda says, her voice trembling with emotion. "He's missing."

Shit. It was bound to hit the news cycle; I'm just surprised it took so long. My father frowns. "What do you mean he's missing?"

He doesn't wait for an answer though. He snatches Linda's phone and starts scrolling through the news article while Shelby lingers next to her desk. "Okay, so, what do I need to do?" my friend asks.

"Go to lunch, it's fine," my father replies. "I need time to figure out how we're going to respond to this. We don't have any details at this moment."

"This is devastating," Linda says.

No shit, Sherlock. Jack Bowman is a huge contributor to my father's political campaign. He's been a Phelps ally for as long as I can remember. Hell, I got my interview with him because of his close ties to my father.

"Lyric, didn't you have an interview scheduled with him yesterday?" my father asks.

Suddenly, one too many eyes are trained on me. I break into a cold sweat, heat spreading through my chest as I struggle to retain my composure.

"I... um... he wasn't there. So I left," I manage.

"Why didn't you call me?" my father asks, his brow furrowed with concern as he points to Linda's phone.

I offer a faint shrug. "I didn't think I needed to call you. I didn't see or hear anything suspicious, he just wasn't there. I figured something must've come up and his assistant would contact me to reschedule."

"I got you that interview, Lyric. If he didn't show up, I would think you would call me."

"For what purpose? Are you privy to his schedule? Do you have a tracker on him?" My father's attitude is irritating me now.

"You know what, never mind."

"Good," I shoot back and look at Shelby. "Ready?"

"Go ahead, Shelby. I'll see you in an hour," my father says.

Shelby gives me a faint smile then follows me across the bullpen and into the elevator. The farther I get from my father and the ensuing chaos surrounding Jack Bowman's disappearance, the better. It worries me, though, now that it's public. It's in the news. What will the cops ask when they inevitably get to me? Even more importantly, what the hell am I going to tell them?

Once we're out of the building and settled in one of the more private booths at Mussi and Joe's Diner, two blocks down the road, I feel like I can breathe again. Of course, this ice-riddled Hugo appetizer cocktail is also quite good at relieving some of the pressure. It tastes great, too, so by the time the waiter comes back with our menus, I'm already ordering a second drink.

"You look pale," Shelby says, flipping through the salad pages of an impossibly large menu. It reads more like a book. "Are you okay?"

"Oh, yeah, I'm just tired," I reply.

"Can't blame you. You put so much time into that algorithm of yours."

"Hey, it's worth it," I say with a half-smile. "It could redefine geopolitics in the long term."

She shakes her head slowly. "I think it's why your dad really wants you to work with him. I still don't get why you won't do it. The pay would be insanely good."

"I can't have my algorithm in the hands of politicians, alone. It's nowhere near ready to be used like that," I say, flipping over to the burgers and fries portion of the menu. "I still have years of fine-tuning ahead. If I am able to test it with the University of Chicago's research team first, and then run a beta model with a large company or a midsized corporation right afterwards, I think I could have a more advanced model ready, in say, a decade. What my father wants is not only impractical, but also not feasible. He wants me on the market with this way sooner than I should be."

"He wants what's best for you," Shelby insists.

I give her a long, hard look. "You used to be against politics altogether. Remember sophomore year? The pink hair? The grungy tees? What the hell happened?"

"I grew up," she says, slightly irritated. "Besides, my doctorate is focused on political science. I majored in it, if you recall. It's a little late for you to be astonished by my choice of career, Lyric, don't you think?"

"I'm sorry," I exhale sharply. "It's just... my dad and I have a strained relationship. You know that. It's always been complicated between us, especially after Mom died. I guess I don't like how close the two of you have gotten and maybe I'm a little jealous."

Shelby smiles softly. "Your dad simply appreciates my youthful enthusiasm and the fresh outlook that I bring to the table. I could never replace you."

"It's not what I mean," I mumble, wondering how to make Shelby aware of my father's tendency to use people without offending her. "Dad tends to drain people. Of knowledge, of energy, of kindness. And when there's nothing left for him to take, he forgets who you are."

"Oh, no, he's been nothing but—"

"Let me guess," I cut her off with a flat tone. "Kind? Personable?"

"What's wrong with him being kind and personable?"

"Under normal circumstances, nothing. But my father isn't normal. Next thing you know, he'll invite you into his inner circle. You'll be rubbing elbows with his Jack Bowmans and other powerful, high-caliber campaign contributors. His fellow political heads and congressmen. His state senator buddies and their Golden Retriever aides. Next thing you know, you're working twenty-four-seven for the man, fetching his coffee and drycleaning. You keep that up until election day, and if he wins, well, you're looking at more of that until your body gives out. If he loses, you get sacked as he cuts his losses. I've seen it before, Shelby. This state senate campaign is insanely ambitious."

"Wow, you have no faith in the man whatsoever," she replies, her brow furrowed with dismay. "I mean, I get that you two have a complicated relationship, Lyric, but I never really understood how much you despise him."

"What? No, I don't despise him. That's harsh," I say.

It's not that far from the truth, but it's not the angle I'm coming from, either. I wish Shelby could understand where I'm coming from. She's been an intern for his campaign for about two months now, and I can already see that she has lost some weight and plenty of sleep. It was supposed to be an informative internship for one chapter of her doctorate thesis. That's all. She wasn't supposed to get in this deep nor this close to my father, and I have to admit, I'm a little worried.

He's not a bad man, but he is an accurate example of a higher politician in the making. I wish I could have a bit more faith in him but I know how natural he is at breaking his promises. He's also remarkably good at making them sound extremely convincing. It worked for local council seats— three times, actually—but the state senate, that's a whole other bucket of fish.

The waiter comes back to take our orders. Shelby goes for a flimsy shrimp salad, while I decide to eradicate an entire burger and sweet potato fries, with a slice of pecan pie at the end. After yesterday's events, I am famished. Max, Ivan, and Artur really gave me one hell of an appetite, it seems.

"Something's different about you," Shelby says as we dig into our plates.

"Define different," I reply, suddenly on edge.

"I don't know. Glowing? Yeah, you're glowing." She pauses and gasps. "Ah-ha! You met someone."

I could tell her the whole story. Shelby is my best friend, after all, and despite the minor tensions surrounding my father, I know she'd keep it a secret. But I don't think I'm ready to hear any of the warnings that would come attached to her reaction. On top of that, I did just have mind-blowing sex with the men who kidnapped Jack Bowman. This is minefield territory, and I really need to be careful with my disclosures.

"Okay, you caught me," I giggle softly. "I met someone."

"Tell me everything!" she says, her eyes widening with excitement.

"There's not that much to tell just yet. We're only just getting to know one another. But I promise, as soon as I have a clearer picture of the guy, I'll spill all the beans."

Or guys.

She nods slowly. "Okay. I get it. But can you at least tell me where he works?"

"He's in the corporate world." It's not as if I can exactly tell her the truth. Besides, I'm not sure myself what it is they do as mobsters.

"How old is he?"

I think of Artur, the youngest of the three. I might as well make this story as believable as possible and with fewer lies to remember down the road. "Early forties," I say.

"Oh, wow. You went straight for a silver fox, huh?" Shelby chuckles softly. "I bet he's handsome."

I laugh. "Yeah, he's handsome. Hell, he's hot. Ripped. I'm guessing he played some kind of sport in his younger days based on his stamina. He may play still. The man can go on and on and—" I pause when I see the look of shock on my best friend's face.

"Lyric."

"Yeah?"

Shelby lets a heavy sigh roll from her chest. "You had sex?"

"Yep."

"And you're just telling this now? After I had to ask? I thought we were best friends."

"We are! But, well, we only just met. Yesterday."

She freezes, fork in midair, staring at me. "Lyric. Are you telling me you met this guy yesterday, and you already…"

"It was instant chemistry," I mumble, my cheeks burning hot. "It's hard to explain, Shelby. It just… it worked so well between us. Neither of us could stop it."

Her phone pings, and she is quickly distracted. I can't help but breathe a sigh of relief—I know she'd keep drilling me on the subject until she gets more information out of me. And that would mean I'd have to tell more half-truths and even full-fledged lies in order to keep yesterday's affair a secret.

"What's going on?" I ask, watching as she feverishly reads through a string of incoming text messages. "Is that my father?"

She nods once. "Yeah. He got a call from the FBI's Chicago field office. They're coming over to talk to him about Jack Bowman."

"Oh, man. It's that serious, huh?"

"It is. Bowman is one of the most powerful people in the United States right now. The fact that he's missing is rattling a lot of folks all over the country, not just here in Chicago."

"And they're asking my dad questions why, exactly?"

"They're close friends and partners," Shelby replies with a shrug. "If there's anyone that knows about Bowman's enemies or has inside information, your dad is a useful resource."

I could be, as well, though I have no intention of telling anyone that.

3

LYRIC

To say that I'm on edge would be a gross understatement.

Jake Bowman is missing and I'm the only one who knows that he was kidnapped. There's been no ransom demands. The cops and the Feds are looking everywhere for him. They haven't reached out to me yet, but it's only a matter of time. I've barely slept since the news of Bowman's disappearance broke.

At least I've got a quiet job here at the library—the hours pass without too much interruption or aggravation. I'm in the middle of rearranging a couple of shelves in the literary fiction section when my phone pings. It's a text from Shelby.

Apparently, the Feds didn't get much out of the hotel's CCTV footage, which tells me that Max, Ivan, and Artur kept their word, scrubbing some, if not all of it. I wonder how they managed to pull that off, but I'm thinking the fewer questions asked is best where the Bratva is involved.

If my father were to learn about my little afternoon tryst with the Bratva, I'd never hear the end of it.

"Miss Phelps?" a man asks, drawing me out of my frazzled thoughts.

I get up and turn around to find a tall, official-looking gentleman in a navy blue suit. "Can I help you?"

As soon as he flashes his Bureau badge, a weight drops in my stomach. I do my best to try and keep a cool exterior in front of Supervisory Special Agent Pete Smith. "I'm here about Jack Bowman," he says. "I understand you met with him the day before yesterday?"

"No, sir. I was supposed to meet him, but he wasn't there," I immediately say.

"But you were in the executive suite of the hotel, correct?"

He measures me from head to toe, his steely blue gaze settling on my face, searching for any clue that might give it away. I suppose everyone's a suspect at this point in time. It doesn't help that I feel guilty; I can only hope it isn't showing.

"I was, yes. But he never showed up."

"And how long were you in the room for?"

"I can't remember, honestly. I checked my phone a couple of times to see if he had attempted to get a hold of me. I tried calling him, but it wouldn't go through. Eventually, I had to leave because I had other things to take care of."

He nods slowly. "What was your purpose for meeting with Jack Bowman in the first place?"

"Mr. Bowman graciously agreed to do an interview with me for my doctorate thesis paper," I reply with a half-smile. "It was going to focus on his rise in the financial district, the tools he used for his company's growth, his plans for the future."

"Did you notify reception that he wasn't there?" Smith asks.

I shake my head, my blood thickening. I take deep, calming breaths as I work my way through one of the most uncomfortable moments I've ever experienced in my life. "Honestly, I didn't think much about it. I just thought Mr. Bowman was a no-show. He's a busy man. I figured he got tied up elsewhere or forgot. I left the hotel and went on about my day. It wasn't until the following day that I heard the news about his disappearance."

"Your father is Councilman Phelps." His quick shift in gears is almost dizzying.

"That's right."

There's a glimmer of recognition and familiarity in Smith's eyes. I'm no mind reader, but I can tell he knows my father. He proceeds to play his part, making me feel a tad uneasy. "I hear he's planning a run for state senate," Smith says. "And that Mr. Bowman is one of his fiercest supporters."

"I guess. I'm not involved with my father's political campaign." All of a sudden, a long forgotten memory pokes at my brain. "Can I ask you something, Agent Smith?"

He simply raises a brow in response.

"If I remember correctly, Mr. Bowman was a federal agent before he moved into the private sector. Right here in Chicago."

"That is correct. He was the director of our field office before he retired," Smith confirms. "I was one of his agents at the time."

"So I assume you know him well."

"I'd take a bullet for the man."

"Who's running the field office now?" I ask.

"I am."

I find that interesting though I'm not sure why. The more information I gather, the more accurate any situational test will be on my algorithm. I do this often, and it has helped me develop some pretty interesting and realistic scenarios.

"Do you have any suspects regarding Mr. Bowman's disappearance?" I continue with my own line of questioning, which gets me a wry smile from Smith.

"Miss Phelps, perhaps you'd like to consider a career in law enforcement?"

"Oh, no," I chuckle softly. "I'm simply curious. Mr. Bowman is a friend of my father's. I know my father is very worried about him."

"We don't yet know if he simply left of his own accord or if he was taken. There's been no ransom demand," Smith says. "I do think we'll hear something soon, though."

"Why do you say that?"

"Mr. Bowman was heavily invested in taking down every organized crime family in Chicago, and one of the reasons why he's been so supportive of Councilman Phelps's run for senate is because of his dedication to eradicating organized crime,"

Smith explains. He then takes out a business card from his jacket pocket and gives it to me. "Please call me if you remember anything else about that day. Even if it seems insignificant."

"Will do."

He gives me one last nod and leaves. As soon as he's out of sight, I feel like I can breathe again. The adrenaline soon wears off, and I'm left shaking like a leaf, my mind darting every which way as I try to recover some focus. But I can't.

I can't be implicated in any of this.

Once I'm done in the literary fiction section, I move over to biographies. There are a few new titles that need to find their place among the existing books, and I need something to keep my mind busy until my shift ends. But there aren't enough titles in this whole damn library to pull my focus away from Ivan, Max, Artur, and the conversation I just had with Agent Smith.

My body remembers every delicious moment of being with the guys. It relives and responds to each second as soon as their faces, their bodies, pop into my head.

I just wish it was only the delicious afternoon I had to remember them by, not the kidnapping of Jack Bowman that comes attached to it. Or the payoff attempt. That was insulting

"You look ridiculously sexy," Artur's voice startles me as if summoned by my thoughts.

I almost fall backward as I spin toward him, but he catches me. His strong arms snake around my waist, and I lose my breath as I meet those grey eyes of his once more. His lips are curled into a playful smile that rattles me to the bone, sending my heart on a galloping race as I try to ascertain what's going on.

"What are you doing here?" I manage as he gently lets me go.

I feel hesitation in his release, and as he takes a step back, I notice he's not alone. Ivan and Max are right behind him, looking just as sexy and intimidating as the first time I saw them.

"I'm digging the naughty librarian look," Artur quips. "You should've worn this the other day. Not that I had a problem with the power suit, that obviously did a number of its own on the three of us."

"What are you doing here?" I ask again, my voice trembling with a mixture of anger and hesitation as I nervously look around. "The FBI was just here, are you insane?"

"We know," Max calmly replies. "It's why we decided to stop by for a minute."

"Oh?"

"What did you tell him?" he asks.

I cross my arms, anger becoming predominant in the flurry of mixed emotions currently swirling through me. "Why? Are you worried I ratted you out?"

"Not at all," he shoots back with a confident smirk that causes heat to gather between my legs. "I'm simply curious."

"Are you okay?" Artur asks me. "You look stressed."

"You think?" I hiss, ignoring my infuriating arousal at their presence. "It's not every day I'm interrogated by the FBI. Of course I'm stressed!"

"Why? You're not the one who kidnapped Bowman," Max replies.

I give him a hard look. "Are you serious right now? Keep your voice down!"

"You need to loosen up," he laughs lightly and comes closer. Ivan and Artur watch, visibly amused, as Max closes the distance between us. His lips are dangerously appetizing, his cologne quick to invade my nostrils as I look up at him. "You had nothing to do with any of it."

"Maybe not but I know who did it, thanks to you," I say.

"So do they," he replies.

I frown slightly. "Smith said he could have walked away on his own, that they haven't received any ransom request or anything else indicating he was taken."

"Smith lied. It's why we followed him here. He knows we have Bowman," Max states.

I shake my head and take a couple of steps back. "Okay, tell you what. I don't want to know anything about it. Plausible deniability is a real thing, and I intend to make the most of it when the three of you inevitably end up in front of a judge. I will not be dragged into the Russian mob's dirty business."

"Actually, you kind of dragged yourself into it the minute you accepted our proposal," Max says. "But you don't have to worry about anything, Lyric. That was the last you'll see of SSA Smith. I promise."

"As long as you keep your end of the bargain," Ivan reminds me.

I'm tempted to give him a proper sneer, but as soon as our eyes meet, I lose myself in the depth of those dark pools. I'm conquered by the memory of him pounding into me, his fingers loosely wrapped around my neck as he bent me over and gave me everything he had.

I take a deep breath and manage to look away, but Max isn't cutting me any slack, either. His hand comes up, knuckles subtly brushing against my shoulder. I can feel his warmth through the white satin of my shirt. His touch sends sparks flying through my core.

"Those are dangerous thoughts you're having," he says, his voice low and burning hot.

"What thoughts?" I whisper.

"You know exactly what thoughts. They're written all over your face, Lyric. What happened at the hotel between us was a one-time only kind of thing. You're too sweet, too pure, for who we are and what we do."

"Then what, you're just here to threaten me?"

"Threaten you? Never. Call it micromanagement, at worst," he replies, the shadow of a smile dancing across his face. "It's best if you forget about us, Lyric. You don't belong in our world."

"It's mightily audacious of you to presume I want anything to do with you," I say.

The three of them give me one last look before they turn around and leave. I hold my breath, waiting for them to walk out the front door. Much like with Smith before, it's not until they're out of my sight that I am able to regain my senses.

* * *

A FEW DAYS pass in relative silence.

I do my best to pretend that everything is okay. I know I am innocent and did nothing wrong. Technically speaking, that is true if I'm to disregard what I said to SSA Smith. Or, better yet, what I didn't say.

It doesn't matter anymore. I'm in the clear. Whatever the guys do with Bowman, it's their business, not mine. I've got an algorithm to hone, a paper to write, a doctorate degree to earn. Bigger fish to fry.

I keep telling myself that but all I can think about is what happened in that executive suite. Whatever switch they flipped on me, I'm starting to worry that they're the only ones who can flip it back off. But do I want that? Max, Ivan, and Artur lit a blazing fire inside of me, and it burns so sweet, so scorching hot, I need more.

Shelby keeps me apprised of the Bowman situation through text messages. Although they know nothing about the information I have, I'm still riddled with uncomfortable emotions. I've added all the data I have on the matter into my computerized algorithm.

It's rudimentary software that needs time to process in order to deliver at least one reasonable scenario. The last time I checked, it was still doing its thing, so all I can do is keep my focus on work and on writing the rest of my dissertation. I'm doing exactly that when Max shows up at my library desk.

This time, however, he's brought coffee and a lovely box of French pastries, along with his debonair smile.

"I figured you could use a little pick-me-up," he says. "Something tells me you skipped lunch again."

"Again? Have you been watching me?" I ask in surprise, trying to keep my eyes on the computer screen. It's hard to concentrate when this mountain of a gorgeous man is standing so close to me.

"Gotta keep our eyes on the prize," Max replies, half-smiling as he looks down at me.

I take a deep breath and muster the courage to meet his wild, green gaze. "What are you doing here, Max? Don't you have a hostage to tend to? A ransom to negotiate? I don't know, people to torment and kill?"

"Is that what you think the Bratva does?"

"Your reputation precedes you."

He scoffs, but he doesn't seem all that offended. "Truth be told, my brother and I are trying a different approach these days. It's people like Bowman and his lackeys who make it harder for us to turn the page."

"The former head of Chicago's FBI field office? He's the one getting in your way?" I let a dry chuckle escape. "It couldn't be the century of crime sprees that you and your predecessors are notorious for."

"Is that playful tongue of yours always that sharp?" he narrows his eyes at me. "I don't remember... oh, wait, it was busy doing something else during our brief time together."

That's enough to bring fiery roses to my cheeks. Heat spreads through my throat as I raise my chin in defiance and hold his gaze. "What do you want from me, Max? I haven't said anything to anyone."

"I know."

"Okay, so?"

He leans forward and his cologne captures my senses again. There must be something in it, some kind of pheromone designed specifically to rattle and distract me. I have no other explanation as to why I seem to melt so easily in his presence. At least my tongue is sharp enough to not make me look like a mumbling fool. I just feel like one.

"Lyric, I'm just being courteous and checking in on you."

"And I'm supposed to believe that's all it is?"

"Truth be told, you're hard to stay away from," Max admits. "Not for lack of trying. I drove around the block three times before I decided to come in."

"You're the one who said I had no place in your world."

"Yet here I am."

"Here you are."

Max smiles again. This time, there's an inviting warmth about him that lingers as he subtly moves around the desk and comes closer. I swivel in my chair to face him, my gaze darting all over the place, wondering if anyone is paying attention to us.

Thankfully, there's barely anybody here. A couple of high schoolers bumbling through the geography section, a few kids on the other side of the aisle, perusing the comic book racks.

"I wonder if the universe brought you to that hotel room on purpose," Max says.

"I had a meeting with Bowman."

"There you go, killing the mysticism right away," he chuckles softly.

I shrug in return. "It's the truth."

"Then it's clear."

"What is?"

"The universe wanted this to happen."

I raise a skeptical eyebrow. "The universe wanted you to kidnap Jack Bowman and potentially get me in legal trouble?"

"No, I mean this," he says and cups my cheek.

A split-second later, his mouth crashes into mine, his tongue slipping past my lips, conquering everything in its path. I moan against his mouth, fire bursting through my whole body as I instantly surrender to him. Max is unforgiving, devouring, consuming, as he claims me yet again. His other hand comes down. I don't even notice until it slips between my legs and under my skirt, finding me hot and wet for him. "Your panties are soaked," he growls against my lips.

"It's not my fault," I manage.

"Your body is naturally reacting to what it wants."

His fingers press against the fabric of my panties, against my overly stimulated clit. My hips buck and sway forward, a reflexive reaction to his devastating touch. His index finger slips over the hem, and he pulls it aside. I'm exposed against his fingertips, burning tenderly for him.

"This is wrong," I whisper.

"Then ask me to stop," he whispers back.

"I can't," I reply and steal a glance to the side, just to make sure that no one can see us.

This is insane. It is shameful and scandalous. Yet all I can do is kiss him, hungrily, desperately, as his fingers work their magic on my tender nub. He takes it one step further, penetrating me while pressing the base of his palm against my clit. I gasp, feeling the pressure gathering in my core. A ball of thunder and lightning threatens to unravel with each stroke.

"You want this as badly as I do," Max whispers in my ear.

"Don't stop," I moan.

"I have to."

"No."

But he does. He withdraws his hand then takes a moment to lick his fingers, one at a time. They're slick with my arousal, his eyes twinkling with delight as he looks down at me. "We should do this again sometime," he says.

"You're devious," I groan with frustration, flustered as I straighten my skirt. "And mean."

"There is something about you that's troubling, Lyric."

I give him a curious look. "You're the one who had his hand up my skirt just now."

"You're dangerously addictive," he says. "We might have to go back on our word. We might have to have you again."

"Not going to happen," I chuckle as I shake my head.

He leans down, maintaining eye contact until I lose my breath. "Don't lie, Lyric. I know you'll give in to your desires."

"You're insane."

"Keep Friday night clear for us. We obviously have unfinished business."

I want to deliver another sassy comeback but I can't find the words. Max gives me one last smile before he straightens his back and walks away, leaving the coffee and the pastries atop my desk.

"Be a good girl in the meantime," he adds.

I huff and plop down in my chair. A minute passes as I sit there, turned on and annoyed by this man's teasing, realizing that I will most definitely be keeping this Friday night open.

4

ARTUR

We're in deep trouble, and we know it.

The minute Lyric walked into that hotel room, we were pretty much done for. It only took us a few days to figure it out as every conversation that followed inadvertently led us back to her. Her presence was brief but inexplicably intimate. We were only supposed to have some fun. To celebrate having managed to get to Bowman without his lackey Smith sniffing us out.

Instead, we ended up deflowering a doctorate candidate with the prettiest smile I've ever seen.

Max and Ivan have been working hard for years trying to steer the family business into a different direction. I've been right there with them, putting my own sweat into it. We were so close to breaking the mold, until Bowman opened his mouth, forcing his federal buddies' attention on us. The dirty bastard.

It had been quiet for almost a decade.

It was supposed to be a simple but effective operation: We tail him. We get close enough to grab him. And then we tell his big kahuna, SSA Smith, to back off our business and independent endeavors. All being things we didn't want to do in order to achieve our goals yet we still had to do them.

Lyric stumbling in on us was an unexpected and interesting accident.

I'm about to approach her. Again.

For the past ten minutes, I've been lingering in the history section of the library, watching her. She has no idea, she's so deeply wrapped up in her own thoughts. We turned her life upside down, even though we should've just let her go. It would've been easier. Cleaner. But we couldn't help ourselves. And neither could she.

"Fuck it," I say, putting the book I've been pretending to peruse back in its place, before making my way across the reading hall. I need to be near her again.

I stop cold in my tracks.

A man walks up to her. A familiar face that fills me with uneasiness. He smiles down at her as she looks at him in slight confusion.

"Dad," she says. "What are you doing here? Aren't you supposed to be at the campaign office? You have the debate in two days."

"Lyric, honey, I need to talk to you," he says.

Matthew Phelps is Lyric's father.

"Shit," I whisper.

If only we had known. Lyric was an innocent bystander. She was supposed to have nothing to do with our scheme, with our persistent enemies. Now she's smack in the damn middle of it all.

"Dad, please, don't tell me it's about the job offer again. I already told you, I'm not interested," Lyric says to her father. "I've already got so much on my plate."

"I know but we could really use you. Your algorithm would give my campaign a definitive boost. I'd wipe the floor with Sanders with or without Sunday night's debate. I need you, honey."

"I don't want to use my algorithm in this way," Lyric snaps. "I've said this time and time again. It doesn't belong in any kind of political warfare. It's a decade away from such an application, Dad. The scenarios it gives me at this point are far too general, too easy to misinterpret. I'm still calibrating its political science analytical tools. It's not ready for what you want it to do."

"But you are," Phelps insists. "Honey, you have such a brilliant mind, and you're wasting it away in this library."

"No, I am resting it in here. Most of my focus goes into my doctorate thesis. I should remind you that degree will get me onto the research team at the University of Chicago."

"I could get you there. One phone call, that's all it takes."

"I don't want your help," Lyric replies with irritation. "I want to be able to do things on my own, Dad, to earn them. You know how much I hate nepotism."

Phelps chuckles. "You never did want to follow in your daddy's footsteps."

"So why keep pushing this when you know the answer will always be the same?"

"My poll numbers are dropping. And the fact that one of my main contributors was kidnapped—"

"Wait, kidnapped? I thought Bowman was just missing," Lyric blurts out.

I slide behind a bookshelf to avoid unnecessary exposure while keeping myself within earshot.

"I got a call from the FBI this morning. SSA Smith received a ransom demand," Phelps says.

"Why did they call you about it?" Lyric asks.

He shrugs and runs a hand through his salt-and-pepper hair. "Bowman is my close friend. He's funding a large part of my campaign. They wanted to know if I could assist them financially. I have cash from the campaign's war chest to dispense. Easier to write up and track."

"Doesn't the Bureau have money set aside for stuff like this?"

"Forget Bowman for a second," Phelps says. "I'll deal with him and Smith. They're not the issue here, my campaign is. I need you, honey."

To my surprise and genuine admiration, Lyric holds his gaze and shakes her head once more. "No, Dad. I'm not going to come work for you. And I will not use my algorithms to help you advance your political agenda. You'll have to do it the old-fashioned way, like every other politician before you. Fundraising, televised debates, phone banks, the whole shebang."

"Wow," he shakes his head in disappointment. "My own daughter."

"I don't owe you anything," Lyric says. "Just because you're my father doesn't mean you're entitled to any of my intellectual property."

"I helped you get here!"

"No, I got myself here. You wanted me to go to Harvard and get into politics, like you did. In case you forgot, and it seems you have, I'm the one decided to go to MIT, instead. I'm the one who designed the algorithm and I'm the one who's building a tool for the next generation. You did nothing, Dad. Hell, even my college tuition was fully covered by the trust fund that Mom left for me."

"Now is not the time to split hairs," Phelps hisses, and I can't help but smile.

Lyric hit a soft spot. She hit it so hard, in fact, that her old man mutters something about her lack of empathy and gratitude before stomping away and bursting through the front doors of the library. I remain behind the bookshelf, analyzing my next steps.

She has a strained relationship with her father, that much is clear, but it doesn't change who Matthew Phelps is. He's one of our most dangerous and influential enemies, one of whom we're looking to crush in order to protect and grow our legacy into the new era of the Bratva. He is one who forces us to remain in the old ways.

Lyric is his daughter. She's fucking nuclear at this point.

It changes everything.

5

MAX

"I did not see that coming," Ivan declares as soon as Artur comes into the office sharing news of Lyric's parentage.

"We never asked her last name," Artur sighs, taking a seat in one of the guest chairs while I walk over to the minibar and pour him a double shot of whiskey. "We saw her, we wanted her, that was that."

"Animals," I mutter as I bring him the drink. "She reduced us to animals. Mindless beasts."

Ivan gives me a cold grin. "And we loved every second of it."

"What the fuck do we do now?" Artur asks.

I sit behind my desk with a drink of my own, watching the amber liquid as I swirl the Bohemian crystal tumbler. It is an unexpected situation, and we do need to figure out a way through it. We are about to begin negotiations and tense conversations with the other Bratva families. We have leverage with Bowman in our possession—the kind of leverage our own father only dreamed of. If we get the others behind us, it'll push Smith into a corner.

"What's the current hierarchy in the Chicago field office?" I ask Artur.

"What does that have to do with anything?" he replies with a furrowed brow.

"Let's take it one step at a time. It'll make sense, I promise."

Ivan grunts and downs the rest of his drink, then helps himself to another while Artur goes through all the known information that we've gathered so far from our meetings and interactions, including our covert research and city-based spies.

"Smith is the supposed ringleader," Artur says. "The minute he took over the Chicago field office, his roaches and under-lings got bolder and louder. Bowman is the cash cow, and Phelps is the PR guy, so to speak."

"We took their cash cow away and we made our demands clear," I reply.

"But they haven't responded," Artur points out.

Ivan scoffs, adding ice to his whiskey. "It wasn't an easy demand. They have to close off all of their investigations into our Northshore and Grimm offices and pull the staties away from our Langdon and Massey properties. That's a lot of manpower that won't be paid overtime for investigating us. Not that they had much to investigate in the first place."

"Northshore and Grimm still need a proper scrub," I remind Ivan. "Let's send some forensic accountants over there to make sure the IRS will never have reason to connect the new companies to the old ones. We're trying to build something clean here."

"Those fuckers won't let us," Artur sighs, pinching the bridge of his nose.

"Which, again, is why we have Bowman. They leave us alone, they get Bowman back. It's that simple. Our men are ready to release him as soon as Smith confirms that they've put an end to their investigations."

Artur nods slowly. "Still no word from him though."

"Not yet."

"In the meantime, Phelps is out there screaming against the Bratva on every possible screen," Ivan says. "He's got a tele-vised debate Sunday night. You know it's going to be one of his main talking points."

"He's dropping in the polls. He can't afford *not* to talk about us," Artur says. "I swear, Max, when you first suggested that we go legit with the family business, I thought it was doable."

"It is," I insist. "We just have a few more hurdles to cross."

"These aren't hurdles, they're fucking behemoths, and they've got money and guns aplenty," he shoots back. "We need the rest of the families' support."

Ivan nods in agreement. "Let's talk to Petrov, first. He seemed the most enthusiastic about a chain of casinos instead of, well, instead of what he's been doing for the past thirty years."

"What about Lyric?" Artur asks, looking first at Ivan, then at me. "What are we going to do about her? We agreed to see her again. Tonight."

"It'll have to wait until we get a firmer grip on Phelps," I say, though it pains me to the fucking bone. I was looking forward to tonight. I was downright excited to bury myself deep inside of her, to breathe her in and feel myself become a new man, nestled between her creamy thighs. But the fact that she's a Phelps has made it all the more difficult. And more dangerous. We've got too much to lose at this point. "We need to play it safe, at least until we get what we need from Smith. Until we release Bowman."

"I wonder what Smith was playing at," Ivan cuts in. "He already had the ransom demand when he spoke to Lyric. He never mentioned it to her."

"Of course," I say, a smirk on my lips. "It would've been self-incrimination. Any defense attorney worth their salt would be able to describe a decades-long relationship between the local feds and the Bratva based solely on our list of demands. We drafted it precisely for that purpose."

An hour later, Imani Petrov walks into our office.

The air is thick between my brother, Artur, and me. It's been this way since we agreed to keep our distance from Lyric. We've gone back and forth on it so many times, it's starting to feel ridiculous. But that is the situation before us. There are greater issues to resolve first, because the last thing any of us wants is to bring the Bratva's war with the feds to Lyric's door.

Petrov has brought tension of his own, judging by the tightness of his rugged, scarred jaw. He straightens his tie as he takes a seat across from my desk, while Artur and Ivan stand near the guest sofa by the window, their shadows growing long across the hardwood floor. Once Petrov is settled, they sit down.

"My birdies have been singing all sorts of scandalous songs lately," Petrov says, his accent thick. "What have you boys been up to? Kidnapping? Extortion? I thought we were trying to go legit here."

"We are," I reply. "We just need to get the dirty Feds off our backs. Bowman was our surest and fastest bet."

"The multibillionaire who controls half of the private security market in the United States?" Petrov laughs. "Well played, boys. I see the Sokolov genius is at its peak."

"I really hope you didn't come all the way here just to insult us," Ivan grumbles.

"No, I'm merely pointing out the obvious."

I lean forward, keeping my focus on Petrov. "It'll work. Smith will come through, and Bowman will get to go home in one piece by the end of the week. Once that's done, we'll be able to go ahead with our original plan. It's why we called you here, Imani."

"Go on," he says, leaning farther back into his chair, as if to keep some sort of distance between us. I'm aware that I make a lot of people uncomfortable. It's in my nature to be intimidating, and I have never tried to suppress it.

"Those birdies of yours, can you train them to look into the south side?" I ask. "There are several properties there that have stirred our interest."

"If you're talking about the White Plains neighborhood, you'll need to get cozy with Larionov again," Petrov chuckles dryly. "That's his turf. But I should warn you, ever since you broke up with his precious Polina, he's made it a point of not dealing with you or anyone aligned with you, Maksim."

I wonder what old man Larionov would do if he learned about the kind of relationship that Polina had with me. With us. She was the only woman who was seemingly interested in building something intimate in the long term with Ivan, Artur, and me.

We shared her in every possible way, and she preferred it. Then, she turned around and almost stabbed us in the back, but we kept things civil to avoid a war with the Larionov's. It's been bitter and quiet between us ever since.

To hear that we may have to deal with Polina's father again makes me feel uneasy on top of everything else. Especially now that we have Lyric rising like the sun on our horizon. Dammit, the timing on all of this couldn't be worse.

"Larionov owns White Plains," I mutter.

Ivan curses under his breath. "That's going to be a huge fucking problem."

"We need White Plains," Artur replies, looking at Petrov. "Why can't you deal with him? He won't say no to an offer from you."

"I don't have the kind of money he's asking for that block," Petrov says.

"We do. Take our funds and go make him an offer," I cut in.

Petrov laughs, almost mocking us. I'm starting to feel irritated by the mere sound of his voice. I grow restless in my seat as I work on practicing restraint. "Larionov will know it's not my money. That bastard is old school. Cold war trained, remember? He's got sleepers everywhere, including in my banks. He'll smell something fishy as soon as I show him the cash, Maksim. It's not going to work."

That's not very encouraging, and given what we're already dealing with, I can feel my stress levels rising. The simple thought of having to walk through Larionov's door and cozy up to a man who still looks at me and sees the bastard who broke his daughter's heart, does not give me a fuzzy feeling.

"We need another way to Larionov, then," I say, giving Petrov a bitter grin. "You're proving yourself useless, uncle."

"Watch your tongue. I still have sway with the other families."

"He's joking," Artur chuckles.

Ruckus suddenly erupts somewhere beyond my office doors. I can hear my secretary, Sophie, arguing with someone. There are several male voices speaking loudly, heavy footsteps thudding throughout the open office area.

I give Ivan a worried look.

"This is a raid!" I hear Smith's voice boom through the closed doors. "And we have a warrant! Nobody move. Cooperate and let us do our job."

"It took him long enough," Artur grumbles, sitting up.

I shake my head slowly. "If he thinks he's taking us by surprise—"

"I got rid of everything he could have, or may have tried to use against us," Artur reminds me.

"Good."

The office doors swing open, and federal agents flood in wearing dark blue windbreakers, their eyes steely and cold, weapons drawn. Smith leads the pack with a confident smirk. As soon as his gaze finds me, however, and he sees that none of us appear to be shocked or worried, said smirk begins to melt into a grimace of raw displeasure.

"Mr. Sokolov," he says, his tone flat. "I have a warrant."

"So you've said. Knock yourself the fuck out," I shrug, leaning back into my seat, while Ivan gives Artur a comforting nudge. "We have nothing to hide."

"What's this about?" Ivan asks.

The Feds start going through every cabinet and drawer in sight. I pull my chair away from the desk so they can access the computer, making sure my phone is in my jacket pocket. Artur is already on his phone with our attorney. It's not our first rodeo.

"Bowman's kidnapping," Smith replies. "We know you're behind it."

"I have no idea what you're talking about, but you're free to look around as much as you want," I shoot back.

"Oh don't worry, I will. In fact, I'll keep raiding every single property that's listed under your name and your associates' names until I find him," SSA Smith says. "If you think we'll succumb to your demands, you've got another thing coming. Hell will freeze over before the Federal Bureau of Investigation bows down to the Russian mafia."

Ivan chuckles dryly. "That's right, you only bow to the Latin American cartels. Isn't that who is favored within your Chicago field office as of late?"

"Don't push it," Smith shoots back. "Hand over your phones, too."

"Sorry, no can do," Artur cuts in, having just finished his phone call with our attorney. "I need to see that warrant first."

"It's perfectly legitimate," Smith insists, but he has no choice. He hands over the signed warrant, and Artur takes a sweet minute to read the whole thing before allowing a grin to slit across his face. "Everything in here is ours to check."

"Everything that's not on our physical person, that is," Artur says, pointing at one particular line. "You fellas need to get your DA's up to speed on these things. This is how you fumble an entire investigation. Do you see our phones out in the open?"

Smith looks around and I can almost hear his blood pressure spiking as he exchanges nervous glances with his agents. They do this every other month. They pick one of our offices, raid it, check it from top to bottom, then seize a handful of our books for their forensic accountants. They've been trying—and miserably failing—to get to us for years. They could never build a RICO case against us, so they're now attempting a more white-collar approach, but even that is turning out to be anything but fruitful. I can see why Smith is frustrated. It doesn't stop me from enjoying the moment though, if only for a little bit.

"Sorry, buddy. Better luck next time," I say with a casual shrug. "I think you need probable cause if you want to get your grubby hands on our personal cellphones."

"This isn't over," Smith replies. "I still have access to everything else in here."

"Like I said, knock yourselves the fuck out," I repeat. "We've been down this road before, Smith. We all know where it leads."

"It's Director Smith, as of next week," he shoots back. "And then, things will be rolled out a bit differently. I suggest you release Bowman before I bring in the hounds of hell."

Ivan snorts. "Let me guess, you're going to split the bill with the fine gentlemen from the DEA and the ATF. You're going to raid another one of our offices and try to get the Department of Defense involved. We know the drill, future Director Smith. We haven't done anything wrong."

Petrov watches him like a hawk. The old wolf would love to blow a hole right through Smith's skull, but he knows we cannot, and will not, go against the Feds like that.

Smith tries a different approach, putting on a subtle smile. "How involved is Lyric Phelps in all of this?"

I freeze. My brain shuts down. Darkness creeps in. I can feel its icy clutches tightening around my throat. Artur and Ivan both give me a hard, loaded look. I take a deep breath and decide to test the waters. Smith didn't bring her up without having a reason or knowledge about something.

"Who's Lyric Phelps?" I ask.

"You know who she is. Witnesses put you outside the library where she works down on Kingston Avenue just a couple of days ago. She was also supposed to meet with Bowman at a hotel you were staying at."

"I really have no idea what you're talking about."

"What were you doing on Kingston Avenue?"

"We have plenty of meetings every single day. Business takes us all over the city," I snap. "Listen, Smith. You're reaching here. It's the mark of a desperate man, and it's going to blow up in your face."

"Or maybe, you three got sloppy. Did you use Miss Phelps as some kind of honey pot?" Smith asks, carefully analyzing each of our reactions.

"Who is Lyric Phelps?" I ask again.

"Matthew Phelps's daughter. Certainly, you're familiar with him, seeing as he's mounting quite the PR campaign against you and your Bratva cohorts."

Petrov exhales sharply. "Oh, right, that stooge who wants to run for a state senate seat. He has a daughter?"

"Apparently," Artur replies with a shrug. "But we know nothing about her, nor have we ever met her. You're barking up the wrong tree, Smith. And last time I checked, it's not a smart strategy to drag your buddy's daughter into your mess. You don't want the future state senator to get egg on his face because of your unfounded allegations."

And there it is. It's sinking in. I can see it in Smith's eyes. He made a play and missed, which means he's got nothing but circumstantial bullshit. He's got a tail on us twenty-four-seven, and one of his guys must've spotted us near the library.

The agents start boxing up files, folders, and notebooks. One of them even takes a deep dive into the shredder. He'll be extremely disappointed when they find nothing except a few pages out of a car-themed magazine and a couple of printer test papers.

"Don't think for a second that I won't be paying more attention to Lyric Phelps. I will find dirt, eventually. And I can say one thing with absolute certainty—let Bowman go, or it's going to get really bad for you."

"We don't have him," I say.

"Let. Him. Go. This is not how you're going to get what you want, Max. Trust me. The people you're after are way higher up the food chain. Bowman can't help you," Smith says.

His words hit me on a deeper level. He knows what we're doing and why we're doing it. He's familiar with our cause, which means he's also familiar with the higher ups who pull his own strings.

We've never received a clear confirmation that Bowman is at the very top of a disgustingly corrupt pyramid, but we know he's at one of the superior levels. Taking him was supposed to be enough to get them to back off and leave us be.

Yet as the days pass, I'm starting to bitterly agree with Smith. Especially now that Lyric's name has been dropped. Maybe this was a misfire on our part. And judging by the sour looks on Ivan and Artur's faces, something tells me they agree.

Whether we like it or not, we may have no choice but to release Bowman and try another approach once everything cools off.

6

LYRIC

I find Shelby waiting outside the library at the end of my shift.

Her smile and bright eyes tell me there are new and positive developments, though I'm not sure in which aspect of her life. But she is holding a box of our favorite macarons, so it must be good news.

"What's up, buttercup?" I quip as I descend the library's front steps.

The sky is a blazing sunset red, while the streets are flooded with endless lines of crimson taillights. It's the early evening rush hour, which means we'll be walking home. The train will feel like a can of sweaty, smelly sardines, and a cab will take forever to hail.

"They released Bowman," Shelby says and opens the macaron box. "So I got your favorites to celebrate!"

"Hah," I chuckle softly. "Pistachio. Love you so much right now."

"Yeah, I figured you'd be glad to hear about this."

"Thanks, Shelby, I appreciate it. And yes, I am glad to hear he's a free man. Please, tell me he's okay."

She nods enthusiastically as we begin our slow walk home. "He's at the hospital getting a full checkup right now. And I'm sure he'll be granting every requested interview once they clear him. But he's okay. Which means you'll be getting your interview with him, after all. It would've been a shame to miss out on such an amazing opportunity for your doctorate thesis, don't you think?"

"To be honest, yeah, I was a little bummed out when he didn't show up. What do they know about his captors?"

That's the million-dollar question.

"I have no idea. The Feds called your dad to let him know that Bowman was safe. He hasn't spoken to Bowman himself just yet."

At least he's alive and seemingly unharmed, which will get the spotlight off me. I was more than just uncomfortable lying to a federal agent and I'm glad it's over. But I have to wonder why they released him.

Did Max and the guys get what they wanted out of him? I haven't heard from any of them. We were supposed to meet up on Friday night, but that never happened.

Not a call. Not a text. Nothing.

It's been radio silence since Max's last visit.

I wish I weren't so anxious about it. Maybe it's for the best. Getting involved with the Bratva is such a bad idea, no matter how you look at it. Hell, I should feel relieved. So why do I feel the exact opposite?

"Tell me about you," Shelby says. "How've you been? Any more sexy time with your new man?"

"No, it didn't work out," I reply, staring ahead while munching on a pistachio macaron. At least I've got the taste of French excellence melting in my mouth to make me feel better.

"Oh, no. Why? What happened?"

"We were supposed to go out on Friday night but I was ghosted. I'm over it," I say. "It doesn't matter."

"I'm sorry," Shelby mutters. "Men can be real pricks sometimes, huh?"

"My dating pool is shrinking, anyway. I'm starting to see those red flags a little clearer these days," I reply with a dry chuckle.

"At least you're not running toward them like me," she laughs.

7

IVAN

It wasn't an easy decision, but we had to let Bowman go.

As soon as Smith dropped Lyric's name, I knew it was only a matter of time before that fucker would find a way to bring her into this. Normally, we wouldn't care. We'd forge ahead, no matter the potential collateral damage. And having a whale like Bowman in our possession could've secured some advantages for the Bratva going forward.

There's just something about Lyric Phelps that tugs at our heart strings. It's a dangerous pull, especially now that we know who she is.

"Bowman's going to be holding a press conference before Phelps's debate," Artur says as he joins Max and me in the living room. We've got a few bottles of whiskey along with plenty of Chinese takeout for comfort food after what we all can agree has been a shitty week. "I want to watch."

"Are we sure he doesn't have any way of pointing a finger directly at us?" Max asks again. "I know we were careful, but—"

"He has no clue," Artur reassures him. "We were more than careful. The guys we hired to guard him were outside contractors. They spoke three different languages, none of them Russian. They were paid handsomely. Two of them are already in Mexico."

"Good. At least there's that," Max grumbles.

"Besides, the cops would've been at our door already," I remind him. "Smith would've been leading the charge with a huge grin on that smug face of his."

"That fucker has some nerve," Artur says.

We're still embittered and downright offended by his approach. It wasn't the office raid that rattled us; we're used to those. It was the hairline distance by which he missed Lyric's involvement. It could've turned out a lot worse. All we can do now is breathe a sigh of relief knowing she's safe.

We were supposed to meet her last night, but we ghosted her because we had no choice. Surely, she must be pissed off and disappointed. She has every reason.

I feel terrible about it.

It's unlike me to experience such remorse. I'm a hard man. Zero empathy, zero care toward most people. I see something I want, I take it. I see someone trying to hurt my brother or my best friend, I take bloody action. When Lyric's name dropped during the raid, I was too close to ripping Smith's head off. I needed every ounce of self-control that I could muster in order to stop myself from splattering him all over Max's pristine office.

"There he is," Max says and turns the volume up.

The three of us sit on the sofa. We're tired and feeling depleted and defeated. Seeing Bowman in front of the camera playing the fucking victim brings the taste of bitter bile up into my throat.

"Thank you, ladies and gentlemen of the press," Bowman says. In the hours since his release, he has managed to get a fresh haircut and a smooth shave. "As you all know, it's been less than twenty-four hours since my release. I needed some time to get a proper checkup, to pull myself together, and to process the entire ordeal."

"Our guys never laid a fucking hand on him," I grumble. "We should've roughed him up a little. At least he would've had a real reason to complain."

"I stand before you tonight as a free man," Bowman declares in front of the camera with the stoicism of Alexander the Great. "What I went through, I wouldn't wish it upon my worst enemy. They took me from my hotel room, gagged and bound. They held me hostage while communicating their demands to the FBI's field office, here in Chicago. This was a power play, but our people are just as good at this game as these monsters and their predecessors. More than once, the federal authorities have managed to put the worst of the worst away. The movies have romanticized the mafia. We don't care about their influence or their dirty money. Over the decades, including the years I spent leading the Chicago field office, we've fought them, tooth and nail. We fought them in the streets, we fought them in court—"

"We fought them on the beaches of Normandy!" Artur mocks him, prompting a chuckle out of Max and me. "My God, the man is so full of himself, he's bordering on delusional."

"He's lucky that Smith tried to drag Lyric into this, otherwise he would still be bound and gagged and whatever else he's yammering on about," I add.

"Today, it ends!" Bowman declares. "I've had enough of these mob families terrorizing members of law enforcement and hardworking Americans. I'm joining forces with the FBI and Matthew Phelps's campaign, effective immediately, in order to put together a program aimed specifically at the city's underbelly. Its Bratva, its Mafia, its Irish Mob, its Triads and Yakuza... we are done letting these rats get away with heinous crimes. We are done with our cautious approach. From now on, we're going hard after every single one of them, until the city of Chicago is clean and mighty again."

"PR shitstorm on the horizon," Artur mutters.

"We're organizing a cross-agency task force, and we're going after the Russians first," Bowman says. "While there is no clear evidence that the Bratva was involved with my kidnapping and ransom demands, those demands would've yielded results benefitting the Russians the most."

Our list of demands was carefully crafted to make life easier for the other families, as well, but Bowman isn't being specific on purpose. He knows it was us. The Chicago Feds have spent the past couple of years persistently harassing us, more so than the Italian or Irish families. He's got the microphone, though, and the nation's ears and hearts.

This really didn't work out the way I had hoped.

"It is my ambition that within the next two to five years, Chicago will breathe freely again," Bowman says. "I stepped down from public service a few years ago, but I can still support our fine men and women in blue with my company and private security resources. We need all the strength and manpower we can get to stand up against these families. And so, it is with great pride that I officially endorse Matthew Phelps's candidacy for a state senate seat. Our city, our marvelous state of Illinois, and our country would be better served with him. His vision aligns with my own, the best interest and well-being of the people at the very center of his campaign and agenda. I stand behind him, as do many of our former colleagues and friends in uniform."

Max curses under his breath and turns the TV off. "This motherfucker."

"It's going to get worse," Artur says. "The press will start coming around more often. They're going to want to know what Sokolov Industries reaction is to all of this."

"We will give them nothing," Max states firmly. "No matter what the tabloids imply, we're running legitimate businesses here. We don't have time for a media war with Bowman or Phelps."

"They won't see it that way."

"I don't fucking care. What I do care about is that we get the rest of the Bratva in line," Max replies. "Which means we have to reach out to Polina and her father. We definitely need the Larionov's support for this."

The idea fills me with cold dread. I had feelings for that woman. Deep feelings. For a long time, I thought she was it for us. The wife we'd always dreamed of. She was eager to be shared. She grew up in the Bratva, so she understood how we operate, what our life is like. She understood the expectations and the risks.

If only she hadn't betrayed us.

Rarely have I felt hurt by anyone in my adult life, but Polina delivered quite the blow. Rage still tests my resolve whenever I hear her name.

I need another shot of whiskey, because we're going into a public war against Bowman and his supporters. It'll take a lot of skill, a lot of diplomacy, and a few unsavory backdoor deals in order to save ourselves and our future. Bowman is coming for our heads, simply because he can and because it'll give Phelps the kind of political win that'll further advance them both.

I reckon Bowman will consider a run for office as well.

Phelps probably sees himself as the next President of the United States.

"We've got an even bigger problem," Artur lets out a heavy sigh as he looks at Ivan and me. "I can't stop thinking about Lyric. I want to see her again."

"You're not alone," Max replies, running a hand through his rich, brown hair. "It's a delicate situation though."

"How many women have we actually met that were so incredibly responsive to the three of us?" Artur asks and shakes his head slowly. "I don't care who her father is. I mean, I should, but Lyric is special."

"We can't avoid her forever," I say. "I mean, we could, but it'll turn into agony soon enough."

Max finally concedes. "I know."

It's quite the shitstorm we're wading into, yet we can't seem to stop ourselves from going deeper. I don't know how this will end, but I do know that I am ready to scorch all of their asses if that's what it takes.

We're building something great here, something that'll take the family away from all these skirmishes with the Feds. It's going to take time and alliances that will make me want to gag, but it's a hard game we're playing, and Bowman just promised us hell if we don't fight back.

8

LYRIC

After Bowman and my father's speeches about their war against the Chicago mob—the Bratva in particular—I am compelled to reach out to Max, Ivan, and Artur. I haven't seen them in a while, and the fact that they never made that Friday night happen has finally begun to make sense. Given the circumstances, and Smith's visit to the library, I'm guessing they were just trying to keep me out of what is clearly becoming a hot, horrible mess.

But I can't stay away anymore, for a multitude of reasons.

I don't have their phone numbers or their social media handles, so one evening, after some Internet sleuthing, I managed to find the address of a house on the Upper East Side that is listed as their official residence.

"Whoa," I mumble, noticing the size of the Sokolov's house as I advance toward it.

The villa is a two-story splendor nestled between giant sycamore trees, with a lush front garden and imposing, black metal gates. Security is stationed outside and judging by the number of sleek Escalades parked in the driveway, along with the sound of electronic music oozing from inside, they've got some kind of fancy event going tonight.

I suddenly feel small as I watch men and women in ridiculously expensive attire walk up to the bodyguards. One of the bouncers checks each guest against a list on his tablet before nodding to his colleague, who then proceeds to scan them with a high-tech metal detector wand.

"Are they inside?" I hear one of the guests ask.

"Yes, greeting folks as they arrive. Max and Ivan, mostly. Artur is by the bar."

"At least I know I'm in the right place," I mutter to myself before working up the nerve to take my spot in the growing queue outside the Sokolov villa, though I have no idea how I'll manage to fake my way inside.

It's a good opportunity to observe. I focus on the older gentlemen. Some have brought female companions, each loaded with flashy diamond earrings and necklaces—displaying the kind of wealth that proves their upper social status. Others have brought what appears to be their young adult children.

The boys look excited but also a little intimidated. If the stories I've read about the Bratva are true, each of these events is an opportunity for the young men to present themselves before the Sokolov's as potential lieutenants in the future, while the girls are elegantly dressed and on hand to inspire possible marriage offers.

That last thought rubs me the wrong way, especially as I watch a pair of beautiful young women sashay past the guards and up the villa's white marble steps, disappearing inside beneath a shower of twinkling chandelier lights.

"Can I help you?" the bodyguard asks when it's my turn. He takes a moment to measure me from head to toe. At least I had the sense to dress in a simple, but tight black dress and stilettos. Had I known they'd have this kind of guest list, I would've sprung for some flashier jewelry.

"My name is Lyric," I reply with a soft smile, my heart racing. "I'm not on the list, but if you would kindly let Max, Ivan or Artur know that I'm here, I'm sure they'll—"

"Get lost," he cuts me off.

Another guest tries to take my place, but the urgency of my situation beckons me to try harder. "Please. Just check with them. It won't cost you a thing."

"It'll cost time," he retorts, still unimpressed.

"Okay. I'll leave. But I hope you have a good excuse prepared for when the inevitable happens, and they ask why you didn't tell them that I stopped by. Best of luck, buddy," I say and turn to leave.

"Wait," the guy replies, then appears to send a text.

My heart's stuck in my throat. I can't believe it worked. The bouncer receives an instant response and gives me a sour look.

"You can go in," he says. "But you have to pass the metal detector first."

"Sure thing. Thank you," I shoot back and let his colleague wand me.

A minute later, I'm inside, marveling at the sight before me.

There are approximately a hundred people in here already, with at least another twenty outside. It's a huge place and absolutely beautiful. I search for one of the guys, but I'm so easily distracted and uncomfortable that I don't even notice Artur until he's mere inches away, his hot breath tickling my cheek.

"What are you doing here, Lyric?" he asks, his voice low while embers burn in his grey eyes. I find myself mesmerized by them, unable to breathe, or even think. "I... I..."

"You, what? You decided to waltz right into the lion's den? Do you have any idea how many of these people wouldn't even bat an eye before shoving you in their trunk?"

He's angry. A split-second later, he takes me by the arm and discreetly guides me up a flight of circular marble stairs. On the upper level, it's quieter. Darker. Glancing back, I realize they've got a security detail stationed at the bottom of the stairs.

"What do you mean?" I ask Artur, then take a moment to silently admire him more thoroughly.

He looks dashing in his dark grey shirt and black silk pants. His ink-black hair is slightly curled and stylishly tousled over his forehead, his gaze glued to my lips. "You're lucky that nobody recognized you as Matthew Phelps's daughter is what I mean," he replies. "Come with me."

"Where?"

He takes me into a large bedroom. This is a man's place. Every inch is masculine and dominant, meant to attract and devour its beholder.

Unsurprisingly, my mere presence in this personal space turns me on.

"How'd you know where we live?" he gives me a troubled look, then narrows his eyes suspiciously. "Did your father put you up to this? Bowman?"

"What? No," I shoot back and yank myself free from his hold, momentarily offended. "No. I went on the internet."

"The internet?"

"Not the regular internet. I didn't use typical search engines," I mumble, trying to keep it sweet and short so I don't incriminate myself any further. But Artur can see right through me, and a devilish grin stretches across his lips. "What have you been playing at, Lyric?"

The door opens and I freeze for a moment. Max and Ivan join us, both of them equally concerned and surprised. And just as handsome, wearing black tie ensembles that make their broad shoulders appear broader, their jaws sharper. I'm starting to think this was a bad idea. I can't even think straight anymore.

"Hey," I manage, along with a shy smile. "Sorry to show up here like this."

"Lyric was just about to tell me how she found out where we live," Artur grumbles, nowhere near interested in cutting me any slack.

"I do a lot of research work online, using a multitude of channels, platforms, and search engines," I sigh deeply. "And since I had no way of reaching you, I started using those tools to find you. I came up with this address, and, well… ta-dah."

It comes out a tad flat.

"You are beyond reckless," Max decrees. But he can't take his eyes off me, either. "Do you have any idea what kind of people we're entertaining tonight?"

"Artur mentioned something about me ending up in the trunk of a car if anybody were to recognize me," I mumble. "And no, I didn't consider any of this until now. I wanted to talk to you. The three of you."

"We're going to have to sneak her out of here," Ivan tells Max.

"Are you not listening? I said I wanted to talk to you."

Suddenly, all three are watching me like hawks. Their eyes are wide and flashing, their lips slightly parted, hunger emanating from them. The tingling in my core intensifies with each passing second of sexually charged silence.

"I saw my dad's campaign rally on TV," I manage to gather some of my thoughts. "I just wanted you to know that I don't condone anything he said. That's his bullshit, his train to ride, not mine. I swear I have nothing to do with him, Bowman, or anything that they promote."

"We know," Max replies.

"Well, I needed you to hear it from me," I say. "I don't like where this is headed. For the record, I don't condone your activities, either. I'm trying to keep my nose clean, to focus on my work, my doctorate thesis, my research."

"And yet you decided to show up here tonight," Artur replies with a half-smile. "You're looking for trouble, Lyric. At least admit it."

"You three were supposed to come see me on Friday."

"Judging by the recent developments, you have to understand why we decided to take a step back instead," Max replies, moving closer.

His cologne, powerful and hypnotizing as usual, fills up my senses. I'm shaken and stirred as he brings a hand up to tuck a lock of hair behind my ear. "You could've at least called me," I murmur, my breath already faltering.

"Fair enough," he whispers as he captures my mouth in a mind-shattering kiss.

Any reservation I had is gone. I'm helpless, defenseless, against these three towering men. All I can do is give in to their power, to surrender, and let them claim me once again. It is the reason why I came here and I might as well admit it.

"We have guests downstairs," Ivan reminds us, though he's staring at me, watching as Max devours my lips while Artur moves behind me. "Fucking hell, you'll be the death of us, Lyric."

"Honestly, I just wanted to talk," I say, gasping when Artur rolls my dress up and sneaks a hand between my legs. "Oh, wow."

Max trails kisses down the side of my neck as he unbuttons his jacket. Ivan begins removing his clothes, as well, enjoying the show as my dress ultimately ends up on the floor.

"You naughty little minx," Artur chuckles and smacks my bare ass. I welcome the ticklish sting with a grin. "You're not wearing any underwear."

"I had my reasons."

"You show up looking like this, what did you think was going to happen?" Artur whispers in my ear.

We lose control of the situation. Quickly. Our minds abandon us, our bodies taking over.

"Looking like what?" I manage in between stormy kisses.

"Like you," Ivan says, and takes me in his arms.

He's naked and hard as a rock. Artur's fingers slide between my wet folds, testing and tempting me into the sweetest madness. Max takes the rest of his clothes off and just like that, I am once more surrounded by three sculpted wonders of men. Ropes of muscle, smooth skin, a plethora of tattoos and scars to behold, and hard cocks twitching, aching for me.

"I don't want you to push me away because of my father," I manage to say as Artur finger-fucks me into a savage frenzy.

The pressure tightens into a ball and my knees feel weak as I hold on to Ivan, my fingers digging into his bulging shoulders. His tongue wrestles with mine, and I taste a lustful haven on his lips as I let him consume me.

"We can't do this forever," Max says. "You'd be in danger, Lyric. We've already crossed so many lines here."

"I don't care," I reply, reaching the edge of reason. "Take me. Please."

"For fuck's sake," Max snaps and takes me over to the bed. "Come here," he commands as he sits down. When I hesitate, unsure of what he wants me to do, he beckons me closer then pulls me down on his lap.

I mount him as he lays back. He fills me to the brim, stretching my slick pussy into sweet ecstasy. He's restless, eager to take me, but I quickly realize there's a new twist as Ivan climbs onto the bed and settles behind me.

"Don't move," he commands, as I glance back at him.

Artur jumps in, positioning himself before me, his long arms reaching until he's holding on firmly to the bed's upper frame. His cock beckons me to taste him just as Ivan works his way inside me.

"Oh God!" I cry out, as Ivan joins his brother.

My pussy stretches, dripping wet and aching with the most delicious torment. I have two monstrous cocks claiming me, and a third that is dangerously close to my lips. This is the next level, and all I can do is follow their lead.

I'm so turned on and burning hot on the inside, desperate for release.

"Take it," Artur tells me, darkness filling his eyes. "All of it, like a good girl."

"You need to know what you're getting yourself into," Max growls, planting his heels into the mattress and ramming into me.

"Ah!" I gasp as Ivan thrusts himself deeper, as well.

It's a slow set of movements at first, as I work to get used to this double girth. Soon, however, my body welcomes every motion. Ivan's hand reaches around, his fingers eager to tease my clit. I'm so close now, I know I'm going to explode. I can feel the pressure building more and more.

"All of it," Artur insists as he glides down my throat.

I relax my jaw and lose my breath as I let him in, as I lick him from hilt to tip, tasting the precum as Ivan starts pounding into me like the beast that he is. My screams are muffled as I suck Artur harder while Max fucks me faster and deeper.

I come hard, tears streaming down my cheeks as they continue to claim me.

Harder, faster, deeper.

I ripple outward like an exploding sun, my whole body convulsing while my pussy aches with raw pleasure. I love the sound of each thrust, of skin slapping skin. I gush all over Max, my juices flowing as I am claimed and devoured. They hold me in every which way, hands roaming up and down my body.

"God, you're fucking perfect," Max grunts as he thrusts himself upward.

My breasts bounce gleefully as he comes hard and fills me with his seed. Ivan growls and plunges into me, rubbing my clit until I can't stand his touch anymore, but he doesn't stop until I explode again, until I'm soaking wet and quivering as he, too, spills all of himself inside of me.

I drink Artur's every drop at the same time.

The madness is simultaneous and perfectly synchronized. The possession is shameless and absolute. I don't want this to end. I need more. I want more. I want it all.

But I can't have it all. Not tonight.

Max, Ivan, and Artur have a slew of dangerous guests to entertain, and I know I can't stay.

"That's all for tonight," Max says, gently kissing my lips as Artur helps me put my dress back on. I'm sore but momentarily sated, unable to wipe this lazy smile from my face. My core is still singing from that string of mind-blowing orgasms. "We'll see you soon, Lyric. I promise."

"You said that before," I mutter.

"It's different this time, although not ideal, given the circumstances. But we clearly have something going on here, and I intend to make the most of it."

"Just as you do," Artur adds.

I watch as they dress themselves back to perfection. No ruffled feathers whatsoever. Not a single hair out of place. Their bounce back skill is unrivaled, while I feel like a spool of string that has been thrown down a long flight of stairs, unraveled and internally disheveled, still reeling from the most wonderful kind of madness.

"I'm not sorry for coming here tonight," I tell them, my heart beating faster with each word of my shy confession. "But I want more."

"So do we," Ivan replies, and pulls me into a short, but hard, reassuring kiss. I taste a hint of whiskey on his lips. "Tonight, however, we have some pieces to move across the chessboard. You can't be seen here."

"I understand."

Max takes my hand. "I'm not sure you do, Lyric. The people downstairs hate your father and what he's trying to do."

"We're not trying to scare you but it's the truth. Those people down there, they're *our* people," Artur adds with a stern look on his face. "We're working hard to convince them to move their businesses into a more legitimate direction, but we're fighting decades of ironclad traditions, not just the dirty Feds or other mob families. We have our work cut out for us, and you, Lyric…"

"I, what?"

"You're our weak spot," Ivan mutters, stepping away to properly gather himself.

"Your weak spot," I whisper, not sure how I'm supposed to feel about it.

The words cause a smile to test Max's lips, but they almost taste bitter on mine. "It's meant to be a compliment," he says, lowering his gaze.

I understand. And since we don't yet fully know what this thing is between us—only that we want to keep at it despite the growing adversity—it's better if we don't give anyone the chance to use me against them. I have enough of a grasp on Max, Ivan, and Artur's plans to recognize that they're in the middle of a massive shift of operations. It's all about to change, supposedly for the better.

But old minds are the ones who resist change the hardest.

So if I want this to go somewhere safe and beautiful, as I dare imagine it could be in my mind, I need to play my part and keep myself safe. Coming here was risky as hell, though I don't consider it a mistake. I didn't know I'd be walking into a mob party.

"Come on, let's get you out the back door," Max says. "I'll have one of my security guys escort you to your car."

"I'm parked two blocks south of here."

"It doesn't matter. You're still under our protection."

My heart grows upon hearing those words.

Carefully, the guys take me out of the master bedroom and down the back staircase. Our goal is to slip past the thinning crowd in the hallway, dart through the kitchen, and out the back door.

"Come with us, Yuri, I need you," Max tells the bouncer who let Artur and I upstairs in the first place.

A big man with eyes of steel and a humongous jaw, Yuri gives his boss a nod and follows along. But as we make our way through the enormous kitchen—currently occupied with buzzing waiters and a rather loud chef with a thick, French accent—a woman's voice causes Max, Ivan, and Artur to freeze in their tracks.

"You invited me here and now you're avoiding me?"

I'm still and quiet as a mouse, partially hidden behind the mountain that is Yuri. Instinctively, Artur's hand comes up and discreetly pushes me closer to him without even looking at me.

I glance around the big guy's arm and see a tall, gorgeous blonde with sapphires for eyes, her slender figure wrapped in a shimmering silver dress, her pretty sights set on the Sokolov men.

I recognize that look. I have it as well where Max, Ivan, and Artur are concerned. I feel it somewhere deep within my bones, and it causes a tightness to thicken in the pit of my stomach as the guys slowly turn around to face her.

She hasn't seen me yet. I doubt she can spot me behind Yuri, so all I can do is stand still and listen. Watch. And hold my breath in fear of discovery.

"Polina," Max says, offering a polite smile. "We were just about to come back to the party. Why don't you wait for us by the bar?"

"Oh, no, darling, I was looking for you three *away* from the party," Polina replies with a charming grin as she steps closer, hips swaying in a seductive manner. She's itching for them, I can tell. It pisses me off. "I'm not interested in talking about the weather with Elena Ratkoff, for heaven's sake. I came to see you three."

"We just need a minute," Artur says.

She reaches out and gently caresses his face. "You look handsome as ever. I've missed you. I can't wait a minute longer."

"You forget yourself," Artur shoots back, his demeanor quickly shifting into something akin to muted hostility. "You forget where we left off, Polina."

"It's why I insist on talking to you away from the others," Polina tells Artur. "We didn't end things the right way, and I understand you've found yourselves in need of my father's support. I think we all know you're not going to get that until we can arrive at some kind of agreement, first." She moves closer to Max and rests both hands on his chest. That sends my blood boiling to the point where I can barely breathe. "Come on, Max. Let's see if we can find a better ending to our story."

"Polina, things are a little complicated right now," Max politely replies. "There's a reason why we organized tonight's party, why we wanted you all here."

"Yes, yes, and all of that can wait. The master bedroom is still upstairs, right?" she asks and gives Ivan a curious glance.

Among the three, Ivan appears to be the most unsettled and affected by her presence, which comes as a surprise to me. He is usually the coldest, the hardest to rattle. Yet this Polina chick seems to have quite the effect on him. The longer it goes on, the uglier it feels. The harder it becomes for me to breathe and remain upright.

"Alright, Polina," Max ultimately concedes. "Let's go talk in my private study."

He gives Yuri a slight nod. I suppose Yuri has just been tasked with getting me out of here on his own, and he knows it. Polina hooks her arm around Max's waist, and I have a mind of tearing the hair off her head, one strand at a time.

"Why don't we go straight to the bedroom. We know where this is going anyway," she giggles.

Hearing that, I want to stick around and see what Max says, but Yuri starts backing away from them and toward the door, automatically forcing me to back away, too. I curse under my breath as we slip past the service staff and out the back door, having left the men and Polina behind.

Outside, it's dark and quiet. Security cameras are mounted everywhere, the automatic motion sensors on the garden lights flicking on as we rush along the stone path leading toward the back gate.

"Who the hell is Polina?" I snap.

"Polina Larionov. She's an important figure in the Bratva," Yuri says without even looking at me.

There's a story there. A past I know nothing about. A degree of intimacy that Polina is clearly trying to rekindle while I was kept hidden behind Yuri. I know they did it for my safety, yet I can't help but feel like I've just been thrown aside after a good romp upstairs. I can't help but feel used and tossed away. It's an irrational emotion, and somewhere deep down I'm aware of that. It doesn't stop the tears from pricking at my eyes, though.

"Keep moving," Yuri says as we walk down the street. I keep hesitating and looking back at the Sokolov villa. "No one can see you."

"How do you even know who I am?" I ask, slightly irritated.

"I'm Max's chief of security," Yuri replies. "I know everything. I'm the one who allowed you access into the house, and I'm also the one who told Max you were coming. Which, by the way, you really shouldn't have."

"Yeah, I get it. I'm the enemy."

Yuri nods once, still nudging me along. "Something like that, yes."

"In that case, thank you for making sure I got out of there safe."

"You are welcome." He pauses for a moment as we reach my car. I have plenty more questions for him, but I'm fairly sure he's not going answer any of them. "You should stay away from the Sokolov's."

I give him a curious look. "Why? I have nothing to do with my father's campaign."

"You're putting them in danger."

"How so?"

"They let Bowman go because of you," Yuri replies, and only now do I hear the resentment in his voice. It sends shivers down my spine. "If anyone learns of your relationship with them, Miss Phelps, you won't be the only one in trouble. There's a lot of filth in this city, and I don't mean just in the mob families. It's also in the heart of the law enforcement system. Do yourself a favor and stay away. Move on with your life. And let them move on with theirs."

"Thank you for the insight," I mumble, giving him a gracious nod before getting in my car.

I take off like there's a tsunami coming after me.

I catch a glimpse of Yuri in my rearview mirror before I turn left and melt into the thickening evening traffic. My nerves are stretched thin. I'm jealous and afraid. I'm confused and constantly aroused. It can't be healthy.

Maybe Yuri is right.

Maybe I should keep my distance.

9

ARTUR

We join Polina in one of our private studies on the ground floor, careful to lock the door behind us. The last thing we need is other folks barging into our conversation. It's already tense and awkward as fuck, especially since I could tell that Lyric wasn't too happy about Polina's interference or her presence as a whole.

Lyric is an intelligent and highly observant woman.

I know she saw it—the invisible thread that was once between Max, Ivan, Polina, and me. The thread we cut once we realized how she was playing us, using us, so she could marry Max and place herself as a stakeholder in the Sokolov Corporation. The betrayal I felt then still stings harshly to this day, though I'm sure none of us loathe her more than Ivan.

"You look good," Max tells Polina, though it's not meant to be a compliment. More of a stale pleasantry, at best. "How've you been?"

"Missing you for the most part," she says, leaning against his desk.

He takes his seat, while Ivan and I linger by the bookcase to his left, keeping a reasonable distance from a woman who damn near tore us apart a couple of years ago.

"It's been two years. You need to get over it," I bluntly reply.

Max gives me a warning look. I know we're supposed to play nice, but I find it hard to pretend with this snake. "Polina, here's the thing. We all know how things ended between us, and I do not wish to revisit the past," Max says. "I'm focusing on the future here. Not only for myself and my family, but for the future of the entire Bratva."

"I'm just teasing," she laughs lightly, seeing that we're not playing her game.

"It's a piss-poor joke," I cut her off. "Considering how we parted."

Her posture changes immediately. "I don't need the reminder," she bitterly replies, hurt lingering in her cold, blue eyes. "I regret it all. It was such a feat of miscommunication, a terrible misunderstanding."

"It doesn't matter anymore," Max reiterates.

Ivan pours himself a drink. "We need allies. The Feds are coming for all of us. We need your father to get on board with our strategy for the entire organization. For that, we need to buy White Plains from him, along with a few other properties. He will be paid handsomely, well above the current market price."

"You're joking," Polina chuckles dryly. "My father would rather gouge his own eyes out than deal with the Sokolov's."

"And whose fault is that?" I ask.

She lowers her gaze for a moment. "Like I said, it was a huge misunderstanding."

"And as Ivan just said, we need your father's support, and you're the only one who can get it," Max cuts in. "Think about it this way, Polina. You fucked up. Big time. And instead of owning up to it, you turned around and poisoned the fountain. You lied to your father about us, fully aware that if we told him the truth, we'd expose our intimate life in the process. But what's coming next is a war. If we don't join forces, we will all suffer."

"Or maybe we'll profit even more," Polina says, raising a devious eyebrow.

"Or maybe you've forgotten that we still have a monopoly on sixty-five percent of all high-end properties in and around Chicago," Max shoots back. "Your father may have his hold on a small percentage of luxury apartments and condos, including White Plains, but they're useless without our support, without our sway in the local councils. He is better off selling to us and supporting our mission. With a little bit of luck, our books will be so clean, the Feds will die of old age before they find something incriminating."

"We've got our own forensic accountants working every fucking registry," I add. "We're working with retired white collar crime investigators. It's time for the Larionov's to join us."

"Listen, I will talk to Papa about this, but I'm not making any promises," Polina says, then gives Max another sweet smile. "What's in it for me, though?"

"You'll survive," Ivan states, his tone flat and deadly.

Polina sneers. "Is that a threat?"

"You haven't dealt with anyone from the FBI's Chicago field office, have you?" I ask her.

She shakes her head slowly. "Am I supposed to be afraid of them? Or that Bowman schmuck? Word on the street is you had him and you let him go. Terrible business decision. What were you thinking? If anything, I reckon the other families will hold the three of you responsible if things go tits up for any of us. How will I convince my father to work with you on White Plains then?"

"You'll think of something," Max replies. "We're making a good offer here. He won't get anything better; I guarantee it."

"Fine, I'll talk to him and see what he says," Polina concedes. For a moment, her gaze lingers on my lips, but then she quickly shifts back into her party-girl mood. "Come on guys, let's go do some shots at the bar. Like old times."

"You go ahead," Max says.

She doesn't appear too happy by being slighted, but she nods and obliges anyway. I can't wait to never see her again—a feeling I wasn't sure I would ever experience, especially in the months after the breakup. Yet seeing Polina now, I've realized I have nothing left in my heart for her. Not love, not affection, not any kind of longing. No respect whatsoever.

The only reason she is still walking and breathing is because of her last name. Because we couldn't afford to go to war with her father and the entire Larionov clan. For better or worse, their presence in Chicago has been useful.

We need to make sure it stays that way.

"That did not go as planned," I say as soon as we're alone.

"No shit," Ivan scoffs, pouring himself another drink.

Max takes a deep breath. "How much do you think Lyric heard downstairs?"

"Ah, the billion-dollar question," I say bitterly. "Pretty sure she heard every drop of poisoned honey coming out of Polina's mouth. We're just lucky Polina didn't see her."

"What the fuck are we going to do?" Ivan asks, looking at his brother, then at me before taking a seat on the sofa by the closed door. "We can't take our eyes off Lyric. We obviously can't stay away from her. We need Polina and her father, and you know Polina's going to try and spin this in her favor, one way or another."

It's a disaster already and we haven't even gotten to the worst part. The Larionov's have been an important part of the Bratva ever since the Russians came to Chicago centuries ago. When the Feds were combing through Al Capone's IRS documents, the Larionov's were buying up properties, including White Plains, bribing local councilors and pushing deeper into Italian territory with veritable impunity on behalf of the Bratva.

Max and Ivan's father never considered buying White Plains from Larionov—then again, he never had to deal with our current shitstorm. For some reason, the Feds kept things slightly more civil with the old man.

With us, it's different.

"We know that Smith and Bowman are pissed off because we've been cutting our proxy ties to the local Feds' office," I say. "It's why they're so determined to nail us. By taking our businesses out of the gutter and into the public domain, we cut off a major money supply for their dirty operations."

"That makes Larionov vulnerable too at the end of the day," Max surmises.

"Not if he decides to work with them," I warn him. "He's always vied for the top spot of the Bratva. What stops him from selling us out to the Feds to get it? We go down, and he gets to step in and take over, despite your father's wishes. If he were alive today, he'd—"

"He's not," Ivan cuts me off. "We're on our own. We've been on our own for years now."

"And Larionov knows it. So does his daughter," I grumble.

"Which means she will try to use it against us," Max says, lowering his gaze. "As if we didn't have enough on our plate already."

I nod in agreement and decide to focus on the only aspect that we can control. "Whatever happens next, we can't lose Lyric."

The words hit deep because we're all on the same wavelength here. Lyric stumbled into our lives and everything changed— our objectives, our limits, our willingness to compromise in aspects of our business and in personal matters.

I don't know if she'll stick around but I do know that I want her, and so do Max and Ivan. That much became clear tonight.

"She's different, isn't she?" Max chuckles softly, a warm twinkle lingering in his eyes.

"I did some research," I confess. "As much as the Internet would allow anyway. Apparently, Lyric is quite the computer whiz with a major in computer science and a minor in finance. I am officially curious as to what her doctorate's thesis is about, considering she was supposed to meet with Bowman."

"Pretty sure she mentioned something about geopolitical repercussions," Max says. "Yeah, she's brighter than most, that's for sure."

"A bit of a homebody," I add. "She doesn't waste nights and weekends at clubs and house parties like many others in her social circle. Generally speaking, girls with political heads for fathers tend to act out."

Ivan smiles subtly. "Pretty sure her way of acting out was cutting most ties with her father. Moved out on her own, refuses to work for him, keeps to herself, and makes her own money. That makes her even brighter, especially given what an asshole her father is."

"And that makes her all the more precious," I reiterate. "This whole thing with Polina tonight is going to get worse. We need to talk to Lyric about it. We need to tell her the truth so she's aware of our history, at least."

"And we need to keep Polina away from her," Ivan replies.

At the same time, we also need to watch our fucking backs, because everybody seems hell bent on gunning for us. I wonder what Piotr Sokolov would have to say about this. Max and Ivan's father ruled over the Bratva with an iron fist, but when we came back from active service and proposed all of these business changes, he was the first to say yes.

It was as if a weight had been lifted from his weary shoulders after decades of playing the same dirty games and getting the same payoffs. He did warn us, though. I remember that conversation all too well.

"Be careful," old man Sokolov told his sons and me. "It won't just be the Bratva families that you'll have to sway in your favor. You will also have to deal with the parasites who have been leeching off us for years and years, and those leeches have grown big and fat. They'll be angry."

Especially the leeches within the FBI's field office in Chicago. I had no idea how deep their corruption went until we started looking into it. Until we started shifting gears, changing business strategies, and stirring the pot at a time when everyone expected us to simply carry on like the others before us.

It will cost us to go legit.

I just hope the price we have to pay isn't too steep.

10

LYRIC

A month passes in relative silence. Then another.

I keep my head down, focusing on my thesis research and my job at the library. Many nights are spent in Max, Ivan, and Artur's strong arms. They either come to my place, or we book a hotel suite somewhere uptown and private. I understand why they're keeping me away from their turf. It's for my own safety, but I have begun to wonder what it would be like if we could just be together, if we could enjoy one another without having to look over our shoulders all the time.

There are permanent shadows lurking over us—the FBI and my father's campaign. Then there are the unseen enemies, the other Russian families who could take advantage of our relationship to turn the tide in their favor, to keep the Bratva where it is. And, of course, there are also the rival mobs, the Italians, the Irish. The Sokolov's have built quite the empire in Chicago, and now everybody wants a piece of the pie.

"Your dad's having another rally this weekend," Shelby says one late afternoon, having stopped by my library desk on her way home with another box of pistachio macarons. For the first time ever, I glance at them and feel a tight nausea building up in the back of my throat. "You should come. I know he'd be happy to have your support."

"He doesn't really have it though," I mutter, my eyes settling on the iced latte she brought along with dessert. "He's well aware. You don't have to try so hard to bring us back together, Shelby. I mean, I appreciate it, I really do. But ours is a more complicated relationship."

"Yeah, I get it. It's a shame though. He's trying to do so much good in this world."

"Careful not to idealize him," I kindly warn her. "He's still a mortal man with flaws and weaknesses. I know he's got a good heart, but I also know what kind of people he aligns himself with in order to get what he wants. My father bends the line of morality, Shelby. A little too much for my taste. Then he walks around claiming the moral high ground. I can't support that kind of hypocrisy, even if he is my dad. I'm sorry."

"He does what he has to do," Shelby concedes with a light shrug. "Politics is dirty, we all know that. It's not for the faint of heart. But your father gets results, and that's why he's already a favorite for that senate seat."

"Oh, I'm not too sure about that. Local councils are one thing. But the state senate? Different bucket of fish, Shelby. He's running up against some massive barracudas. The rival party is coming in hard on conservative policies, and with the way things are going across the entire state, my father's petty feud with the mafia families might be his undoing."

She gives me a confused look. "Your father is determined to clean the streets of Chicago once and for all. How is that a bad thing?"

"It's not a bad thing. It just goes against the interests of a lot of powerful people, many of them way above my father on the food chain. That's the hard truth." I take a deep breath and try my hand at one of the pistachio macarons, determined to enjoy a bite. I've been feeling sickly and lightheaded almost every day for the past week. Constantly tired, somewhat bloated. Suddenly ravenous, then five minutes later, close to puking. "Like I said, I'm sure my father means well, but I don't think he'll get too far in the current political climate. Enough about him, though. I want to know about you. How've you been?"

Shelby smiles softly and leans against my desk with a bright look in her eyes. "I think I'm in love."

"Oh. Okay. I'm listening," I giggle. "Tell me all about it."

"I can't. Not yet anyway. We didn't expect it to happen. So for now, we're just trying to figure out what it means and where it might lead."

"So you're keeping it on the down low."

"Yeah," she lowers her gaze, sounding almost disappointed.

"You'll tell me about it when you're ready," I say.

"That's right. How is everything going with this mysterious lover boy since you decided to give him a second chance after ghosting you?" Shelby asks, offering a playful smile, while I struggle to chew and swallow what used to be my favorite dessert.

"It's great. The chemistry is there, we're getting to know each other better. I feel safe when I'm with them. Physically, emotionally. It's all there."

"Them?"

"Him. I mean him," I blurt out, my blood suddenly running cold. "My head's a frickin' mess these days. Oh, shit," I pause, feeling the sweetness turn into something acrid on my tongue. "I'm going to be sick."

A split-second later, I bolt for the bathroom. I almost miss the stall altogether, making it just in time to hurl my entire soul out. Heaving and panting, sweating and feeling hot and cold at the same time, I realize that there may be something more serious going on here.

Shelby's footsteps startle me. "Lyric, are you okay? You went white as a sheet of paper."

"Yeah, yeah, I'm okay. My stomach just got really upset all of a sudden," I say as I manage to pull myself back up and flush everything down. "I could use a drink though. I'm so thirsty."

"Here," she replies, and I find her waiting by the sink with a bottle of water ready for me. "You sure you're ok?"

I nod slowly. "Stress, most likely. Work. My thesis. Everything is starting to pile up. I'll be okay, I promise. I just have to be more careful with what I eat."

"When's the last time you got your period?" Shelby asks, narrowing her eyes as she analyzes my immediate expression. I reckon she figured it out barely a moment ahead of me as I'm trying to do the basic math in my head. "How about we stop by the drugstore after you finish your shift? I don't have any plans for the rest of the night. Your dad said I deserve some time off before the next rally."

I can't say no. Shelby has been there for me through everything. She's the one I turn to when I need someone to just listen. Even if I haven't told her the whole truth about Max, Ivan, and Artur, she knows enough to offer reasonable and sound advice. And this right here, I can't possibly shoulder it alone. If she's right with her suspicion, I want her by my side when the result comes.

A few hours later, we're both staring at the plus sign on a pregnancy test.

"Well, shit," I say, my tone flat, my eyes tired.

Shelby takes a deep breath while I take another swig of cold water. I feel hungry. Maybe I should eat something before the nausea returns. It's been a rollercoaster all day and now that I know why, it'll probably get worse before it gets better.

"You should see an OB-GYN," Shelby suggests. "Just to confirm."

I exhale sharply and toss the test in the bathroom bin, then go straight into the kitchen. There's a tub of peanut butter and chocolate ice cream that's got my name on it. "Man, this is not the right time."

"I get it," Shelby says. "But you know, you do have options."

"I've always wanted to be a mom and have a family of my own. I just didn't expect it to happen so soon." I pause and take the ice cream tub out of the freezer, ready to confront my shortcomings on the whole matter. "Truth be told, we weren't careful about it. At all. I never stopped to consider it."

"Love does that to people."

I give her a startled look. "That's a charged word."

"It's obviously the right word," Shelby chuckles. "Look at you, all flustered and pregnant, ready to keep a baby in the middle of a doctorate thesis. Your life's work is waiting for you, yet you're willing to become a mom. If it wasn't love, we wouldn't even be having this conversation."

"We've only been together for a couple of months. It's too soon to call it that."

"It's too soon to have a baby, too, yet here you are."

"You're not helping," I huff and grab a couple of spoons. We sit around the kitchen counter island and dig in, one scoop at a time. Fortunately, this particular taste seems to offer me soothing comfort and genuine delight.

"What are you going to tell your dad?" Shelby asks.

I shake my head vehemently. "Under no circumstances can he know, Shelby. Please, this is my issue, my body, my life. Please."

"Okay, but you know, if you're keeping the baby, you won't be able to hide it forever," she tells me.

I sigh. "I know, but I just need some time to sit with it myself first, okay?"

She nods. "Okay. What about the father?"

"Right. So, here's the thing," I say, then let another scoop melt in my mouth before I decide to tell Shelby the whole truth. "It's not just one guy."

Shelby stares at me for a hot second, then bursts into laughter. "You're dating different guys? Oh, wow. And you're still complaining about how you don't have time to do much else. No wonder! Wait," she pauses, slightly confused. "Which one are you in love with?"

"All of them."

"All of them?"

I take a deep breath as I try to find the right words to explain the situation. "I'm dating three guys."

"Three."

"Yes but not at different times. I don't keep a schedule for this. I'm dating all three at the same time. They're... well, they're sharing me."

Shelby nearly chokes on her ice cream. "Holy shit."

"Yeah. Honestly, I get it. I couldn't believe it either when they proposed the whole thing, but then, curiosity got the better of me."

"What was it like?" she asks, her eyes wide with a mixture of shock and fascination. "I can't even wrap my head around a threesome with two guys, let alone a foursome."

"It's amazing, if you really want to know. Being with three men who are so intimately in sync and wholly connected is amazing. And it's hard work, I'll admit," I add with a chuckle. "But it's incredible. I don't think I'll ever be able to come back from that."

"So, let me get this straight. You've been in a relationship with three guys," Shelby concludes, nodding slowly as she tries her best to process the information. Another scoop of ice cream seems to help. "And they were your first, right?"

"Right."

"And now, you're pregnant."

"Yeah."

She starts laughing. "And you obviously don't know who the father is. Oh, Lord have mercy, this is amazing. Somebody needs to make this into a movie, it's too rich."

"Tell me about it." I can't help but laugh along with her.

It's insane. It's terrible timing. It's scary and then some, and I can see why Shelby would find it funny. It kind of is. It's ironic on so many levels, a screenwriter wouldn't have been able to come up with something like this. But it's real. It's my new reality, and it's starting to sink in.

"Lyric, you're going to be okay," Shelby determines, noticing the concern darkening my face. I can feel it—the worries, the what if's, the worst case scenarios quick to unravel in my mind. "You're not alone in this. Besides, there's three of them. Surely, at least one will come through for you."

"I can't tell them," I blurt out. "Jesus, Shelby. We're just hooking up. I know you and I were talking about love and all that, but truthfully, I don't know where we stand or if this is even meant to last."

Shelby thinks about it for a moment. "It sounds like you need to talk to them about the status of your relationship before anything else. Ask them where they stand."

"The age-old question that either gets you dumped or ghosted in this day and age," I mutter, suddenly afraid of that happening. "What if I ask them and they end it? Where will that leave me?"

"A single mother at twenty-three," Shelby shoots back. "Lyric, you also have responsibility in this. You have to accept it, and you have to be able to consider every possible outcome. What you're missing now is clarity. Talk to the guys. See how they feel about you. But under no circumstances will you go through the pregnancy, the birth, and the subsequent child-care by yourself. You hear me?"

I stare at her for a moment. "I hear you."

"I'm serious, Lyric. I'm with you all the way, I promise. I'll keep quiet about the whole thing, until you're ready to share your news. You have my word. But you need to talk to the guys about this. See where you stand and how they see the relationship working in the long run."

How long will that run be, though? What's the life expectancy on such a complex relationship? And most importantly, how will we make it work?

11

MAX

It's been strange. Beautifully strange.

Lyric is becoming an essential part of our lives, and none of us were ready for it. We thought it would be a one-time only fling. She seemed curious and eager enough, but then we delved deeper, and now we find ourselves enthralled, entranced, and unable to pull away from her, even knowing it's the reasonable thing to do.

Every time we tell ourselves that this is it, this is where we draw a line and put some kind of distance between us, we find ourselves getting even closer. One day we're talking about doing everything in our power to protect her and keep her close, the next we're coming up with ways to push her away because the sharks are circling closer.

"We know where this conversation will go," Ivan warns me as he comes into my office.

Artur is already helping himself to a second cup of coffee. My secretary made sure we were fully stocked for this so-called business meeting with Polina Larionova. "Where is Polina?" Artur asks, then takes a sip of his coffee. "She's already five minutes late."

"She's on her way up. I beat her to the elevator," Ivan scoffs. "She didn't see me, though."

"Is she alone?" I ask.

He nods once. "I've got a bad feeling about this."

"I never have good feelings about anything pertaining to Polina, but we need to have this conversation with her. We asked her to speak to her father, and she did. We owe her this courtesy," I reply.

Lyric has been dodging our calls and messages for the past few days, blaming the thesis research. I'm starting to think there's something else going on, but with everything we're trying to manage and keep away from her, I figure if she needs a bit of space, we can give her that.

"I miss her," Artur mutters, as if reading my mind.

"I know. We haven't seen her in a week," I reply.

"Which is way longer than what we're used to," he insists.

Ivan sighs heavily, pouring a coffee for himself. "What we're used to. Would you listen to us? Head over heels with a twenty-something, who also happens to be the daughter of one of our enemies."

"*One of* our enemies," I repeat after him with a bitter smile. "The fact that we have multiple enemies is a huge red flag in itself, don't you think?"

"We're screwed either way," Ivan shoots back.

The office door opens, and in walks Polina, looking quite modest in her cool grey pantsuit, her platinum blonde hair pulled into a perfect bun, gold loops hanging from her ears. "Good morning, gentlemen," she says, taking a seat in the armchair across from my desk. As soon as she's settled, I'm bombarded by a whiff of her perfume. It's almost sickening, an overload of sandalwood that makes me somewhat anxious. "We need to talk," Polina says, looking at each of us.

"I presume it's why you're here," I bluntly reply.

"How have you been?" she asks with a pleasant smile. Years ago, she would've had me at hello. Now I can barely stomach her presence.

"As well as can be, given the circumstances," I say. "But we're sticking to the plan, working on our strategies, and forging ahead. We're seeing a growth in support from the other families, so we're optimistic."

"And the Feds?"

"Still as obnoxious as always," Artur sighs. "But we're clean. Our books are clean. They have nothing on us, nor will they find anything."

"That's good to hear."

"What about your father?" I ask, eager to get straight to the point. The longer Polina sticks around, the more uncomfortable we all seem to get. "I understand you spoke to him about our bid for White Plains."

She gives me a long, curious look. She has thoughts she'd like to voice, but she decides to keep them to herself, choosing to follow my line, instead. "Yes, we talked about White Plains. And I come bearing both good, and bad news."

"You don't say," Artur mutters, and I give him a warning look.

Out of the three of us, he is the least receptive to Polina's charms. The most inclined to put a bullet in her head if he has to. The most determined to keep her out of our lives forever, and therefore, the least comfortable whenever we have to entertain her.

"You see, my father's anything but a fool," Polina says. "He recognizes the value of your proposal, and he agrees that the price you offered is well above the market value for White Plains."

"Okay," I reply, with a tone that urges her to continue.

"However, he also recognizes the importance of tradition, honor, and respect. All three, he says, were lacking when you ended our relationship, Max. At least, that's how he sees it."

"And I suppose you didn't give him all the spicy details about that breakup," I say, half-smiling. "Or about the relationship itself."

"For everyone's safety, obviously not."

"So basically, we're still stuck at this stalemate, with your father thinking the worst of us, even though you're the one who ruined everything," I reply.

Polina offers a slight shrug. "I guess you choose to remember things differently."

"You betrayed us, Polina. There's nothing to remember differently," Artur snaps. "Now, what does your father want for White Plains, other than money? Out with it."

"He's proposing an alliance," she says. "A business alliance, between our families."

Ivan, Artur, and I remain quiet for a long moment, exchanging wary glances. Ivan was right. We know where this is going, and I dread that I have to even consider entertaining what's about to come out of Polina's mouth. I should've seen it coming since the house party.

"An alliance through marriage," she continues. "I marry you, Max, and in return, not only will my family sell you White Plains for the price you offered, but we'll also give you our full support within and outside the Bratva. We're prepared to renounce our own ties to Bowman's people, if you agree to these terms."

Ivan snorts. "You're out of your fucking mind."

"Am I?" she asks, giving him a long, slightly amused look. "I would've imagined you being the most eager to rekindle this fire. I may be marrying Max on legal paper, but intimately, it would be the four of us again."

"That'll never happen," Artur cuts in. "You made sure of it."

"Why dredge up the past? I'm offering you a better option for the future," she replies, still irritatingly confident in her proposal.

I don't know what upsets me more, the audacity of the proposal, or the fact that it does—at least from a business perspective—make a lot of sense. Were it not for Lyric, I probably would've considered it, if only for a moment. But as things are, it's an absolute no from all three of us.

However, we can't just shut Polina down either. We still need her and her father's support, and both Artur and Ivan know it, which is why they stay quiet and let me do the talking.

"Polina, you're well aware that no matter how you try and sugar coat it, you wronged us in the past. You made us out to be the villains because of our complicated relationship, and we allowed it because we couldn't—and still can't—afford a scandal of such magnitude. Not when we're skating on thin ice while trying to move the Bratva into more legitimate fields of business," I say. "It doesn't change the truth, though. You betrayed us. I hope you don't think you're going to play us again."

Polina shakes her head slowly. "My father was the one who suggested it. Not me. In fact, I spoke against it, but he said I should ask you, either way."

"Why do I find that hard to believe?"

She laughs lightly. "Oh, Max, believe what you want. But these are the only terms he is offering. Do not blame the old man for wanting to marry me into the Sokolov dynasty. It would bring the Larionov's nothing but prestige and future wealth. Combining our bloodlines would make us stronger against everyone, including the smaller families of Chicago."

"And I'm guessing that your father's connections within the legal system would suddenly become available and useful to us against the Feds once I put a Sokolov ring on your finger?" I ask.

Polina nods once. "Of course."

"We'll think about it," I say.

"We will?" Artur gasps, giving me a troubled look.

"We will," I insist, keeping my gaze glued to Polina's. The air is so thick between us, almost unbreathable. Years ago, I would've given her the moon. Yet now, I just want to get her out of here, sooner rather than later.

She stands up, a perky smile curling her scarlet red lips. "You're seriously considering it? That's wonderful news."

"Give us time," I say. "You'll have your answer soon."

"You know where to reach me."

She walks out, her chin up and stiletto heels clicking defiantly across the hardwood floor, as Ivan, Artur, and I watch her get into the elevator. Once the doors slide shut, and she's out of our sight, Ivan rushes to close the office door, then turns around to glower at me.

"Are you fucking kidding me? 'We'll think about it?'" he hisses.

"What did you want me to say? Fuck no, straight away?" I ask him, feeling my blood pressure rise. I'm angry because Polina has found a way to make our lives harder at a time when we desperately need the opposite. "We need her and the old man. We need White Plains. We need to think about it."

"We're not going to say yes," Artur chimes in. "Right?"

I shake my head. "I'd rather die, but she doesn't need to know that yet."

"What if we have to?" Ivan mutters, as he slides down onto the sofa. He runs a hand through his short hair, his breath heavy and faltering. "What if there's no other way?"

"There's always another way," Artur says. "We just haven't found it yet."

"Why did we expect better results?" I ask, leaning back into my chair. "Ivan said it well before Polina even walked in. We knew this was coming."

We were hoping for better results. That's where the dismay stems from. From the hope that maybe Polina would do the decent thing for once and set our record straight with her father. Of course, she couldn't do that without implicating herself, without soiling her own image in front of daddy dearest. Her ego is too big. Polina would rather burn alive than stop being his perfect princess.

Either way, it's a ginormous fuckery. We need to figure out what to do with it.

We need to transfer White Plains into the Sokolov consortium sooner rather than later, for a multitude of reasons, some of them legal. Our accountants insisted upon it, since it is key in keeping all of our businesses clean and clear of any additional federal interference. Had I known that going legit would be so fucking tedious, I would've stayed in the Navy.

But then we never would've crossed paths with Lyric. I can almost smell her hair. Taste her lips. A sweet reminder that despite everything that we've been struggling with, Lyric has been a wonderful, soul-rejuvenating constant. And I intend to keep her around.

"Obviously, not a word of this to Lyric," I say after a heavy pause.

"Obviously," Artur replies. "How would it even sound?"

Awful. It would sound awful.

A few hours later, Ivan and I are visiting one of our north-side offices. There have been some logistical irregularities reported where the transportation department is concerned. We need to make sure everything is in accordance with the most recent regulations, since this particular building is smack in the middle of Matthew Phelps's council district.

He's been sending inspectors to bother our employees on a weekly basis, slapping us with fine after fine.

This time, however, one of our administrators caught whiff of an issue before another inspector's visit and called us.

"We're missing several documents, including the last three manifests for July," our eager logistics administrator, Trent, says as we walk back into his office.

"What do you mean we're missing transport manifests for July?" Ivan asks Trent, his brow furrowed with genuine concern. "That's a fifty-thousand-dollar fine right there."

"I'm well aware, Mr. Sokolov, but I swear I don't know how it happened. We usually keep everything right here in this office. The manifests, the travel logs, the passes, everything. And my assistant is good at labeling it."

"When did you notice they were missing?" I ask.

Trent sighs heavily. "That's the thing. I don't think they were ever submitted. Not on paper, anyway. But we need them to explain some discrepancies in fuel consumption for that period, otherwise the inspectors from the city council will have a field day with this. Like you said, sir, fifty grand."

"Fucking hell," Ivan mutters. "Let me see the ledgers."

Trent is a good guy. He's been under our employ for a few years now. He's a fair man with a good work ethic. His father worked for our father, and Trent inherited his position, though he did start out in the loading bay, first.

I don't trust anyone fully, except Ivan and Artur, but I do know that Trent wouldn't allow such issues to arise, especially during such a stressful time. If anybody hates city inspections more than us, it's him. Without hesitation, he unlocks one of the file cabinets and takes out a heap of ledgers for Ivan to sift through.

"We need to figure out what happened to that missing fuel," my brother says.

"One of our employees could intentionally be responsible," I add.

Voices boom beyond the wall of glass. I look out and see a familiar, yet disturbing sight—a river of FBI windbreakers spilling into the bay, manhandling our employees while waving a search warrant for everyone to see. "Oh, for fuck's sake," I scoff and leave the office, running down the metal steps to get ahead of the situation. "What the hell are you doing here?" I ask the agent waving the warrant.

"Search warrant for your premises," he replies with a dry tone.

"Yeah, I figured that part out. For what?"

"Suspicion of trafficking and other illicit activities."

I snatch the warrant from his hand to read it. The legal jargon is all there. Nothing but circumstantial garbage at first glance, which tells me that this is just another attempt from Smith and his cohorts to bully us.

"My lawyers will need to verify the validity of this warrant before we let you search anything," I try my luck.

The agent gives me a broad, overly confident smile. "Knock yourself out. They'll tell you the same thing they told you the last time we paid you a visit. Suck it up, buttercup."

"Your audacity is spectacular," I reply, my fists itching to wipe the smirk off his face.

Ivan steps in. Shit. I didn't even see him coming. I don't like the darkness in his eyes. I know it all too well. It's muted rage that is about to get really, painfully loud. The agent, however, doesn't immediately sense the threat. It will be his undoing, and I'm not sure I can help him.

"This is harassment," Ivan says.

"We have a warrant. Back the fuck away and let my people do their job," the agent replies.

I wonder if he's one of Smith's lackeys or if his arrogance just comes with the windbreaker and the badge. But Ivan doesn't care. He's got close to a foot on the guy and he didn't join me down here to play nice with the Feds.

"You do your job and whatever the fuck else you need to do, but our employees deserve to be treated with respect," Ivan says, then nods to the side where two agents are shoving a few of our drivers into a corner, tossing and turning everything over in their path. "It doesn't look like they're searching for anything. It looks more like shit-stirring and destruction of private property."

"You need to mind your own business and let my people do their job," the agent says, one hand already on his holstered weapon.

Ivan's eyes grow wide with amusement and not the good kind. "Are you seriously threatening to shoot me?"

"Ivan, come on." I try to get in between them, but my brother has reached his breaking point. Even I can't stop him. "Ivan…"

"If I feel like my life is in danger, I will shoot you," the agent says. But it's that constant smile of his that has the hairs on the back of my neck stiffening with irritation. Ivan is right to call him out, I'm just not sure about his choice of attitude. "Back away—now."

One of our drivers cries out in pain when an agent twists his arm behind his back. A skirmish erupts a few yards to our right, and Ivan immediately jumps in to put an end to it. The agent watches him, fingers nimbly grasping his gun, ready and almost eager to unholster it.

"Ivan!" I call out, but it's too late.

My brother throws the first punch, resulting in one agent falling backward, completely disconnected from reality. Fuck. The other two Feds try to tackle Ivan, but he's not an easy man to take down. He swings left and right, dodging punches and delivering one blow after another, until a taser hits him in the back.

"Ivan!" I shout again and rush to help him, but I'm pulled back by more windbreakers.

"Stand back!"

"Don't move," one of them says to my brother.

"How the fuck is he going to move, you're electrocuting him!" I snarl, struggling to get free. Granted, I could throw some punches of my own and break a couple of jaws, but the situation is fucked up enough as it is. I can't risk making it worse. "Somebody help him!"

Ivan is on the ground, twitching, until the handler of the taser finally turns the power off. Two of his colleagues get on top of my brother and cuff his hands behind his back. This just went from bad to worse in the span of minutes.

"Don't move!" the goon on top of my brother shouts.

"You people are incredible," I gasp, barely able to believe my own eyes.

I can almost feel my brother's pain coursing through my body. This is one of those moments where I wish the old Bratva rules could be applied. The Feds would've never dared to walk in and do something like this. They would've had a smidge of common sense, at least, knowing that we could easily find out where they lived, where their kids went to school…

But it's not within our moral code to function according to the traditional values of our organization anymore, which is both a blessing and a curse. In this situation, it feels more like the latter than the former.

"Alright, I got him."

"Ivan don't say a word. Don't fight them. I'll get you out quickly, I promise."

"Good luck with that," one of the agents says with an irritating smirk. "You'll have to wait until he's transferred to jail and arraigned. Quickly doesn't apply here."

It's at this point that Ivan completely freezes, looking up at me with a mixture of dismay and concern. We've had our occasional brushes with the law over the years, but nothing that needed more than a night's worth in county jail. My brother can't spend an hour in such a space without losing a bit of himself in the process.

Ivan is a hard man, riddled with the kind of darkness that he's had to become particularly adept at controlling. Confinement brings out the worst in him, his composure and self-control greatly tested.

If I don't get him out quickly, I fear he'll unleash his anger and distress on whoever's unlucky enough to share a cell with him. My hand is already reaching into my pocket and pulling out my phone as I watch Ivan get dragged out of the loading bay in a most unceremonious fashion. To make matters worse, a handful of reporters have gathered outside, snapping photos, asking stupid questions, filming Ivan as he's escorted to one of the FBI's black vans.

This will hit the news within the hour.

Smith and Bowman have kicked things up a notch.

12

LYRIC

On the less busy days at the library, I get to whip out my personal laptop and add more lines of code into my algorithm. It's a lengthy and tedious process. I often end up working for hours just to tweak a single parameter interpretation within the entire program—yet that small change can make a world of difference from one prediction to another.

If I'm to hand a version of this over to a company someday, I can't risk any errors, not even by a fraction. I'm insanely proud of how far I've come with this already, and it drives me to keep pushing.

It's also the only thing that seems to keep me focused in the middle of the shitstorm that has somehow become my life. I tell myself that maybe it was meant to happen this way, but I still feel guilty. I'm scared. I want this baby, and I intend to see everything through to the end.

I just don't know if I'll do it alone or with Max, Ivan, and Artur by my side. It's such a weird situation and it makes my brain hurt just thinking about it, let alone trying to make sense of it.

I take a break from coding and go into one of my news apps to check recent events. I need to stay on top of what's happening in order to further calibrate the algorithm; I've already started running a few possible scenarios regarding Chicago and its mob families.

I take a few minutes to go through several recent videos. The violent crime rate has dropped since the city council implemented some of the new measures they had voted on earlier last year. An Italian-American lieutenant of the Camorra family was found dead in his pool last night. A Sokolov...

"What in the ever-living fu—" I swallow that last word as I watch Ivan being arrested on camera, dragged out of a shipping company's loading bay infested with federal agents. I catch a glimpse of Max in the background on the phone, eyes wide as he spots the camera filming him. I see the smirks on some of the Feds' faces.

The news chyron makes it unclear as to what they were raiding that location for in the first place, but there's an article link for me to follow.

My blood runs cold as I realize that the motive expressed by the Bureau to the press sounds shoddy, at best. "Suspicion of illegal activity, are you kidding me?" I blurt out, anger quick to set in. "This is ridiculous!"

I need deep breaths for the fire in my veins to settle. I grab my phone and call Artur. He doesn't pick up. I try Max next. Still, no luck. I get anxious, restless in my seat as I immediately go into my "focus on the solution, not the problem" mode, which has me digging deep into my list of contacts.

Since my father is a politician and a darling of the media, I've had my share of interactions with reporters and journalists from pretty much every outlet in the Greater Chicago area and beyond. I saved many of their numbers over the years, thinking they might come in handy someday.

And here we are.

"Hi, Lindsey. Sorry to disturb and call you out of the blue like this. It's Lyric Phelps," I say then pause, waiting for her to remember me. "That's right. Listen, I'm wondering... I saw something on the news about Ivan Sokolov being arrested. Ahh, yes. Did you or one of your colleagues run that story?" I take a deep breath as she tells me all about it. "Okay. So, you were there. Okay. Do you have any idea where they took him?"

She doesn't, but she sends me the number of someone who followed the Feds' van across the city after Ivan was picked up. Ten minutes and five calls later, I'm finally on the phone with the guy.

"They haven't released him yet?" I croak upon hearing the news. "Boy, it sounds like they're really sinking their claws into him, huh? Why do I want to know?" I need a decent, reasonable lie for this. "I'm a reporter for a small, independent online newspaper. Just trying to break into the game, ya know?"

Finally, after another ten minutes, I get a location.

At about the same time, Max calls me back, and my heart practically jumps out of my chest as I answer. "Are you guys okay? I just saw the news."

"Yeah, for the most part. The Feds have done quite the number on us," he says.

"I saw. What happened?"

"I'm sorry, Lyric, I can't talk about this over the phone. Right now, I'm dealing with another issue because I can't get Ivan out of jail. Not today anyway."

My stomach drops. It can be so easy to upset the balance of an otherwise sturdy ecosystem if you know which buttons to push. The Feds were pretty smart and organized with this particular stunt.

With trembling fingers, I enter new data into one of the algorithm's ongoing processes, listening as Max tells me about how stuck he and Artur are, for the time being.

"So, until we figure something out, Ivan has no choice but to spend the night in jail," he says.

"That's just insane. What about the other families?" I ask.

"None of them will touch this. As soon as the incident hit the news, they all went radio silent. I can't exactly fault them. The Feds expect a reaction from us, which is precisely what we're not giving them. It's messed up, but I know Ivan understands. I just don't like the idea of him sitting in jail, not even for another minute."

"They are doing this on purpose, aren't they?"

"Yeah."

"Divide and conquer, I'm guessing."

Max lets out a heavy sigh. I can almost feel his anguish. I'd give anything to be there, to hold him and run my fingers through his rich, brown hair, comforting him. But I know they want me to stay away from this whole situation. It makes sense. I'd want me away, too, especially after SSA Smith's last visit.

"I'll be in touch once I know more," Max says before excusing himself and hanging up.

I can't just sit here and do nothing. However, I can speed up the algorithm's process for a few possible solutions, so I do that instead. An hour passes before I manage to come up with a reasonable resolution. I'll have to explain it to the guys when it's done, but I decide to do it anyway. There's a lot that Max, Ivan, and Artur don't know about me.

Maybe it's time I start letting them in.

After all, if I'm to have their baby, there should be a higher degree of intimacy between us on every level of an already insanely complex relationship.

When I arrive at the precinct, I recognize members of the press gathered outside. I approach them tentatively, thankful that I'm not easily recognizable. My dad may be a camera sweetheart, but I 've done my best to stay out of their range ever since he first ran for public office. Wrapped in a camel brown overcoat, I make my way up the steps and chat up one of the photographers.

"Who are you all waiting for?" I ask with a soft smile.

He gives me a hard look at first, but when I refuse to budge or stop smiling, he softens, ever so slightly. "What's it to you?"

"Just curious," I reply and slip a one-hundred-dollar bill in his jacket pocket.

"Ivan Sokolov. One of the uniforms from the reception desk tipped us off," he says, softer and a hundred bucks richer. "They set bail, but apparently all of the Sokolov accounts have been frozen, and the Feds are doing their best to stop Sokolov's brother from getting him out."

"That's pretty bold of them, don't you think?"

The guy shrugs, checking his camera settings. "I guess. I don't know what they expect to gain, though. You can't take the Bratva down, not like this. It's never going to be that easy."

"Because of their influence?"

"Because of their history. The Russian mob were here long before the FBI was even founded. These are hard bastards. A warrant and a couple of nights in jail won't make any of them crack. These Bratva folks will kill you if you look at them the wrong way. And no one will even know you're dead. They'll just make you disappear. Poof. Like you never existed."

I know this as well, yet hearing a stranger tell me such stories causes shivers to run down my spine. We're talking about the three men that I am profoundly intimate with. I'm pregnant by one of them. And in a few moments, I'm going in there to help them.

Frankly, I don't really know how I feel about that.

I bid the photographer farewell and go inside.

The inside of a police station is the last place I had on my bingo card for this week's city travels, but as the situation beckons, I have no choice but to take a deep breath, keep my cool, and do my best to navigate what comes next. These are murky, perhaps even dangerous, waters.

More than once, I've heard Max and the guys talking about the level of corruption within law enforcement. More than once, they've let slip that they can't trust the local Feds with anything. And if they can't trust the federal government, how can they even think about trusting the local police?

"Hi. I'm here to post bail for Mr. Ivan Sokolov," I say matter-of-factly to one of the uniformed officers at the reception desk. I manage to muster up a flat smile but I'm burning up on the inside, my stomach the size of a pea. Hopefully, they can't tell.

"You're here for what?" the guy blurts out, giving me surprised look.

"Bail. For Mr. Sokolov. I understand he's being held here. I'm here to bail him out."

"And who are you, exactly?"

I shrug. "Does it matter?"

"You're in a police station, miss. When an officer of the law asks you to identify yourself, you are obliged to do so."

"Actually, no, I'm not. Not unless you are charging me with something. I know my rights, officer. But since I would like to get out of here sooner rather than later, my name is Lyric Phelps."

"And you're here to post bail for Mr. Sokolov," the officer reiterates, tapping away at his computer with a permanent frown in his brow.

"That is correct."

"Why?"

It's my turn to give him a cold look. "I'm not required to disclose that information, either."

Silence falls between us, and with it comes the glares of several of his colleagues. The mild ruckus up to this point of cops and felons buzzing around, admins shouting and phones ringing seems to have slowed down. I suddenly feel pressure bearing down heavily on my shoulders.

I do not yield, however. My head stays high, my heart still in my throat, but I power through every soul-crushing second until the officer concedes with a slight nod.

"Bail was set at four-hundred and fifty-thousand dollars," he says, a smirk testing the corner of his mouth.

"Great. I suppose cash will work?" I instantly reply as I set a black bag on top of his desk.

He stills at the sight of it, eyes round with pure shock. "Cash?"

"Taxes already deducted, and I can provide a full paper trail for every single bill, if needed," I say, half-smiling. "I'm a city councilor's daughter, officer. I can't afford to play dirty while my father advocates for righteousness in this great city."

He nods slowly and hands the bag over to one of his colleagues. "There's a money counting machine in Rhonda's office," he tells the guy. "Double-check that it's all there while I draw up the paperwork."

"Why would you do this?" his colleague asks me with an expression of sheer disgust. "These people are the worst. Russian mobsters. Criminals. Killers. And you're Matthew Phelps's daughter. The man who's trying to put them away."

"I'm just here to pay Mr. Sokolov's bail," I insist with the same flat, pleasant smile. The less I say, the less I entertain this clearly tense conversation, the easier it will be for me later down the road. "Will there be anything for me to sign?"

They don't like this, but they are compelled to oblige.

The money gets counted in a back room, while I go through a slew of paperwork with the reception officer. Signature after signature. Initial after initial. Approvals, agreements, receipts. Everything needs to be accounted for, so that nobody has any questions left to ask at any point in the future.

Once it's all done, I sit patiently in a corner, watching the buzz of the precinct continue.

"Lyric?" Max's voice startles me.

I didn't see or hear him coming. I glance up and find him standing so close to me, I can smell his heady cologne. I can almost feel his heart thudding against mine. "Oh," I mumble and get up. "I didn't know you'd be here."

"What are *you* doing here?" he asks.

"You're angry," I mutter.

"I'm frustrated. They're hell bent on treating us like criminals," he replies.

"Well, you did... you know, do that thing with Bowman," I shoot back with a low voice, careful so no one can hear me.

Max lets a sigh leave his broad chest. "Yeah. I guess we had it coming. I just didn't think it would be on such flimsy warrants. Our law firm is halfway done dismantling every single piece of paper that they've been throwing at us lately. It's the bank accounts that really set us back, though, even if it's just for a couple of days."

"Oh, I took care of that. It's why I'm here."

He gives me a confused look just as the reception officer comes over with a final receipt. "You're all set, Miss Phelps. The money has been counted, every penny there. I'll have someone send Mr. Sokolov up in just a few minutes," the guy says.

"Thank you," I reply.

The officer backs away, stealing a dark glance at Max in the process, but he doesn't say anything else. Max, on the other hand, is positively and understandably befuddled, unable to take his big green eyes off me.

"Lyric, what is going on here?"

"I paid Ivan's bail."

"You *what*? Are you serious?"

Shock is the first thing to hit. But then relief rushes in, softening his features before discomfort comes along. All I can do is gently touch his forearm and smile. "Yes. It's taken care of. I didn't want Ivan in jail for a moment longer, either."

"That's a lot of money, Lyric. I know your father's well-to-do, but he's still a public servant. Where in the hell did he get that kind of cash?"

"It's not his cash. It's mine."

Max is even more confused now, while I grow increasingly uncomfortable being in this police precinct. My anxiety levels rise as I notice more and more people looking at me, watching me, trying to listen and pick up on anything that I say.

I've captured the attention of every uniform in this place. It shouldn't come as a surprise; I knew it might happen. But I didn't expect Max to be here. It will make it easier for the cops to associate us.

"Lyric, where did you get that kind of money?" Max asks in a low voice, a muscle twitching nervously in his square, bearded jaw.

"That is not a story that I can share with you here," I say.

"What the hell just happened?" Ivan cuts in as two officers bring him over to us. They both look clearly displeased about the whole thing, throwing daggers at my face, while I have the urge to shrink into something the size of an ant and disappear. All of my earlier bravado seems to have fizzled away, now that I see how rattled the vipers' nest really is. "Lyric?"

"Not here," I insist before heading out the door, Max and Ivan trailing me in confusion.

I'm nervous and quiet in the back seat of Max's car, sitting next to an even more befuddled Artur, while Max gets behind the wheel, Ivan in the passenger seat. None of us say anything for a minute or two, the situation still sinking in. It had seemed simpler in my head, even as I analyzed the algorithm's possible scenarios. Then again, maybe I let my heart lead me with this particular move, finding ways to justify my decision.

"Lyric, we owe you a great debt of gratitude and money," Artur says, his grey eyes searching my face while I try to understand the emotions that glimmer across his. "The longer Ivan stayed in that cell, the worse it would've been. But we obviously need to talk."

Ivan turns around in his seat. He's confused. Conflicted. Torn between anger and frustration, yet his gaze remains soft upon mine. "Where'd you get that kind of money?" he asks.

"And cash at that," Max adds, gripping the wheel so tight that his knuckles are turning white.

"So here's the thing," I begin, trying to find the right words to explain myself and my eerie capabilities in a way that makes sense. "You are already aware that I'm rather good in computer programming. Computer science, to be specific, with a specialization in finance"

"It doesn't explain four-hundred-and-fifty large in cash," Artur insists.

"I'm getting there," I chuckle nervously. "It's my money. I earned it fair and square. I paid taxes on it, too. It is perfectly legal, if that's what you're worried about."

Max starts the engine and pulls the SUV out into the steady flow of traffic. The farther we get from the police station, the more relaxed I begin to feel.

"As you also know, I insisted on gaining my financial independence as soon as I went away to college, not wanting to have anything to do with my father in that sense. I didn't want to depend on him for anything. In order to survive throughout college, to buy my own apartment, to be my own person, I needed a hefty revenue stream. I suppose I've told you enough about my algorithm project. I used its earlier versions to check odds on several online betting websites."

"You've got to be kidding me," Artur laughs. "You did what?"

"I went to five major betting sights. I did my research, checked the odds, introduced every megabyte of data into my algorithm, and went over its proposed win scenarios. It worked. I achieved seventy-five percent accuracy. I made a lot of money betting on pretty much everything. Soccer matches in Europe. Football and baseball in the states.

Horses. Boxing and MMA fights, including the UFC. I made it as far as Thailand with the higher bets. Over the years, I managed to put together well over three-and-a-half million dollars. That's how good my algorithm was then. It's only gotten better since, which is why I'm using it for my doctorate thesis."

"Holy shit," Max mutters while keeping his eyes on the road. "Lyric, we clearly don't know nearly enough about you."

"I manage on my own. Quite sure I said that more than once," I reply with a shy smile.

"This is more than managing on your own," Max says. "Jesus, Lyric, you're a fucking genius aren't you?"

"I was approved for Mensa, yes."

Ivan laughs, looking infinitely relieved as a free man. "Damn. I did not see this coming. I was ready and bracing myself for another night in jail and a heap of bloody trouble ahead. I feel like I'm the fucking damsel in this story."

"No, you're not. You're my man. You're all my men," I reply, raising my chin in defiance. "I did what I did because I understand now. I understand the risks you took when you freed Bowman to keep the FBI away from me. Don't think for a second that I wasn't aware. All I did was repay the favor."

"Does your father know?" Artur asks me.

I shake my head. "Not yet. He'll find out eventually. I was hoping I might be able to post that bail anonymously but the cops weren't having it."

"We're VIPs to those bastards," Artur sighs. "They were so thrilled to have caught one of us, even though they all knew they didn't have a leg to stand on. They've been trying so hard to get to us."

"I know. I'm sorry."

"What are you sorry for?" Ivan shoots back. "You're not responsible for your father's sins."

"No, but she very well may have just tanked his chances at the senate by bailing you out," Artur cuts in.

I cringe. "Yeah, that's something I'll have to deal with, I'm sure. Just another great disappointment."

"Wait, a minute. Let me get this straight," Max begins. "Circle back to that algorithm of yours, because I'm curious. You said it gives you possible scenarios of how events might turn out based on the information that you feed into it, right?"

"Right."

Artur glances behind us. I follow his gaze. "We have a tail," he says. "Grey sedan, two cars back, second lane."

"What do we do?" I ask.

"Don't worry about it," Max says. "We have nothing to hide. They're desperate to find something, so they've been keeping a detail on us twenty-four-seven. Lyric, the algorithm, talk to me."

"That's pretty much it. I've spent years developing it. I started my junior year of high school and it's been advancing ever since. The clearer the parameters, the more information I can feed it, the more accurate the predictions."

"Could you apply it in a situation where a certain organization is looking to shift gears and change its business model altogether?"

I give Artur a wry smile. "For the Bratva, you mean."

"Yes."

"It could definitely have an application there, yes," I answer. "I would need a lot of information though. And it would take weeks to build a viable set of future models. But yes."

"Could it help us spot potential situations? Say, traitorous associates, FBI raids, that kind of thing?"

I nod. "Anything law enforcement related would need a ton of details such as arrest records, warrants, a thorough history of yours and your predecessors' activities, etc. But again, yes. It's doable. I need more research and more years to develop it, but I'm sure I can pull off a level of accuracy never seen before."

"This feels like something out of a sci-fi movie," Max mumbles.

"I guess it kind of is. But sixty years ago, robots were the stuff of sci-fi movies, and yet here we are," I reply.

"We got ourselves one hell of a woman, fellas," Ivan cuts in, giving me a playful wink. "You're just full of surprises aren't you?"

We reach a side of Chicago I've not seen in a while. It's one of the most affluent parts of the city, with high rents and an even higher cost of living. I know this because I was originally interested in moving here after I finished high school. I had yet to make my money though, and I was on a slightly tighter budget at the time.

It's a nice area, clean and quiet, with a string of coffee shops and fro-yo cafes on every corner.

As we get out of Max's SUV, I look around. "Do we still have a tail?"

"No, it's why we took the tunnel," Max replies. "They were expecting us to go straight ahead but we lost them when we turned."

A massive luxury apartment building towers to my right, its front façade made of white marble and steel, mirrored glass, and open terraces. "What is this place?"

"We have a penthouse here," Max points upward at the high-rise. "I figured we could all use some peace and quiet for a couple of days. They'll have eyes on the mansion for sure."

"The boys are keeping an eye on the place," Artur reminds him. "But I would imagine the Feds have run out of bogus warrants by now. We should be able to enjoy a respite for at least a week before they find something else to pick on."

I follow them into the building and past the polite and impeccably dressed doorman, then into a large, round elevator that takes us all the way up to the top floor. "How can you live like this?" I ask in a low voice. "Constantly dealing with this kind of harassment. Because that's what it is. Harassment."

"We brought this on ourselves the minute we decided to stop funding local corruption," Max says, his brow furrowed. But the glances he gives me are soft, almost spicy, in their intensity. "It's the price of trying to do better than our father and the men who came before us."

My heart skips a beat when Ivan's hand rests on the small of my back. Everything had been so tense and stressful up to this point, that I'd almost forgotten myself as a woman, if only for a minute or two. But now that I'm in this enclosed space with my men, the elevator working its way up, I'm bombarded by lustful sensations as I quickly begin to realize where we're headed.

Their penthouse.

Their bedroom. Oh, God, I'd missed this.

"You're doing the right thing," I look at Max. "You said it yourself. How many people are willing to go through hellfire for that?"

"Few. Very few."

"Thank you, Lyric," Ivan says, then pulls me closer, wrapping his arm around my shoulders and planting a soft kiss on my temple. "I didn't see you coming, but I'm glad you took this chance."

"I know you guys would've worked it out eventually," I reply, resting my head on his shoulder for a sweet moment. "I just couldn't bear the thought of you being stuck in that place."

Artur chuckles softly as the elevator dings and the doors slide open. "Yeah, like you said, we're your men."

"I meant it."

Artur takes me by the hand while Max and Ivan go ahead. We follow a narrow, burgundy and gold hallway until we reach the door at the very end, for which Max takes out a special keycard. I find comfort in Artur's touch, the kind of comfort I need, now more than ever.

"I just didn't expect to hear those words from you," Artur whispers with a hint of a smile. His gaze deepens as it becomes locked on mine, and I feel my breath faltering. There is something in the darkness of those grey pools that creates a tingling sensation in my chest while heat begins to gather in my core. "We don't yet know where this is going, Lyric, but we do know we want you here with us."

"I don't want to be anywhere else."

That's not a lie. There's a chance I'll suffer one way or another for today's deeds. But right now, in this moment, I feel like it's all worth it. I'm safe again, in a sense, because I've brought my men back together. I did what I had to do.

I'll face the consequences later.

Artur closes the door behind us, then promptly proceeds to remove my overcoat. Max takes his jacket off, while Ivan pours himself a drink from the bar in the lounge area. There's a giant, cream-colored sofa that stretches out in a half-moon shape, a fire burning in the digital wall-mounted fireplace, its flames crackling and flashing orange, yellow, and red.

"You're one hell of a woman, did I ever tell you that?" Max says, coming closer.

I can feel Artur lingering behind me. I can hear him as he takes deep breaths, his nose brushing against the back of my neck. He inhales me deeply as shivers dance along my spine, his fingers nimbly working around my hips to unzip my jeans.

Max kisses me first, our tongues fighting for dominance until I surrender, while he and Artur peel the clothes off my body. Ivan joins us, wearing only the hint of whiskey on his lips as he captures my mouth in a ravenous kiss next. I taste him. I breathe him in. I lose myself in the moment as their hands move up and down.

I gasp when Ivan removes my pink lace bra and takes a nipple in his mouth. "Oh, yes," I hiss as I feel Artur's fingers dig into my buttocks.

Slowly but surely, we move closer to the sofa. Lips collide. Tongues swirl. Minds are lost until I find myself laid onto my back, knees up as Ivan goes down on me. My eyes glaze over with raw desire as I feel his tongue sliding between my wet folds, fingers eagerly priming my entrance for one hell of a meaty feast.

Artur and Max flank me on the sofa, and I eagerly take each of their hard, pulsating cocks in my hands, gazing deep into each pair of eyes before I lick the tips and suckle most voraciously. I taste the precum and swallow every drop as Ivan's fingers curl inside me, thrusting faster and deeper as his lips close around my swollen clit.

"Oh, don't stop," I cry out before I let Max slide all the way down my throat.

"Fuck," he groans, while Ivan works me over.

Tension gathers in my core, the pit of my stomach tightening as every muscle in my body contracts to the highest point. "I'll never stop," Ivan moans and sucks my clit until I finally come, crying out as my juices cover his face.

I stroke Max and Artur's cocks, reveling in the feel of their veins throbbing against the palms of my hands. I devour them both before Max switches places with Ivan. Heat burns through me, ecstasy rippling outward as I shudder, melting in my orgasm just as Max drives himself deep inside of me.

"Yes!" I hiss as he fills me to the brim, stretching me into the realms of sweet madness.

"Take it all, baby," Artur beckons me to deep throat him and I do exactly that as Max starts pounding into me.

Before I realize what's happening, I'm shifted on my axis.

I ride Max, while Artur comes up behind me and joins him inside. Ivan takes the top of the couch so I can taste him, so I can stroke his magnificent cock with both hands while I lick and suckle on his delicious tip. "Tastes like heaven," I say, then relax the back of my throat and let all of him in.

"I'm your man," he replies, lovingly gazing down at me, watching as I devour him. Watching as I ride Max like there's no tomorrow, as Artur fucks me harder and faster, slapping my ass with every vicious thrust. My pussy clenches, a second orgasm blowing through me as I beg them to fuck me harder until I feel nothing and everything at once.

"Please!" I beg.

"Fucking hell Lyric, you were made for this," Ivan gasps as he thrusts himself deeper.

All I can do is stare and hold my breath until I feel him come, shooting his seed down my throat, moaning in sheer bliss. It's music to my ears, as Artur and Max join him at the pinnacle of heaven itself. Harder. Deeper. Deeper, until they explode inside of me. Until I finally feel nothing and everything at once.

Sweat drips down my face. I taste Ivan on the tip of my tongue as he pulls back, leaving one last salty drop behind. I swallow it and give him the laziest smile I can muster, while Artur and Max give me their last pumps, panting and twitching in a sweet afterglow.

"I was made for this," I whisper. "For you."

"Yes, Lyric. And although it puts us in a line of deep trouble," Max replies, gently caressing my breasts, "I'll gladly suffer the consequences."

"We'll all suffer the consequences gladly," Artur jokingly corrects him, then plants a string of kisses down my back.

I soften in their hold, coming down from my own perfect cloud, my pussy aching yet yearning for more as I briefly glance out the window.

It's not even nighttime yet.

Perfect. It means we have plenty of hours left before sunrise.

13

LYRIC

A week goes by and it's still quiet in Chicago. I don't know what to make of it. Ivan thinks it's the calm before the storm. I stay on my toes with my head down, buried in my work.

I carry this little secret in my womb every day, working up the courage and waiting for the right time to talk to them about it.

One morning at the library, I'm logging a daytime shift while combing through several files to consider for an algorithm scenario regarding the Bratva. That entire conversation with the guys sparked my curiosity. Whatever I input now, however, is barely skimming the surface, and therefore, I expect some loose predictions at best. I still want to know how things might turn out for them though. It could be telling of how things might turn out for me, too, since our lives have become so tightly intertwined.

I spend my nights at their penthouse. The Feds have yet to come around, most likely due to the fact that it's still in

Max's father's name. Besides, there's an unmarked cop car watching my apartment building. Another drives past the library every couple of hours.

I see it parked across the street as I do my work. I can't see who's inside, but I can almost feel them looking at me through the window.

My phone rings, startling me.

"Miss Phelps," a woman's voice comes through. "I'm sorry it has taken me so long to follow up after the missed interview with Mr. Bowman."

"Hi."

My blood runs cold.

"He's back in the saddle, as you may or may not have heard, following that horrendous ordeal," she says, her tone mellow and honey-sweet. "I spoke to him about the interview and he asked me to extend his apologies."

"Oh, please, no apology needed. It's not like he stood me up," I nervously chuckle.

"True, but even so, Mr. Bowman also wanted to know if you'd be interested in trying again for that interview. Given that he is close friends with your father, Mr. Bowman wanted to give you the courtesy. If I remember correctly, the interview is meant to be part of your doctorate thesis right?"

"Yes, that's correct."

"How does next Monday sound? Six p.m., in his office?"

"Yes, that should be fine."

I don't know why I said yes to this. Perhaps saying no would've made Bowman suspicious. At least this way I can try to pretend that I don't know anything.

"I'll call back on Friday to confirm the appointment if that's alright with you?" the assistant asks.

"Thank you, that would be perfect."

My stomach churns incessantly, no matter how much clean food and water I give it. Then again, there's no amount of clean food and water that can help reduce the stress level of the situation I've gotten myself into. I can only own it, deal with it, and roll with it. Once my shift is over, I put my laptop away, leaving my colleague to take over the desk, then head out, eager to get home and fix myself a scrumptious dinner. Ivan sent me several pieces of prime beef from their dedicated butcher shop—one of the least expected perks of dating a Russian mobster, it seems.

A man waits next to my car. I stop when I spot him. I can't make out much from where I'm standing, but he seems to be casually leaning against it. The view is rather offensive.

"Cocky bastards," I murmur and start walking again.

"Miss Phelps," SSA Smith says, a smile stretching to reveal two rows of eerily white and perfectly straight teeth. Veneers, most likely. Fake. Like him. "I was hoping I'd run into you today."

"Run into me?" I bluntly reply. "You're waiting for me."

"Figure of speech. How've you been?"

"Fine, thank you," I am so nervous, tension cuts through my muscles as I work overtime to keep a straight face and a calm demeanor. I can't let this man see that I'm afraid. "Can I get in my car, please?"

Smith chuckles dryly. "You know that's not how this goes."

"How does it go then?"

"I have a few follow-up questions, Miss Phelps. It's in your best interest to answer them, believe me." He pauses and glances around. There are plenty of people out at this hour, most on their way home from work. Tired and weary. He seems tired and weary, too. "You paid Ivan Sokolov's bail. Why? I thought you had no idea who the Sokolov's were."

"I'd rather not answer that question."

"I could take you in for an official interview, Miss Phelps, yet here I am, being nice and discreet about it. Please, do not test my patience. It's already wearing thin."

I take a deep breath, my synapses firing rapidly as I try to find the right thing to say. I can't incriminate myself. "We met after your first visit, under completely separate circumstances. They paid me for IT services I provided for them. And then, last week, they called to explain the rather delicate situation in which you and the Department of Justice put them in, asking if I would kindly use the money they paid me with to bail Mr. Sokolov out."

"What did they pay you for, exactly?" He narrows his eyes at me. I'm sure he doesn't believe a word that's coming out of my mouth, but everything is purely circumstantial at this point.

"Like I said, IT services."

"What kind of IT services?"

I can't help but scoff. "I'm sorry, but I don't disclose the delicate type of work that I provide for my high-paying clients."

"Fair enough, but they paid you four-hundred and fifty-thousand dollars for a so-called IT job? I'm curious."

"If you really want to know, the work I did for them is adjacent to the project I'm currently developing for my doctorate thesis. I can send you the introductory chapter of my dissertation if you want. Anything more might be too complicated for you."

Smith raises an eyebrow. "Are you calling me stupid?"

"It's an algorithm designed with specific parameters and computations, meant to analyze an existing scenario, based on detailed information which it then translates, runs through an AI interface, and ultimately outputs in the form of predictive scenarios. It has distinctive applications across different fields, including business and finance-related industries. Which is what the Sokolov's were interested in."

I hope I've hurled enough technical jargon at Smith to befuddle him and stop him from digging deeper. If I have to slap him with my entire thesis, I absolutely will.

Smith nods slowly. "And you just decided to give them their money back."

"Agent, I understood the situation they were in. And they promised they would transfer the same amount back to me once their accounts were in the clear. Including a bonus, for the inconvenience. I did what any person would do in this situation, especially since I would like to retain them as clients."

He chuckles, shaking his head, processing and rejecting every layer of this lie with the condescension of a man who knows the truth, and the frustration of a man who can't prove it.

"Miss Phelps, I will only say this once. Whatever it is that you're doing with these people, you should stop. Your father's career will be negatively affected. Not to mention your own career, your future, your entire life, for that matter."

"Are you threatening me, Agent Smith?"

"Not at all. But you clearly don't know who you're dealing with. I warned you before. The Sokolov's are dangerous Russian mobsters. They will kill anyone who stands in their way. They build their empires on the bones of innocent people. Corruption. Trafficking. Most of Chicago's high crime rates occur because of them and the other mafia families. You have no business aligning with them."

"As far as I'm concerned, all my work with Mr. Sokolov is legal and fully certified," I reply. "It pertains to the financial sector. I have nothing to do with whatever it is that you're accusing them of."

"You keep telling those lies, Miss Phelps. Maybe somebody else will believe you."

"Agent, I would appreciate it if you'd stop harassing me. Bringing my father into the conversation won't yield the results you desire. He and I have nothing to do with each other when it comes to business. He's in the political field, I'm in academics. I'm just a doctorate student trying to do my best with what I know."

Smith curses under his breath and straightens himself, moving away from my car and coming closer toward me.

Instantly, my muscles tighten and my temperature rises as I try to keep my composure.

"I know you know more than what you're saying. One way or another, I'm going to take down those fuckers. Let's get that clear right now, so there's no misunderstanding later," he says, giving me a hard, mean look. "Anyone who gets in my way will understand why it's the worst fucking idea to mess with me. And I'm not a Supervisory Special Agent, anymore, Miss Phelps. You will address me as Director Smith from now on. I lead the Bureau's field office in Chicago, and I've got my sights set on the Sokolov's. They're going to burn. You should be careful so you don't end up burning with them."

"That definitely sounded like a threat."

"It isn't. It's a promise. Don't fuck with me, Miss Phelps. Don't get in my crosshairs, because not even your daddy will be able to save you if you do." With that, Smith walks off, leaving me a quivering mess.

"Son of a..." I mumble, barely catching my breath as the adrenalin begins to wear off. My muscles turn to jelly. I'm sweating through every pore as I fumble through my coat pocket for the damned car keys.

My phone rings. It's my father. "Oh, for fuck's sake."

He wants to meet with me. I jump in my car and drive to a café close to his campaign offices. I'd rather get this over with than postpone it, because there's already enough tension in my life.

It's not a coincidence that my father called on the same day that Smith showed up and Bowman's assistant reached out.

There's a play happening here, and I need to be particularly careful with how I handle it.

I find my father sitting at a corner table, out of sight, sipping slowly from his cappuccino. He looks exhausted, shadows lurk under his eyes, and a three-day-old stubble grayer than the last time I saw him covers his jaw.

I guess it's true what they say about politics eating people alive.

"Caffeine at this late hour?" I quip, taking my seat across the table from him.

"I have to be back in the office after this," Dad says, eyeing me closely. "You don't look so spry. Are you okay?"

"Yeah, I had a long day, that's all."

"I imagine you did. With a federal agent coming to see you."

I stare at him for a long, heavy second. "You called right after he left. Did you have me followed, Dad?"

"Not followed. I just asked a few folks to keep an eye on you to make sure you're okay."

"You could've asked me," I reply, anger sending a noticeable tremor through my voice. "What is going on here? What's this whole cloak and dagger nonsense?"

"Cloak and dagger nonsense? Lyric, you're the one associating with dangerous criminals! Did you think I wouldn't hear about it?"

He's furious. I see it now. Absolutely furious.

"I figured you would hear about it, but you don't know all the facts yet," I say. "I'm not associating with dangerous criminals."

"You posted Sokolov's bail."

I roll my eyes and tell him the same thing I told Smith, though the lie does roll off a tad easier from my tongue the second time around. "So, you see, it's nothing to worry about. All I did was give them their money back."

My father studies my face with the curiosity of a mad scientist about to crack a body wide open, a muscle twitching furiously in his jaw. "You know the difference between Director Smith and me is that I raised you, right Lyric? I know you better than most. And I know I didn't raise a bumbling idiot, so why are you trying to play one?"

"What do you mean?" I'd blush and take it as a compliment under different circumstances.

"There is something going on with you and the Sokolov's, Lyric. I don't know whether or not you're engaging in some kind of liaison with one of them, or if it's something else. But whatever it is, it needs to stop."

"Dad, forgive me, but where do you get off telling me what I can and cannot do? I'm an adult."

"Sooner or later, those bastards are going to get what they deserve. They will be arrested, and everyone around them is likely to go down with them. It's part of my campaign promise. I intend to make it happen, and I've got Bowman and Smith's support. The FBI is behind me on this, along with several other divisions of the Justice Department. Lyric, this will not end well for them, and I certainly don't want you getting caught in the crossfire. Do not let this moment of, let's call it temporary insanity, steer you away from your true calling."

I can't help but scoff, shaking my head in disappointment. "Do you even know who it is you're teaming up with? Do you have any idea as to who's got your back or who the Sokolov's really are? Because I've got a feeling that you're just parroting popular campaign promises to get votes, but you don't know what you're truly signing up for."

"And you do?" he laughs. "You, the kid who has her nose stuck in books and computer programs all day? I've been working in politics since you were a baby. I know more about this than you ever will, which is why I'm here talking to you. Father to daughter, adult to adult. Be reasonable."

"I don't think I'm the one who's being unreasonable."

Truth be told, I can't trust my father. I understood that long before the Sokolov's came along. He's let me down in so many different ways over the years, especially after Mom died. This is just one of the many instances where I can see that we're fundamentally different people.

"Lyric, I love you more than anything in this world," he leans forward, a gentle gaze scanning my face. "I promised your mother I'd keep you safe. I offered you an opportunity to work with me, to stay close to me."

"You just want to use my algorithm for your own political benefits. Please, don't pull the Dad card. Like you said, I'm not a bumbling idiot."

"Regardless of my reasons, you still have that choice," he insists. "You can stay close to me, or you can pull yourself farther away. But I've got a feeling you're not going to like where the latter takes you, honey. And when the shitstorm that's about to hit the Sokolov's engulfs you, I'm not sure I'll be able to help you out of it."

I've had enough. It's been a long day, made only longer and more insurmountable by unexpected interventions. The last thing I need right now is a lecture from a man whom I could never follow, whose example I was never inspired by, regardless of our blood ties and affections.

"Thank you for your concern," I mutter and get up. "I'm going to go home now. Take care."

"Lyric, don't take it the wrong way."

"How else am I supposed to take it?" I snap, drawing attention from other patrons. Curious eyes linger on us, making me uncomfortable. "You don't think I'm capable of making sound decisions with my life unless it involves doing your bidding. Working for you, to be specific. Let's just leave it at that, Dad. Have a great evening, and good luck with your campaign."

"Lyric—"

He doesn't get any more out of me. I'm out the door and fuming as I stalk back to my car and get behind the wheel. I'm starting to think that this is just part of the process. The payment for everything that I've been doing with Max, Ivan, and Artur is coming through. That must be what this is.

Smith has his eyes on me, he made that painfully clear.

And now my father is trying to meddle in my life as well.

14

LYRIC

Over the next couple of days, I find myself growing increasingly frantic and restless. My pregnancy keeps swinging from one weird craving to another. I'm trying to stick to a healthy diet, even though every fiber in my body is screaming for some peanut butter and chocolate brownie ice cream.

Max and the guys have been made aware of my conversations with both Smith and my father. Respectfully, they declined to comment about Dad, but they had plenty of curse words about the local Bureau Director.

It has made them even more determined and more tightly wound, which, in turn, has made it harder to find that perfect moment to tell them about my pregnancy. I don't think they're ready to deal with that just yet, not with what's coming. Because something *is* coming. My father and Smith both said as much.

The sound of heels clicking in an otherwise quiet library has me looking up from my lunch. The woman I see walking toward me seems familiar. The closer she gets, the tighter the dread in my stomach gets as I recognize her.

"Shit," I mumble to myself.

Tall, blonde, vaporous, and so entitled that no space is big enough for her. A goddess walking among mortals is how she carries herself, and it's all visible in the way she looks at me.

"This is clearly not my week," I whisper, praying to all the gods for patience, because I've got a feeling it's about to get worse from here.

"It took me a while to find you," Polina Larionova says upon reaching my desk. "You're Lyric Phelps."

"That I am. Who might you be?" I ask, though I already know the answer. I just want to see how she presents herself. She came here for a reason, and this is one of the few moments where playing the idiot might work to my advantage. Remembering everything that Yuri told me about her, I brace myself.

Polina smiles coldly, ever the confident vamp. "You know exactly who I am."

"I have no clue whatsoever."

She gives me a hard glare, waiting for me to admit it, but I refuse to give her anything. I simply stare back, my eyebrows arched upward in innocent curiosity. "Polina Larionova. Maksim's fiancée, to be specific."

"His fiancée," I chuckle dryly. "Getting ahead of yourself a little, aren't you?"

"So you do know who I am," Polina replies, irritated that I wasted a few extra seconds of her precious life as she nervously taps her gel nails atop the desk counter.

"I don't give a shit who you are. What are you doing here and what do you want?"

"I see. So you want to do this the hard way," she says, eerily calm and composed all of a sudden. "That's fine. I can nip this in the bud right now, not a problem. You need to stay away from Max, Miss Phelps. You need to stay away from Max, from Ivan, from Artur. You don't belong with them. Go back under your daddy's protection, because otherwise—"

"Are you threatening me, Miss Larionova?"

"Otherwise, the wolves will eat you alive. No, I'm not threatening you, I am stating a fact. You American girls, you think the world owes you everything, that you can just get whatever you want when you want it. It doesn't work like that."

It's my turn to give her a hard look. "That's rich coming from you, while I'm here, working in a public school library and nowhere near eager to throw my daddy's name around in order to get people's respect."

"You're not cut out for them," Polina hisses, inching closer while her blue eyes shoot daggers at my head. "You're just the flavor of the week, Miss Phelps. A plaything for them in my absence, nothing more. We have history, Max, Ivan, Artur and I. History that runs deep. And we have a future together, as well. Their success, their very survival, depends on our marriage. You should cut your losses and leave them be. Consider it a great experience and move on."

She clearly knows more about me than I do about her, and it makes me feel vulnerable. But there's a reason why they left her behind. And there's a reason why Max assured me that they have no intention of rekindling their rapport. Ever.

Problem is, I also know what Polina is talking about regarding the benefits of their supposed marriage. It has everything to do with her father's support, which the Sokolov's desperately need. But it doesn't mean I have to roll over for this stuck-up bitch. Not when I'm so deep into it with the guys, not when I'm carrying their child in my womb.

"I understand that you're bitter about the past," I calmly reply. "But from what I'm told, that's on you and nobody else. And while an arranged marriage would sway support toward the Sokolov brothers, it's not my place to discuss any of this here with you. I don't know you, Miss Larionova, and you don't know me, so how about we let the guys decide who's who and what's what?"

"I'm just trying to spare you future humiliation," she sneers. "Soon enough, our engagement will be announced. Max has no other choice if he wants to remain head of the Bratva. The elders are not happy with his projected legitimate businesses. They stand to lose a lot of money with such a move. No matter how you feel about them, you'd best be on your way. You don't belong here."

"The only one who needs to be on her way right now is you, Miss Larionova," I say, raising my chin in angry defiance. "Whatever Max decides, whatever Ivan and Artur decide, it's up to them. I'm not walking away from anything unless they ask it of me. Until then, I suggest you mind your own fucking business and get the hell out of my library so I can finish my lunch."

Polina stares at me for what feels like forever, clearly at a loss for words. "Excuse me?" she finally manages, shaking her head slowly.

"Get the hell out of here," I reply with a shrug. "You've said your piece and I don't give a shit. You'll never see me quaking in my boots, so you might as well get on with your life. I have a lunch to finish and work to do."

"You will regret this," Polina says.

"I now regret coming into work this morning, that much is for sure," I reply. "Had I known you'd show up, I would've intentionally overslept."

"This won't be the last you'll see of me."

I roll my eyes, having lost the last thread of patience I had left. "I sincerely hope it is the last I see of you because you're boring me."

She walks away but I know she'll think of something to retaliate. Polina is the kind of woman who doesn't take no for an answer, who bullies anyone she deems inferior to her. But my heart is already tightly bonded to Max, Ivan, and Artur in more ways than one. I'm willing to fight for what we have, even if it means making enemies of people like her.

My stomach still churns, thoughts of unsavory scenarios roaming through my head. Polina is barely out the door, and I'm already wondering if agreeing to an arranged marriage with her is the only way for the guys to truly forge ahead and save everything they've worked so hard to build.

What if she's right and I am in over my head?

When evening comes, I wrap myself in the arms of my men, though I don't tell them about Polina's visit until after we make love, until after we're sated and tired, basking in the afterglow and splayed across the bed like puppets.

Max draws invisible circles around my nipple, his gaze soft and warm. Ivan is half-asleep in my lap, one hand still kneading my thigh, while Artur gets up to pour himself a glass of scotch, naked and gloriously hung.

I adore this sight. I adore the feeling I get when I'm with them. This right here is my safe haven. My paradise. As weird as it may sound, as taboo as it may seem, it's my Eden. I don't want to lose it. Least of all to someone like Polina Larionova.

"Has your father said anything lately?" Max asks, planting a delicate kiss on my shoulder. I'm wrapped in their scents, a heady mixture of cologne, sweat, sex and cum. My favorite fragrance ever.

"No," I lie and instantly feel bad, but I don't have the nerve to bring it up yet. "It's been quiet, for the time being. How are things looking on your end?"

"Murky, at best," he says. "But there's something you need to know Lyric, something we have to inform you about. It's the right thing to do."

I give him a startled look. "What is it?"

"Your father," Ivan says, raising his head so he can properly look at me. "He's dirty, Lyric. Dirty as they come. We can't let him win that senate seat, which means we'll have to start digging through his past, his partnerships, his everything."

"I get it," I say, a heavy sigh rolling from my chest. "In a way, I think I've always suspected he was. I think deep down I always knew with some degree of certainty."

"You're a brilliant woman," Artur chimes in, having brought me a glass of scotch, as well. "It's obvious that you would've figured it out by now."

"No thanks," I politely reject the drink. "Max can have it."

Artur's eyes narrow for a second, but he doesn't hesitate to hand the glass over to Max, who takes it without a second thought. "Matthew Phelps is tied to Bowman and Smith, somehow. We'll have to look at his campaign and his campaign contributions. We'll have our people search— they'll be able to dig up some skeletons."

"Something tells me you'll find plenty of them," I grumble, staring at the ceiling for a while. "It pains me to even say it."

"I know, babe. But if we're to survive this, if we're to take our whole business into legitimacy, we have to obliterate those who want to drag us down into the gutter with them," Max says. "If we can take Phelps down, if we take Smith and his whole field office down, hell, if we manage to take Bowman down too, we won't need any familial alliances within the Bratva. No favors, no negotiations. They will all understand precisely how we roll."

"And they'll either tag along or get left behind," Ivan adds.

I chuckle nervously. "Speaking of alliances within the Bratva. Polina Larionova paid me a visit at the library today."

Heavy silence falls over the bedroom as the men stare intently at me.

"What?" I ask.

"You don't drop a bomb like that and not give us any details," Max mutters. "What happened?"

I leave nothing out and they quietly listen, occasionally exchanging nervous and irritated glances. Ivan's nostrils flare. He's angry. Artur becomes restless. Max, on the other hand, sets his glass on the night table and sneaks his arm around my waist, pulling me closer.

"Polina was out of line," he says. "We'll make sure she never bothers you again."

"She was pretty adamant that you're going to marry her," I reply, searching his face for any hint that my worst nightmare might come true. But all I find is ironclad reassurance as he peers deep into my eyes.

"I'd rather die a thousand deaths before I put a ring on that woman's finger."

Artur sits on the edge of the bed, lovingly gazing at me. "Didn't we just tell you that we're going to throw your father's political career in the trashcan just so Larionov can't pressure us into marrying his daughter, among other things? If that's not a declaration of love, I don't know what is."

"Love?" I hear the word and repeat it for myself, my heart eager to stop and drink it in.

"We're just getting started," Artur says, inching closer beside me. "We were already on a different path when you came along, Lyric. All you did was speed things up. We're trying to adjust to it as best we can, but if there's one thing that the three of us have come to agree upon completely, it's that we want you in our lives. We want you, all of you, every wonderful facet of you."

Tears prick my eyes as I try to process his words, to wrap my head around what he just said and the ensuing implications. "Glad I'm not the only one who feels this," I say, nestling my head in the warm space between Max's stern jaw and muscular shoulder. "So glad."

"We don't know how this will end, and we certainly don't want to make promises that we can't keep, promises that we could unintentionally end up breaking."

"We don't want to disappoint you in any way," Artur adds.

Ivan looks at me. "But you are ours, Lyric. Polina can stomp her feet all she wants. She's never getting between us."

15

IVAN

It was only a matter of time before Lyric would be harassed by Polina. She's trying to hurt and control us. Max warned about this. Artur knew it would be coming. I did, too, I just didn't think I'd react to it the way I did.

I'm not the share-your-feelings type of guy, yet Lyric tapped into that side of me the other night.

We have work to do if we're to build a future with Lyric, if we're to steer the Bratva away from the old ways without the city of Chicago swallowing us up whole.

Matthew Phelps needs to be knocked down a couple of pegs. Either we completely destroy him, leaving Bowman and Smith without an important political voice in the media, or we turn him, getting him to give us all the information he's got on those bastards. Either way, Phelps isn't jumping into that senate seat anytime soon.

With Artur and Max both busy with errands of their own, I take a long drive around downtown one afternoon, attempting to lose my federal tail before I switch gears and delve deep into the south side. I meet with an associate at a boxing club close to one of the last surviving community centers in the area. It's a beat-up dump, but kids and adults still come here to blow off steam, to steer clear of the gangs, and to do something better with their spare time.

"We could've met somewhere else," Paul says. We're sitting on one of the wooden benches next to the boxing ring, two tweens going at it while their coach barks directions at them. "This isn't our usual cup of tea."

Paul Kozlov once ran bets for my father. A small man with beady eyes and one too many knife scars, he made a living by getting to know people's deepest, darkest secrets. Now, Paul is one of our best hidden and most dangerous weapons against anyone we might deem adversarial.

"It isn't, but I've got Feds watching my every move," I tell him, my gaze wandering around the room. "How've you been, Paul?"

I slip him an envelope with an obscene amount of cash in it. Once our accounts were unfrozen, we took everything out and switched back to good old-fashioned paper, just in case Smith is able to bamboozle another judge before we can take him down.

"Better now," Paul nods and grins with gratitude, putting the envelope in his inner jacket pocket.

"I'm glad to hear that. And the kids?"

"Ten and twelve, Ivan. Not a day goes by that I don't thank God for giving me boys. They're easier to deal with, believe me," he says. "My sister, the poor woman, she's dealing with three adolescent girls. It's chaos at her house, all day, every day."

"I can imagine," I chuckle softly, still scanning the room.

"You weren't followed?" Paul asks me.

I shake my head slowly. "It took me thirty minutes to lose my tail."

"That's a long time. You're getting old, Ivan."

"Fuck you, Paul. I'm still younger than you."

He chuckles dryly. "You're past forty, brother. We're all old past forty. Law of nature."

"By the same law of nature, we're still alive in our forties and still active in the Bratva. What does that make us? Really good mobsters or really pathetic ones?"

"We're fucking geniuses because we get to watch our children and grandchildren grow up," Paul replies, his brow furrowed as he watches the tweens spar. "Which is why I'm here, brother. I admire what you, Max, and Artie are trying to do. I'm with you, one hundred percent."

"I'm glad to hear it."

"If you fellas lose leadership, Larionov will jump in. That fucker is too old school for this day and age, Ivan. He'd throw us all back into the dark sixties, and like I said, I want to watch my boys grow up. I want to sit at Markie's wedding and criticize the menu. I want to poke fun at Lee's future wife the minute she gets pregnant and starts complaining that she's fat."

It's my turn to laugh. Paul has a way of laying it down that makes him seem both ridiculous and hilarious, briefly making me forget about how shrewd and dangerous he actually is.

"You said you could get me intel on Matthew Phelps," I say after we finish catching up.

"I did say that, yes."

"And?"

"Well, what do you want to know? That two-bit politician thinks he covered his tracks, but he and his cohorts were no match for yours truly."

I give him a long, curious look. "I need dirt, Paul. The worst kind of dirt. I can't let him win that senate seat."

"Which means you have to tank his polls. The only way you're going to do that is if he winds up in jail, or if you reveal something about him so awful, it'll keep the news cycles busy until election day."

"So what do you have?"

Paul smiles and takes out a small thumb drive. "Courtesy of one of my many little birds scattered across the city. One of my guys knows a guy who knows a girl. Heard a whisper there. Logged anonymously into a few social media accounts to verify and double check certain details. Paid off a hooker or two, you know, the usual. Anyway, this right here is gold."

"What's on it?" I ask, slipping the drive into my coat pocket.

"Most of what I got is pretty circumstantial and likely easy to spin with a good lawyer and a PR team. It would bury him eventually, but you need to move fast with this guy. What I can give you that shows short-term promise is Annie Knowles." He looks at me as if I'm supposed to know who that is.

All I can do is shrug in sheer ignorance.

"Annie Knowles is a former employee of Phelps's city council campaign. A disgruntled employee, might I add. She was Phelps's PA during that time. Her contract ended abruptly and she tried to go to the press with her issues on the matter. Only one obscure publication had the balls to print something, the others buried the story. That obscure publication was quickly bought by a massive media corporation and shut down. It took a while to get my hands on that article."

"What does it say?"

"Nasty stuff," Paul sighs. "About Phelps. But you need to talk to Annie Knowles yourself. Somebody scared her out of Chicago. She's now living in Grand Rapids, Michigan. I tracked her down and got all the information available on this chick. Legal filings state that she has an active NDA with Phelps's campaign, so tread carefully and see how much it costs for her to break it."

"What are the odds that she'll want to break it?" I ask. "As far as I know, NDAs can destroy a person's life if they're broken."

Paul glances around, a smile testing his thin lips. "I have it on good authority that Annie Knowles's son is knee deep in shit with one of my bookies. Knee deep. And apparently, she hasn't been able to reach Councilor Phelps, although she's been trying for the past couple of weeks. This might be your chance to swoop in, Ivan. Find out how much she loves her son. Maybe she's willing to sacrifice that NDA in exchange for—"

"Saving her son from your bookie."

"That's right." He flashes a cold grin.

He's as ruthless as ever. Always happy to work in the shadows and squeeze money out of people. I need all the help I can get, and as unpleasant as this whole business with Annie Knowles may be, it seems like both Paul and I stand to earn something if I play along.

Paul gets his money back through me. And I get the information that I need to destroy Matthew Phelps.

IVAN

Arriving at Annie Knowles's address in Grand Rapids, I quickly realize that she was generously paid off on top of that tedious NDA. Her house is the biggest and grandest on the block, settled in the middle of a notoriously affluent neighborhood.

Cautiously, I get out of my car and walk up to the front gate.

The gardener spots me and comes over. "Can I help you?" he asks, his black brow furrowed slightly, beads of sweat trickling down his tanned temples.

"I'm here to see Mrs. Knowles. I'm her lawyer," I reply, wondering if it'll do the trick.

"Okay," the guy replies and opens the gate for me.

A minute later, I knock on the front door. I can hear the sound of footsteps approaching from inside while a golden retriever rushes up to sniff me. I get a wag of the tail as a sign of approval, so I grab his tennis ball and toss it. Like lightning, he bolts away to catch it, just in time as Annie Knowles opens the door.

"Who are you?" she asks, suddenly alert, her gaze bouncing back and forth behind me. She sees the gardener working on her bushes and realizes what happened. "Did that idiot let you in?"

"Mrs. Knowles, be kind. The man is innocent. I may have deceived him," I reply with a polite smile.

Now she looks worried. "What do you want?"

"I mean no harm, I just want to talk," I say. "About a friend we have in common. A certain Matthew Phelps."

Annie Knowles appears young for her mid-forties though I can tell that she has had some work done. I can see the faint lifting scars on her eyelids. The lip filler. Definitely some Botox involved. But if there's one thing that she couldn't cut away, it's a deep frown line as she measures me from head to toe, understanding the position she has just found herself in.

"Who are you?" she asks again. "I'm calling the cops."

"I'm a friend of Paul's," I say. "You might know him as Rooker's boss."

"Rooker?" Annie gasps, turning pale.

"As it turns out, I have something you need and you have something I need. How about you invite me in for a cup of coffee so we can discuss this in peace and out of sight. I doubt you want your nosy neighbors to learn about your son's gambling proclivities."

She thinks about it for a moment, briefly glaring at the gardener again. Something tells me the guy's going to be out of a job after I leave, but I cannot afford to feel responsible about his fate. My own fate concerns me more.

It takes another five minutes before I'm with a cup of coffee in hand, sitting across the kitchen table from Annie Knowles. The house is ever more beautiful on the inside, but there are signs of wear and tear, layers of grime and dust everywhere. By the looks of it, she could only afford to keep the gardener to maintain the outside appearance. Indoors, the place appears to be too much work for a woman who clearly ran out of money.

"You know Rooker," Annie mutters, watching me while I sip my coffee with slow and deliberate gestures.

"I don't. I know Paul, his boss. And I'm offering to pay your son's debt, interest included, in exchange for some information."

She cocks her head to the side. "That's a lot of money, mister…"

"Mr. Sokolov," I politely supply.

"Mr. Sokolov." My name sounds familiar to her, I can tell, but she doesn't immediately register who I am. Good. I've got a few more words before the real dread sets in, when she becomes aware of who's in her kitchen, casually drinking her coffee. "It is a lot of money. Seven-hundred thousand, if I'm not mistaken."

"Plus interest, another two-fifty," she sighs deeply.

"Your son went all out, didn't he?"

Annie scoffs and shakes her head. "I did my best with Henry, I swear, I really did. I paid for everything, his school, his courses, I made sure he had everything he ever needed, and how did he repay me?"

"You gave him too much," I reply with a wry smile. "Henry never learned the value of money, the effort one puts into hard work. Then again, all of this," I add, motioning around us, "it didn't come out of any hard work either, did it?"

"What do you mean?" she sounds offended.

"It's hush money. How can Henry appreciate hard work when you never set a good example for him?"

Annie's frown deepens. "Are you here to help me or are you here to insult me?"

"It's the truth, isn't it? You can't even afford a housekeeper anymore," I say. "And judging by the house—the expensive furniture, the high-end Italian light fixtures, the work you had done on yourself and what you just told me about your son's every whim having been satisfied—there's only one conclusion I can draw. You came into a shitload of money and you squandered it, one penny at a time, without any real consideration for the future. You never invested in anything, you simply let your son turn into a monetary black hole. And now, you're at your wit's end, desperate and broke, probably looking to sell some of the stuff in the house so you can put gas in that outrageously glossy Escalade parked in your driveway. How am I doing?"

"Who told you all of this? Was it Phelps? The prick wouldn't even take my calls. What's this about?" Annie grumbles, crossing her arms. Judging her is finished and it's time to move on to the next stage of this conquest.

"Mrs. Knowles, I need information from you. In exchange for that information, I will pay off Henry's debt. That's all you need to know. And it stays between the two of us. You'll never get a sweeter deal than this, I'm sure you're aware."

I can almost hear the wheels in her head turning, screeching loudly until she reaches the inevitable conclusion. "What do you want to know?"

"Why did you leave Matthew Phelps's campaign? What happened?"

Her jaw drops. "Oh. No, I can't talk about that."

"The Meridian Observer published a story about it," I continue, watching her closely. "They promised a follow-up with more details, having already done an interview with you at the time. But then they were bought and shut down. Said interview never saw the light of day, and you signed a non-disclosure agreement in the meantime. Shortly afterward, you moved here. I have eyes, Mrs. Knowles. I can see what happened. I just need to know the whole story."

"No. You just said it. I signed an NDA. I can't break it. They'll sue me. They'll ruin me."

"But Henry will be debt free and no longer in danger of losing his life. Isn't that a price worth paying? Your son's life? Because we both know Rooker will start cutting body parts off that boy until he's paid."

"Can't you talk to his boss?" Annie asks, growing increasingly desperate. There must be quite the conflict unraveling inside of her. "Can't you give Henry more time?"

"Why would I talk to Paul or anyone else about your son's misfortunes? The only way I help you is if you help me."

She's reached the dead end that she's been dreading. It's written all over her face in tiny pearls of sweat. "That stupid boy," she mumbles, closing her eyes for a moment. "He did it. He fucking ruined me."

"I think you ruined yourself with your lack of foresight. Henry's problem didn't emerge overnight," I say. "Anyway, these are the terms of the deal I'm offering. Henry's life and physical integrity in exchange for information."

"Mr. Sokolov, you have to understand, that NDA—"

"Was signed after you gave the interview with Meridian. I just want the content of the interview. That's all."

Annie blinks several times. For a moment, she looks relieved. But then another bout of despair takes over. "I don't have the tapes. I don't have a transcript, I don't have anything. They destroyed every single document and recording at Meridian after they were bought out. I know, because I tried to get copies when I heard about the takeover. I needed an insurance policy."

"Why?"

"Because Matthew's fixer was waiting for me to sign that fucking NDA and take his dirty money, and I wasn't sure what to do. I figured I could cover my ass somehow, but it didn't work. I had no choice but to sign and take the cash."

"You sound real broken up about it," I reply flatly.

Her lips twist with bitter contempt. "You had no idea what I went through, what I had to deal with. I was a single mother, living from paycheck to paycheck. I believed Matthew when he promised me the fucking world, when he…. No, I can't. I can't do this. I'm done covering Henry's ass. I have to sell the house, he's on his own."

"He's your son," I insist. "Rooker won't forgive him."

She's crying now. Struggling not to, but the tears flow freely, anxiously down her overly tanned cheeks. "I did the best I could."

"Mrs. Knowles, you need to understand something. No matter what you do or say, even what you don't do or don't say, somebody is going to get hurt. If you help me, I promise that Henry won't be the one, and that you'll have something to fall back on."

"What do you mean?"

"I can throw in an extra couple hundred grand to make your life easier. But if you keep saying no today, Henry will get hurt, and so will you," I say, leaning back into my seat.

Finally, her shoulders drop in shameful defeat. "I could tell you a lot of things about Matthew Phelps, but I wouldn't be able to prove it. He was rather good at covering his tracks over the years, even when I was working for him. But I heard rumors through the grapevine while I was trying to reach out to him recently."

"Rumors?"

"Yes. That's he's getting a little too close to one of his aides. Shelby something," Annie says, and I catch a hint of bitterness in her voice. I know the Shelby working for Phelps that she's talking about. Lyric's best friend. "And if I know Matthew, I'll say this—when he gets close to someone, when he gets intimate, he lets his guard down. There's plenty of incriminating material in his private study. You'll know it when you find it. But you have to find it first. And if the Shelby thing is real, she can tell you where it is."

"Look at you, singing like a little bird," I reply with a cocky grin.

"I can't breach that NDA, Mr. Sokolov. I'm afraid of those people. If my life sucks now, it'll suck even worse if they find out I'm talking to you. Please, understand."

"No, no, I get it," I say.

I get up and text Paul to confirm, along with a screenshot of a wire transfer. "Your son's debt is cleared."

"Thank you," she mumbles, relief changing the color of her cheeks ever so slightly.

"Just do yourself a favor and send that boy to rehab, otherwise, you'll keep ending up in the same place."

I walk out of the house with a weird sense of accomplishment. It didn't turn out exactly the way I had hoped, but I still got something out of it. Technically, it's a rumor, but rumors aren't born from thin air.

Someone in that campaign office saw something. Someone heard something. Conclusions were drawn, whispers were cast into the wind until one of them made it into Annie Knowles's ear. The woman is bitter and disgruntled, desperate enough to pass it on.

Whether it's accurate or not remains to be seen. It's better than nothing. We've got a different starting point for what comes next, and I intend to see it through to the end. I need this nightmare to be over. I want our lives to be ours again, without the Feds tailing us everywhere. I want Lyric to feel safe with us. She deserves love and happiness, peace and room to flourish. We can't give her that, not with Smith, Bowman, and Phelps grilling us from every direction.

They came after us, looking for a fight.

We're coming to them now, and we're bringing the war to their doorstep.

I'm done playing it clean and safe.

1 7

MAX

We've been making encouraging progress on our side of the problem. Ivan is following up on that intel regarding Shelby—unbeknownst to Lyric, of course.

We agreed that there's no point in causing strife between the two women without any concrete proof. We need evidence that there's an actual affair going on there. Fortunately, Ivan's street connections are panning out, and we've got plenty of useful and discreet eyes focused on Phelps's campaign.

Artur and I are having trouble getting the Bratva elders on board. Old man Larionov is adamant about marriage. We've had two conversations with him already, both in Polina's absence, and both have ended in a stalemate and a promise to think about it some more. The other families are split evenly between the traditional ways and the new ways that we're trying to implement.

"Unsurprisingly, it's the younger generation that's more eager to get on board," Artur mutters as we drive through the city. Ivan is in the backseat, checking CCTV footage of

Phelps's office on his phone, having tapped into the system with Lyric's remote help. "Amir, Vlad, the whole Petrovski clan, they're all happy to try new business ventures."

"They're tired of having to clean up after these other relics," Ivan says. "Gone are the days of making people disappear without a trace for the tiniest inconvenience or slight. It's the age of the internet, fellas. It's no longer easy for people to go missing with cameras everywhere."

"That, and the fact that the Feds have gotten better at boxing us in," I say. "It simply doesn't work like it did in the old days, but we can't exactly do everything we want to without the majority's support."

"Has Lyric said anything about Shelby lately?" Artur asks, changing the subject.

The neighborhood rises ahead, with Lyric's apartment building sparkling against the sunset sky. I shake my head slowly.

"She hasn't been saying much these days," I reply.

"Yeah, she's been quiet," Ivan adds. "Not her usual self. I wonder what's going on."

"I don't know. It's what I'm hoping to figure out tonight."

Artur gives me a worried look. "We've got eyes on the building, right?"

"Oh, definitely. We're going through the back door anyway just to be safe."

"We could've had dinner at the penthouse," Ivan says.

"True, but Lyric never confirmed. So I figured we'd bring dinner to her instead."

I can feel Artur and Ivan's gazes drilling holes into my head. All I can do is let out a heavy sigh as I keep my eyes on the traffic. It was a last-minute decision and I'm not a fan of popping up unannounced either, but Lyric's noticeable absence has me thinking unpleasant and confusing thoughts. I need to see her.

"Are we sure she's home?" Ivan asks.

I nod again. "Yeah. The boys confirmed that her car is parked out front."

Twenty minutes later, I park the SUV behind the apartment building. Ivan, Artur, and I sneak through the back door and make our way up, carefully checking every floor. There's no sign of hidden agents lurking in the shadows, so we stop outside Lyric's door and knock.

As soon as the door opens, the look on her face has my heart racing.

There is definitely something wrong.

"What are you guys doing here?" she asks, her bright blue eyes wider than ever. She nervously dips her head into the hallway. "Did anyone see you?"

"No, we're in the clear. Provided you let us in," I chuckle, trying to break the tension.

Lyric sighs and steps back. We walk in and make ourselves comfortable in the living room. Her laptop is on, lines of code running up the screen while a freshly brewed cup of tea rests beside it. I'm trying to analyze as much as possible before I shift my focus back to her. She's nervous, that much is obvious.

"Okay, so what's up?" Lyric asks, anxiously sitting in the armchair closest to the window, as if to keep a certain distance from us.

I don't like it. Every second that passes adds tension, straining my nerves beyond their reasonable limits. "I could ask you the same thing," I say, stealing a glance at Ivan and Artur. They're quiet, watching her like hawks, but I know they see what I see. "We figured you were busy since you haven't been very responsive lately. Is everything alright?"

"Yeah," she says, averting her eyes. It's irritating. "Just busy, like you figured."

"We could order in," I say. "Maybe Chinese? You loved Zhang's menu, didn't you? The spring rolls were your favorite, if I remember correctly."

She sighs heavily, finally gathering the nerve to look me in the eyes again. "I don't think so. I still have work to do," she says, pointing at her laptop.

"We'll wait," Ivan replies. The air thickens between us. I don't like being lied to, but Ivan, he *hates* it. The slightest scent of a lie turns him inside out, transforming him into a bloodhound. He won't let her be until she tells us what's going on. "Unless you want to skip past the bullshit and tell us what's really going on."

"What do you mean?" she asks, her pitch subtly higher than usual.

"Lyric, we're not idiots. There is clearly something affecting you," I say, trying to remain as calm and as courteous as possible, even though my blood is starting to boil. "What is it?"

It takes a while for the words to come out but she finally says them.

"I think we need to take a break."

My stomach feels heavy. Deep down, I think I saw it coming. The situation we're dealing with was bound to lead us here, no matter how badly we wanted it to turn out differently.

"What is this about?" I ask, mustering every ounce of patience I have left.

Ivan leans back into the sofa, his eyes never leaving her. Artur shifts uncomfortably in his seat but stays quiet.

"A series of events, I guess," Lyric replies. "Maybe I should've told you about it sooner, but I thought I could handle it on my own. I didn't want to add more pressure to an already boiling pot."

"What. Is. This. About?" I ask again, adding emphasis to each word.

She gives me a pained look. "Smith approached me outside the library last week. He warned me about you. Kept asking questions about the bail. I lied, obviously. I told him you paid me for an IT project in advance and you asked for that money back to cover Ivan's bail because your accounts were frozen."

"That obviously didn't fly," Artur mutters.

"No, it didn't. But he didn't have any proof against me, either. He had no choice but to leave me alone, for the time being."

"You definitely should've told us about this sooner," I say.

"That same day, my father asked to see me," Lyric sighs heavily. "He also warned me about getting involved with you. It was an unpleasant conversation, but I pushed him away, telling him the same lie I told Smith. I'll stick to it until the end of days, for what it's worth."

"With a little bit of luck, you won't have to," I try to sway her softly back to us. The mere thought of not having Lyric with us makes me feel unpleasant and uncomfortable things. I wasn't ready for this, even though an inkling of it had been testing my thoughts since I noticed her distance in our text conversations. "Lyric, we're close to getting the dirt we need on your father. That's the first step in our crusade, and we're almost there."

"Polina also came to see me again."

Ivan shakes his head slowly. "It never fucking stops, does it?"

"She was adamant that you and she are about to be married, reminding me that I don't belong in your world, and that there will be consequences if I don't back off. I know you don't want it, but if Polina could track me down so easily, I reckon she can also make me disappear with a simple snap of her fingers, if I keep being an inconvenience to her plan."

"She wouldn't dare," I say. "It would be the death of her."

"I'll wipe the Larionov's out myself," Ivan snaps.

Lyric frowns. "You wouldn't be able to save me, though. You'd only be able to avenge me. What good will that do if I'm dead?"

Fucking hell. This conversation is the result of days' worth of mulling it over for Lyric. It's not a decision she made lightly, but I can tell from the look in her eyes that she has made up her mind, and it's tearing her apart on the inside.

Her fingers quiver nervously over her knees. Her lips part slowly with each heavy breath. Tears glisten in her eyes as she tries not to look at us too much, knowing she might break down completely. I can almost feel her pain because it mirrors mine, and I know I'm not the only one who feels this way.

"We can protect you," Artur says. "Now that we've been made aware, we can take precautions."

"You're fighting a difficult war already," Lyric replies. "I'll only hold you back. It's not safe for you. I am your weakness and those around you are starting to pick up on it. It's my fault. The minute I posted that bail, I knew we'd end up here, sooner or later."

"Lyric don't do this," Ivan says. "We can work something out."

"I'll help however I can, remotely. I'll help you take my father down," Lyric sighs. "I'll gather all the information we have so far and run it through the algorithm. I'll give you the odds on every possible scenario until you have a solid strategy to win, but I need to keep my distance. I'm sorry."

She is sorry. I know she is.

But it doesn't stop my heart from bleeding with every beat as I stand up and give her a long, meaningful look. "Are you sure about this?" I ask in a low voice. "The last thing I want to do is keep you somewhere that doesn't feel safe."

"What are you doing?" Artur cuts in, clearly befuddled by my decision. "No, we have to—"

"We have to let Lyric decide," Ivan cuts him off. He doesn't like this either, but he's following my lead as my brother has always done.

"I'm sorry you feel this way," I tell her, working hard to keep an even tone and my eyes on hers without my soul twisting itself into an agonizing pretzel. "But if it's what you want, we'll oblige."

"Honestly, it's not what I want. However, it's what needs to happen because they're circling us like vultures, and it's only a matter of time before one of them finds an opportunity to blow it all up," she says.

I am at a loss for words. Every fiber in my body screams, begging me to fight for her, but I know and I understand where she's coming from. Ivan and Artur can see it as well.

The truth is, we are fragile.

When we're with Lyric, we're fragile. Vulnerable. We let Bowman go because Smith paid her a distressing visit. Bowman. We had him, and we let him go. I should've known then that it would come back to bite us in the ass. And here we are.

As I walk out of Lyric's apartment flanked by Artur and Ivan, I make it my mission to pay those fuckers in kind for everything they've done, for everything they tried to do, and for everything they're about to do.

"We're taking the war to them," I state to my brother and best friend.

"Burn it all down," Ivan agrees.

18

ARTUR

The following days feel like an agonizingly slow torture.

I can't sleep. I can barely eat. I keep checking my phone, looking to see when Lyric was last online.

We're worried about her.

As long as Smith, Bowman, and Phelps are on the loose, I don't think Lyric will ever be truly safe.

"She's inside." Max's voice knocks me from my thoughts.

It's a chilly evening, close to midnight, and the city's hustle and bustle has dwindled with the late hours. My nerves are fried and everyone I see feels like a potential enemy. It could be paranoia on account of everything that has happened over the past few months, or it could be the simmering anger morphing into anxiety, playing tricks on my mind in Lyric's absence.

Either way, I'm fucking miserable, and my brain is working overtime to keep me focused.

"Phelps's secretary, you mean?" I ask, looking around, making sure we weren't followed.

"Yeah. We've had eyes on the building since the last volunteers left a couple of hours ago," Max confirms. "I'm not sure what she's still doing up there."

"She'll tell us," Ivan replies.

"You'll make sure of it," I chuckle dryly.

We make our way up the steps and through the front doors, stopping by the night guard's desk first. I flash the guy a fake badge—one of the many we use for more covert operations such as this. "We're here to speak to Miss Sullivan. I understand she hasn't clocked out yet," I say.

"Fourth floor," he replies, not giving us a second thought.

I give him a thankful nod and lead Ivan and Max to the elevator, occasionally glancing back to find the chunky guard with his feet up on the desk, flipping through a smut magazine.

"If only all our missions were this easy," Ivan mutters as we step into the elevator.

"We haven't gotten to the hard part yet," Max warns.

The elevator doors slide shut. A minute later, we walk into the bullpen of Matthew Phelps's campaign office. Posters of him hang everywhere, his white plastic smile plastered over every damned wall.

He appears charming and handsome at first glance. No wonder he's got the support of the middle-class so tightly in his grasp. He looks like the friendly next-door neighbor who will water your plants for you while you're on vacation.

To my dismay, however, the place isn't as empty as we'd thought.

"Shit," I mumble as I see Phelps's secretary coming out of his office. She's not alone. Two men in dark suits accompany her, and they've spotted us. "Guys…"

"It's cool. I've got this." Max takes the lead.

We keep walking but I'm no longer sure what we're walking into. Four FBI agents come out of an office to our left. Four more from the right. My heart starts beating faster, my eyes zooming all over the place to register every possible detail. Beads of sweat bloom on my temples.

"I thought the place was empty," I whisper.

"Our guys were clearly wrong," Ivan replies, a muscle twitching in his jaw. He's pissed off. "This isn't going to end well."

"Keep cool," Max mutters.

Director Smith is one of the two men with Phelps's secretary, and the grin slitting his face is enough to make me feel nauseated. "I was wondering how long it would take you to get here," he says with a casual and unconcerned tone. "We've been waiting for you, gentlemen."

"Waiting for us?" Max asks.

We meet halfway across the open area in the middle of the bullpen. Stacks of flyers and manila folders cover almost every workspace. Dozens of phones. Computers. Stickers with Phelps's mug everywhere.

"What are you doing here?" Max asks Smith.

"I could ask you the same question," Smith replies. "Actually, my first question is how'd you get up here?"

"The night guard let us through," I calmly cut in with a nonchalant shrug.

Smith gives me a hard look. "Hm. Guess somebody's getting fired tonight. I told that idiot not to let anybody in."

"What do you want, Director Smith?" Max draws his focus away from me, while the secretary watches our exchange with tense and weary interest.

"Are you deaf? I'm asking the questions here," Smith shoots back. "What do *you* want?"

"We were hoping to speak to Councilman Phelps. Alone. I take it he's not here?"

His agents inch closer, almost unnoticeably so at first glance. They have their hawk-like eyes fixated on us, hands on their holstered weapons. They can't be stupid enough to open fire in the office, so my guess is they're going for good old-fashioned intimidation.

"You know he's not here," Smith says. "And we both know it's not the reason for your visit."

"What other reason is there?" Max asks with a raised eyebrow.

Smith scoffs, raising his chin in sheer arrogance. "Miss Sullivan here is the object of your attention. Go on, ask her what you want to ask her, then be on your way."

For a split second, I'm speechless. I see Max's gaze narrow. How did these fuckers know we were coming to see Shelby? As if reading my thoughts, Smith continues. "I know everything that you're doing. I know where you go, who you meet with, what your endgame is. I know it all, and it's time for you to understand that. You have nothing to surprise us with. Nothing to scare us with. And rest assured, you're never setting foot in this building ever again. You're not to come anywhere close to Miss Sullivan. If I so much as catch a whiff of you in the air, I'll—"

"You'll what? Get a restraining order? Arrest us? For what?" Max chuckles dryly. "You've run out of reasons, Director. You've run out of warrants. And soon enough, you'll be running out of excuses and support, too."

Smith takes a step forward. He's about half-a-head shorter than Max, but he's well-built and bold enough to stand up to the three of us. My guess is that the badge and gun give him a certain kind of false confidence. "I will do whatever it takes to see you and your whole organization burned to the ground," he says. "If you think you're going to reinvent the wheel, you've got another thing coming, Mr. Sokolov. The world doesn't want change. Even your own people agree."

"No number of threats will stop us from what we have to do," Max replies. "Your threats, however, are proof of repetitive harassment. I will be filing a complaint directly with Quantico about this."

"You go ahead and do that. See how many more raids you can withstand before one of you finally breaks and you let things stay the way they're supposed to stay."

"Nothing stays the same forever. Change is inevitable. Adapt or die, Director. It's been the way of the world since long before this great country was even founded."

Smith laughs lightly. "You must be delusional to think that you three have what it takes to institute real change in a system designed precisely against it. I will enjoy destroying you, that's for sure."

"Max, let's go," Ivan cautiously places a hand on his brother's shoulder. "They're itching for a fight. We're not going to give them one."

To my surprise, Ivan is the one talking sense and advocating against any form of violence. Then again, he's got two good eyes and he knows how to use them. We are outnumbered and outgunned, two to one. And I'll bet there are more agents waiting in a van or two somewhere outside.

"I know, I know," Smith says. "You were hoping to come in here, take Miss Sullivan by surprise, and maybe squeeze her until you get your dirt on Matthew Phelps. We're just here to make you understand that you, Mr. Sokolov, are not ahead of us in any way. If anything, we're ahead of you."

"Is that why you haven't been able to make any charges against us stick?" Max replies. "Because you're eons ahead of us?"

Smith is getting angry. I firmly grasp Max's arm and pull him back. "Come on, let's go."

"It's a matter of when, not if," Smith says.

"Let's go," I say to Max again.

"That goes both ways," he tells Smith, then turns away.

Shelby is wide-eyed and quiet. I think she's scared, but not necessarily scared of us. She keeps staring at us, hope twinkling and dying slowly in her gaze, while Smith's lips twist into a sickening smile as he savors this minor victory.

We walk back to the elevator, constantly aware of the number of federal agents just waiting for one of us to make the wrong move, to justify the unholstering of every gun on these premises.

"We're not giving them that satisfaction," Max grumbles as we go into the elevator. "This is fucked up."

"And then some," Ivan sighs. "They knew we were coming. They were waiting for us."

Downstairs is no longer empty either. A dozen more agents have entered the building, standing close to the doors and watching us as we leave. The amount of discomfort that I'm experiencing has my senses flaring every which way while I keep my sights ahead and hope to make it back to the car without an altercation.

"Somebody told them," Max replies.

His steps grow faster and heavier as we get closer to his SUV, parked just across the street. Next to it is a black van, the side door half open, revealing a snippet of a fully-equipped SWAT operative. These bastards were ready to come in, guns blazing, if we got even a single inch out of line.

"Somebody told them," Max says again when we're back at our office behind closed doors and with double the security downstairs.

"Heard you the first time," Ivan replies, pouring himself a drink. "But who?"

"Who knew?" I ask as I sink into one of the guest chairs across from Max's desk while he gets behind the computer, rubbing his temples. "The three of us knew. And nobody else."

For the briefest of seconds, Ivan and Max give me a long, curious look. I become heated as I sit up straight and shake my head in dismay.

"You do have a history of oversharing," Max sighs.

"I told Polina about our moves all those years ago because we were in a relationship with her. I thought we could trust her. You both thought we could trust her too," I shoot back, anger coursing fiercely hot through my veins. "Dammit, Max, are you ever going to let me live that down?"

Ivan clears his throat. "In Artur's defense, we were just as stupid at the time, brother. He's right. We can't point fingers at one another here. It would mean that Smith has already won."

"I'm sorry," Max says to me. "It's just, who would've told them? We have a mole in the organization. The Feds knew too much already, long before the events of tonight. But Smith clearly had inside information."

I keep looking around the office, trying to find something, some inanimate object to focus on while I attempt to figure out what happened. It's better than dwelling over a past that none of us can change. Polina screwed us over once, and we each played a part in that miserable situation.

We can't let Smith or a potential mole threaten our bond. What Max, Ivan, and I have is more than a simple friendship. It's more than a brotherhood. It's a connection that will survive anything as long as we never forget where we came from, and where it is that we strive to get to.

"We talked about approaching Sullivan over the past couple of days while at the penthouse," I say, deciding to focus on the solution rather than the problem. "Maybe they found out that we own it and they bugged it."

Ivan shakes his head. "We sweep for bugs every two days."

"Long-range mics, then? From a neighboring apartment?" I suggest.

"We own the whole floor," he casually reminds me.

"We talked about Sullivan in the car," Max chimes in. "Never mind, that gets swept for bugs on a daily basis."

"Hey," I mumble, chills running down my spine. "We had a conversation about it not long after our meeting with the Larionov's the other day."

And there it is. The flicker of realization, flashing hot-white in Max and Ivan's green eyes as they both look at me, a half second before Max starts digging through CCTV footage. We have cameras mounted everywhere, including hidden ones in tricky angles for anybody who's aware and determined enough to try and bug our office.

It takes a few minutes, but Max pulls the footage from our Larionov meeting, while Ivan and I join him in front of the screen.

"Okay," he says, hitting the play button. "Here's Larionov and Polina, coming into the office. His guards stayed outside."

"Right," Ivan replies. "Fast forward a bit."

We watch the footage at triple speed and I notice something odd about Polina. "Hold up, slow it down," I say, then point at the screen. "Look at her."

"She takes off her ring," Max mumbles, eyes narrowing as he leans forward toward the screen. "Let me zoom in."

A couple of seconds later, the three of us bear witness to the greatest insult that a Larionov can commit against the Sokolov's and the Bratva itself. In the video, it's clear that Polina had a small recording device hidden underneath her dramatically large, pink quartz ring.

I remember cracking a joke about it being potentially classified as a blunt object and deadly weapon during the meeting —a meeting that none of us wanted to be in but had to— because the Bratva needs the Larionov's, unfortunately.

"Look," I say. "She leans forward here, to straighten her shoe strap, supposedly."

Ivan immediately moves away from the desk and kneels next to the chair in question. He leans all the way down while Max and I listen to his hand patting the bottom of the upholstery. He comes back up holding a small device the size of a penny, just a little bit thicker, disgust giving his face a pale hue.

"Our sweeps didn't find this," Max says. "Why? We have detectors for this kind of stuff."

"It's ceramic plated," Ivan replies. "Next generation, Quantico-developed. Only the upper echelon of the FBI's division has access to this type of tech."

I blow out a breath, quickly putting two-and-two together. "You've got to be kidding me."

Max leans back into his chair. "Polina's working with the local Feds? It can't be."

"The Larionov's working with the local Feds isn't the craziest scenario," Ivan surmises. "Not when Larionov is still so keen to keep the Bratva in cahoots with local law enforcement, to keep the corruption and bribery machine well-oiled across Chicago."

It makes my stomach sink like a lead weight.

"Polina planted a fucking bug in our office," I say. "This is insane. This can't be happening."

"Oh, but it is," Ivan replies. "She's probably doing her father's bidding."

"It's in her best interest as well, to keep us from accomplishing what we're trying to do," Max says. "She should be ready to embrace the consequences of her actions, though. She knows how this game is played."

"Now we have an even bigger problem," I say, as the whole picture comes into sudden focus. "This bug has been recording for what, six days?"

"Yes," Ivan says.

"Six days' worth of private conversations have reached federal ears," I reply. Ice courses through my veins, tension thickening in the pit of my stomach as the possible repercussions begin to emerge, one awful layer after the other. "They know way more than just our intended visit tonight."

Max frowns deeply, staring at the screen. "Yet it's Sullivan they decided to focus on. Why?"

"They want us to stick to our original lane," Ivan says. "They want the Bratva right where it is, laundering money, paying their people off, making back door deals and feeding into the great machine that the chuckleheads at the FBI's field office have put together over the past few decades. They want us running the same illicit affairs, the same under-the-radar businesses while they continue pretending to hunt us down, to keep up appearances. That's it. That's the whole gist."

"The Larionov's want the same," I conclude. "Hence why Polina did this."

"All that wedding crap is nothing more than her own personal whim. A whim that old man Larionov decided to indulge, if only for her to be rejected again while she planted a bug and made herself useful, anyway." Max groans and pinches the bridge of his nose. "Jesus Christ, they're a twisted fucking family."

"We need to close ranks," Ivan warns. "And we need to update our security measures."

We need to do a lot more than that. There were several sensitive topics that may have reached Smith's ears aside from our intention to privately accost Sullivan and get access to Phelps's secret documents.

There were conversations about Lyric, too. I desperately try to remember what was mentioned about her. Hopefully, nothing important, only trivial stuff that might've gone unnoticed.

Then again, what are the odds, given the shitstorm that we walked into earlier?

Slim-to-fucking-none.

19

LYRIC

It's been quiet for the past few days. On the outside, anyway.

On the inside, however, a storm has been raging. Thousands of thoughts blowing through, crackling and clapping, making it impossible for me to focus on pretty much anything.

I need to pull myself together. I finally made it to my interview with Jack Bowman after several instances of rescheduling in the span of a week. I'm nervous and terrified for multiple reasons, but I need to go through with this in order to maintain appearances.

"He'll be ready for you in a minute," his PA tells me as she comes out of his office.

I give her a slight nod. "Thank you."

Glancing around, I see the man spared no expense to make his HQ as sleek and as luxurious as possible. I recognize the Italian lights and the Tuscan, handmade furniture—it must've cost him a fortune. And to think he started out as a government employee, putting white collar criminals away. Now, the guy turns billions over like it's just another walk in the park.

He lives and breathes money, which is why I'm interviewing him for my doctorate thesis in the first place.

But knowing what I know now, I see him in a much different light than I did when I had the original interview planned.

I don't admire him; there's nothing admirable about a man who is at the top of a pyramid built on schemes, corruption, and bribery. There's nothing admirable about a man who played the victim and manipulated the media to wage a war against the Sokolov's, just as they're working to turn their Bratva businesses legit.

He's a monster. I need to be careful and approach him as such, no matter how successful or how charming he might be.

Oh, God, I want to puke.

Today's bout of morning sickness has been more acute than usual. My OB-GYN said it's because of my high stress levels. Unfortunately, I don't see them coming down anytime in the near future.

"Lyric!" Bowman exclaims as he steps out of his office with a broad smile. "I'm so glad we're finally able to do this interview!"

"Mr. Bowman," I greet him, getting up from my seat.

He reaches out to shake my hand. "Please, call me Jack. Come in."

I follow him into his office and he closes the door behind us, my heart thudding as I cautiously approach the guest sofa. He takes a seat next to it, then gingerly proceeds to pour a cup of tea for me. "Thank you," I say and help myself to a tentative sip.

"Given that it's raining cats and dogs out there, I figured you'd enjoy a smidge of ginger and lemon," he chuckles softly, then leans back into his chair, ever so smug.

It pisses me off. Why can't he actually be the good guy that he's been pretending to be? Instead, he's a human farce, a monster, pulling the strings of others for profit and influence. I actually thought he wanted to make a difference in the world, only to learn that his entire business profile was built on lies.

I'll have to amend my algorithm accordingly, which means another month of data input before I'm able to extract realistic scenarios for my thesis.

"I'm glad we were finally able to do this," I say, struggling to smile. "When I heard about what happened to you, with the kidnapping and all—"

"Oh, terrible thing, I know. But I'm bouncing back. How's your dad? I haven't spoken to him in a few days now."

"Busy with his campaign. I reckon you talk to him more than I do, actually."

"He's going to be president someday. You know that, right?"

God, I hope not. I hope the truth comes out. I hope there is some justice left in this world, because I don't want this baby to be part of a future where the evil hide in plain sight, corrupting innocent souls purely for the love of money and influence. It sickens me to even think about it.

Instead of an answer, I change the subject. "Have you had a chance to look over the preparatory emails I sent by any chance?"

"Yes, I did. I'm ready. Hit me," he laughs, then runs a hand through his hair, fine lines sharpening at the corners of his tired eyes. "I'm eager to answer and help you put together one hell of a doctorate thesis. Assuming, of course, that you will give me a chance to test that algorithm of yours when it gets to the next stage of research."

"It would be my pleasure." I lie. If he's not rotting in a jail cell by then.

He smiles and nods delightedly. "When do you think you'll be ready for the first round of trials?"

"Hopefully, next year, if I get my desk at University of Chicago. Their research department is at the forefront of this—"

"You won't have to worry about that. I'll make a few calls—" he tries to cut me off.

"Jack, please don't," I politely stop him. "I'll tell you the same thing I told my father, I'd rather get there on my own. On proper merit. It's the right way, especially for an algorithm that may reshape the future altogether. I need to make sure I'm worthy of it, if that makes sense."

Jack pauses for a moment, tilting his head slightly as he carefully analyzes my expression. "I must admit Lyric, I am genuinely impressed by you already."

"How so?"

"Well, you're a beautiful young woman, first and foremost."

"Thank you."

"You are obviously brilliant. Your IQ and Mensa membership speak volumes on the matter. Your father speaks highly of you, despite what he described as a complicated father-daughter relationship in the absence of your mother."

He's going for the feels now. Hitting me where he knows it might sting a little. Luckily, I saw this coming. I spent the past few days running different scenarios through the algorithm regarding this meeting and its potential outcomes, just to practice a few more volatile parameters. I wonder how many of the results I got will turn out to be accurate.

I nod slowly. "Yes, well, politics and I never got along."

"Nor should you," Jack says. "Unlike your father, I think you need to remain non-partisan. You're a scientist, Lyric. I don't believe you belong anywhere near politics. The same can be said about your algorithm, despite what Matthew says."

"I'm surprised you think that way."

"Well, I've met my fair share of politicians, and while I love and support your father, your technology is crucial in other aspects of life. It shouldn't serve as a tool for congressmen and senators to win elections and get more donations for future campaigns. The whole political machine is precisely that, a never-ending cycle of pumping money into advertising. Matthew can handle himself fine, he doesn't need your algorithm."

I give him a wry smile. "I'm pleased to see how much faith you have in him." I'm getting better at lying.

"And I have just as much faith in you, Lyric. Which is why I'm glad you're here. I'm glad that we're able to have this conversation, and most importantly, I'm glad you ended it with the Sokolov's. They were a terrible influence on you."

The words whizz past me and I barely register them.

Yet when I do, my entire world comes crashing down around me. I freeze in my seat, staring at Bowman in disbelief. I shouldn't be shocked. Of course he knows about my involvement with the Sokolov's. He's the head of the snake that Max, Ivan, and Artur have been working so hard to cut off. Smith is his henchman. My own father is his crony.

Bowman most likely knows about me and my connection to the Sokolov's because I posted Ivan's bail. Once I did that, I was fair game for these monsters.

"You don't have to worry about a thing," he tries to reassure me, though I can tell he is subtly pleased by my reaction. "I understand. Some men can be charming. They can entice you and use you as they see fit," he says. "But I'm glad your wisdom prevailed and you ended it."

"I'm not sure what it is you think I ended with them, though."

"Whatever it was, it's none of my business," Bowman replies. "I just want them as far away from you and your father as possible. Don't forget, they kidnapped me. They held me hostage for days."

"I thought you said you didn't know for sure it was them?"

His lips twist into an arrogant smirk. "You may be a genius Lyric, but I'm pretty high up on the IQ scale as well, if you remember."

"My apologies, I didn't mean to offend you." I sense the need to tread carefully here.

"You need to understand something, Lyric, and I'm glad we have the opportunity to talk about this now. The Sokolov's are going down for a multitude of reasons. Their expectations of the future are unrealistic. You can't polish a turd and call it gold, and that is precisely what they're trying to do. The Bratva serves its purpose as is, the same purpose for over a hundred years.

"The mere fact that they think they can push it into a different, more legitimate direction isn't just a wild dream, it's pure delusion. The Sokolov's are fighting a system designed by their fathers and grandfathers. They're fighting a system designed by *my* father and grandfather. They will never succeed."

"You give them little credit," I say. "According to my algorithm…"

I pause as Bowman bursts into a bout of copious laughter. "You ran them through your algorithm? You sweet, naive child."

"I'm not sure I understand what's funny here."

I'm also not sure how much longer I can keep this fake pleasantry up. Bowman clearly isn't interested in partaking in an actual interview with me. He's more interested in showboating and teasing me about the Sokolov's. There's a play here, and it seems that I am meant to be one of his pawns, which makes me wonder what his endgame is, at least where I'm concerned.

He knows I'm not seeing Max, Ivan, and Artur anymore, regardless of the nature of our dynamic. It's his way of telling me he stays informed about his enemies.

"Okay, let me try to put things in perspective for you," Bowman says. "You're a brilliant woman, a mastermind about to change history in many ways. Your father is a good man and a sharp, promising politician. Yet somehow, you managed to get involved with the Bratva and have seen more law enforcement in a month than most people do their whole lives. Is this how you wish to fail, Lyric? By associating yourself with the worst of the worst?"

"Jack, forgive me, but I had a business relationship with the Sokolov's. Nothing more, nothing less."

"Let's assume I believe that" he replies dryly, "and that you weren't getting in deep with them. It's beside the point, anyway. Even a business relationship could spell doom for your academic career. They're toxic, they're dangerous, they're the scourge of our society, and I will do everything in my power to take them, and all of their associates out for good. I've got your father's support in this, along with the Bureau."

"Is that what you're determined to do?" I ask, my tone flat. I'm getting kind of tired of hearing the same crap, over and over again. "Or are you just determined to make sure they stay in their lane and do nothing about a system that has brought you colossal profits and influence?"

"I'm offended."

"*I'm* offended by the amount of self-righteous bullshit that you and my father and Director Smith keep trying to feed me. You all shower me with compliments, saying that I'm so intelligent, that nothing gets past me, yet all I hear coming out of your mouths are layers upon layers of shameless lies. I must really look stupid to you." I pause, giving Bowman a moment to blink and gather his thoughts. "Why did you call me here today? It obviously wasn't for an actual interview. You couldn't give a rat's ass about my thesis. You know damn well that I can finish my dissertation without any of your precious quotes."

"There she is," Bowman chuckles, increasingly satisfied with my reaction. "The kitty does have claws. Smith was right about you."

"I just want to be left alone."

"And that is precisely what I called you in for, my apologies for the slight deception," he says. "I wanted to make sure that you are, indeed, done with them."

"Why?"

"Because they're about to get wiped off the face of the earth and I promised your father that I would at least try to keep you out of it. You can't stop what's coming, Lyric. You can't change a world that has no interest in being changed. Personally, I doubt your algorithm will get anywhere, because no one really wants things to be different. If they did, the streets would be burning, day in and day out. The whole planet would rebel. Nations would unite. But nobody wants that utopia that you and the Sokolov's envision."

"*You* don't want it. You and those who profit from the chaos."

He smiles broadly. The sheer sight of him makes me sick to my stomach. "Consider this your only warning. I sure hope you're truly done with the Sokolov's, Lyric. Because you don't want to be anywhere near them when we go after them. The Bratva as a whole will remain as it is, serving the same purpose as always, until they are deemed useless.

"If you don't keep your distance, you will find yourself engulfed in something neither I, nor your father, will be able to save you from. Matthew may not be Father of the Year, but he does love you. I'd like him to get the opportunity to see you grow old."

Slowly, I grab my bag and get up, only to realize that my knees have gotten weak. "Will that be all?" I ask, trying to keep my voice from trembling.

"Send me those interview questions in an email and I'll reply with some nice quotes for your paper. Let's keep it civil until the end, shall we?"

I simply nod.

He watches, still smiling, as I walk out of his office. I glide past the PA, barely mumbling a goodbye as I head straight for the elevator. By the time I'm downstairs I'm virtually running out of Bowman's building. My heart is thudding and my breath comes quick as the world spins all around me.

Having lost control over my senses, I shudder and stop for a moment, waiting for a semblance of clarity to return. Whatever it is they're planning against the Sokolov's, it's going to happen soon. I broke it off with them because I need this baby of mine to be protected, but I did promise to help them from afar and I intend to keep that promise. I've already supplied them with all the information I had about my father, and I still have some scenarios running through the algorithm. I need to speed that process up and start looking deeper into it.

Bowman thinks he's got me figured out. He also thinks that he cannot be stopped. It's precisely this level of over-confidence that caused greater men throughout history to fall. Empires have crumbled on account of a leader's obtuse vision. Bowman isn't some fresh-minded entrepreneur.

No, he's just more of the same, simply wrapped up in a different style and color.

20

LYRIC

Hours pass slowly as I stare at two different screens of data. Scans of various documents, photographs, records, strings of code and text notes. I'm dealing with police files, public information, webpages, forums, webchats. I had my algorithm tap into the world wide web itself—a dangerous gambit since it could return too many results, but so far, so good.

I'm building a series of parameters to deliver a clear and immediately available scenario. For that, I need insane amounts of details, and it's something I need to do manually. Fortunately, there's enough food in the fridge to keep me sated at least until the weekend. I don't want to have to leave my computer unless it's to eat, sleep or shower. I'm way too invested.

"I need a connection between Bowman and Phelps," I speak into the microphone that's connected to my laptop. The algorithm's AI assistant picks up my request and inputs it through its program. "Something specific and verifiable, to tie Jack Bowman to Matthew Phelps. Go as far back as college or high school. I never learned how my father and Bowman met."

The software chirps in response while I go back to perusing various police records. Nothing I've come up with has managed to bring me closer to a satisfying conclusion, but I have a feeling that the truth lies somewhere in a much greater picture, one of which my mind isn't able to process. A computer, on the other hand, if dealt with correctly, could be a game changer.

"Now add all the information we've gathered about my father's campaign contributors," I say. "We need to find a link between the campaign donations and the Chicago FBI office. Include employees of the field office, please. All of them. Payments were made, from proxy to proxy most likely, until the paper trail was lost. We have to find it."

As the program continues its work, I make myself another cup of tea and walk over to the window, briefly checking my phone. There's a message from Max that I haven't had the courage to read. It's been in my inbox for an hour.

Are you okay? he asks.

With trembling fingers, I type a reply. *Thanks, I'm okay. All good.*

I know they have eyes on me. I don't see them but I'm aware that I'm being tailed by at least one of their bodyguards at all times. It does give me a sense of security. I sleep better at night knowing that despite the way we ended it, they care about me and they still look after me.

How'd the Bowman interview go? Max texts back.

I don't know how to answer that. They're already aware that he's gunning for them, and Bowman didn't give me any details that they might find useful.

It was weird for me but I got all the information I needed.

Are you sure?

I promise.

"Processing complete," the AI machine beeps and delivers a vocal notification.

I freeze, mug in hand, and stare at the screen for a while.

"This is the first time you've moved so fast," I mumble. "What gives?"

Slowly, I pull my chair closer to the desk and start reading through the report. The algorithm is correct at a glance. The lines of code are there, all the parameters I fed into it. Processing time is shorter than ever, which is quite the accomplishment. I should pat myself on the back, but the scenario and conclusions that my own work has delivered sends shivers down my spine.

Each concluding statement comes with visual and sound attachments. Photographs collected from the obscurest corners of the world wide web. Documents. Scanned newspaper articles. Police reports. Receipts. Absolutely everything I need to confirm with remarkable confidence that...

"My father and John Bowman go back over thirty years," I say with a shuddering sigh. "They met early on in college, same fraternity, same parties and clubs. Jesus, they even dated the same women over the years, my mother not included."

The more I read, the more appalled I become.

Bowman and my father stayed close over the years. Small business endeavors on the side. Joint charity organizations. Weekends away with cops and federal agents.

Holy shit.

This is an old and well-oiled machine, and my father stands somewhere on the higher level. He's been there for years while Bowman has been its de facto leader since day one. Smith joined later. The organization itself has a wide reach, but Max and the guys were right, from what I can tell. It's all concentrated within the Bureau's Chicago field office, which has gathered the most complaints.

The majority were shelved, only to be made available to the public many years later through the FOIA. The few that were investigated turned up little to nothing, and only a handful resulted in penalties of any kind.

My father benefited aplenty from Bowman's movements. There were investigations opened against his campaign at another field office, but the Chicago boys stepped in, taking over and shelving those, as well.

It's true—my father is one of the main players on the board. Everything makes sense now, and it scares the hell out of me because I already have a difficult relationship with the man. At this point, I'm not even sure I ever really knew him.

What does he want?

How far is he willing to go in order to get it?

And where does that leave me?

I don't have an answer. I only have more questions as the algorithm continues to produce results, updating the scenario with each passing minute. With trembling hands, I pick up my phone and text Max again.

We need to talk about my father.

21

———————————

LYRIC

As evening settles in and the city becomes shrouded in darkness and twinkling lights, I open the door to my apartment for Max, Ivan, and Artur. It's been a while since we last saw each other, and the atmosphere is noticeably tense and awkward between us.

They get settled on the sofa and I bring out some sodas along with cheese and crackers, mostly out of courtesy.

No one here has an appetite. Not even me.

"Are you okay?" Max asks, giving me a long and curious look as I sit in the armchair closest to the window. It seems to be my go-to spot the last few times they've been here.

"I'm fine, just really tired. You?"

They look great. Sharp as always. Seeing them now makes me realize how badly I've missed them.

Heat is already pooling between my legs. My heart feels like it's beating a million beats per minute. This is going to be the most difficult platonic sit-down of my entire life.

"We're taking it one day at a time," Max says. "The Feds won't leave us alone. They're opening one investigation after another, but they haven't raided any of our places of business lately."

"There's a rumor going around that they're putting together a massive joint RICO task force," Artur adds. "Some kind of interagency alliance, led by the Chicago field office and aimed at us in particular."

"Oh God," I mumble, my blood running cold.

Max chuckles softly. "It's okay. We've had RICO crosshairs pointed at us before, and they had more evidence then as opposed to what they're trying to pull now. They can't touch us."

"What about the other Bratva families?" I ask. "Aren't they your allies?"

"Most of them, yes, and they know to close ranks when they start recognizing surveillance drones and vans," Max says.

"And the ones that aren't allies?" I inquire, crossing my arms. My breasts feel a bit more tender, a sign that my body continues to adapt to its new, secret little tenant.

Ivan leans forward, his eyes drilling holes into my soul. "They are stupid and they will pay. Right now, they're feeding the Feds all kinds of false intel. We made sure to plant some bad seeds in the garden so it'll be easier to weed them out later."

"Good grief."

"You said you wanted to talk about your father," Max says. "I suppose it's related to our current issue, yes?"

I nod slowly and point to the tablet on the coffee table. "I loaded everything there. My algorithm yielded some pretty interesting, albeit unsavory, results," I say. "It's all accounted for. Every scenario, every conclusion, every statement. I've got receipts for everything."

They exchange brief glances, then Artur picks the tablet up and starts going through the main file. The more he reads, the darker his grey eyes become as he, too, goes through the motions of discovery, shock, outrage, and determination.

"Matthew Phelps is as dangerous as Jack Bowman himself, except Phelps has more to lose and is likely easier to indict," Artur says, passing the tablet to Max and Artur next. "He and Bowman are tighter than I had suspected."

"Fucking hell," Ivan mutters. "It's not just campaign contributions either."

I shake my head. "No, no, it's way more. Squashed investigations, witnesses strong-armed into recanting their complaints or testimonies altogether. Over the years, Bowman and the local field office have been actively shielding my father from a grand jury, while my father has been actively lobbying for all of Bowman's businesses. Most recently, he went hard and all in at every major political meeting to get Smith appointed as director for Chicago."

"I'm sorry you had to find out this way," Max mutters, warmth in his gaze.

All I can do is shrug. "It's okay. I mean, I always suspected that he had a dark side of sorts. You know my general opinion of politicians. It stems from him, from the way he conducts himself. This, on the other hand, is something else entirely. Worse. Darker than anything I imagined. I don't know how he will ever recover when the truth comes out."

"See, that's where the trick is," Artur smirks. "*If* the truth comes out. This is why they're so hellbent on keeping our organization tethered to theirs. Once they lose the Bratva, the other mob families might want to follow suit. Next thing you know, nobody is afraid of the local Feds anymore, leaving their precious illicit network weak and unprotected. Vulnerable to complaints and IA investigations. Right now, they're untouchable, and your father seems to have played quite the role in creating this environment."

"How do we undo this?" I ask.

Max shakes his head. "We can't undo anything. You shouldn't be anywhere near us for what's going to happen next."

"What do you mean?"

"We've gathered some intel of our own. This right here," he says, pointing at the tablet, "this is exceptionally useful to narrow down some leads. We'll know what to look for when the time comes."

"What intel?" I ask, growing increasingly anxious and confused.

Ivan exhales sharply. "We found one of your father's former staffers. It wasn't easy or cheap, but we managed to get a lead on where we might be able to scoop out actual proof of your father's crimes. It's clear that he has committed his share of misdeeds, and that he will continue unabashed well into the state senate. He must be stopped."

"I agree," I say with a heavy, painful sigh.

"We know this isn't easy for you," Max says. "He's still your dad, he's still family. There's love there, no matter how strained the relationship is. It lands an even harder blow because he's pretty much all the family you've got left."

My eyes sting a little. Tears keep testing me, but I manage to hold them back, determined not to let any of this get to me again. There's been enough crying. I can't save my father, not without hurting the men I love, and that is what pains me the most. Making such a decision and having the power to implement it in the first place.

"I will do what needs to be done, which is why you have that," I point at the tablet. "I uploaded every piece of relevant evidence on there. Make sure it stays safe. The District Attorney will need it. My guess is you'll have to convene a secret grand jury to indict my father, and I think that what you have so far will sway a reputable judge in your favor."

"We just need to find one, a good judge, that is," Artur says. "It's not just the law enforcement that's crooked. The Justice Department has worms of its own."

A thought crosses my mind. "I think I can help with that as well."

"How so?" Ivan asks, his brow furrowing slightly as his gaze drops onto my lips. It thickens the tension between us, making it harder for me to breathe. Without even realizing, I lick my lips to quell the growing sensation of thirst that's turning my mouth into a dry cotton pit. It is enough to cause Ivan's gaze to darken and his nostrils to flare. "The algorithm, you mean?" he asks, clearly eager to cool his heels.

"Yes. I can have it scan the justice system, the circuits as a whole," I reply. "I can have it analyze court rulings, political affiliations where known or declared, that kind of stuff. I can even have the algorithm produce reports based on each ruling to tell you which judges might be better suited to see this through to the end."

"It's not just the judge," Max says. "The District Attorney needs to be brought on board first and foremost. He's the one who convenes the grand jury."

I nod. "Can you trust him?"

"We're not sure. But we haven't found any dirt on the guy either. He might be squeaky clean and genuinely righteous."

"Or he could be really good at hiding his true face," Artur points out. "We will need to do more research of our own on the matter. Thank you for doing this, Lyric. I know it's not how you wanted things to turn out."

I smile softly and get up. Big mistake.

The world starts spinning all of a sudden, the view before me dissolving into a puddle of milky colors as my consciousness slips away from me. I feel Max's strong arms close around me as he helps me remain upright. I didn't even register the moment he jumped from the sofa to reach me in time.

"Are you alright?" he asks, his voice low and gentle.

"I'm sorry. Yeah, I'm tired and overwhelmed."

"And worn out," Artur sighs as he, too, comes over and stands behind me. "You look a little stressed, Lyric."

My vision begins to clear as the blood flow intensifies. His touch is all it takes to get my engines roaring as he proceeds to squeeze my shoulders, a tentative massage designed to loosen me up.

It's loosening me a bit too much.

I'm soaking wet, my cheeks burning pink with reckless desire.

"God, Lyric, I can read you like an open book," Artur chuckles and plants a kiss on the side of my neck. All I can do is suck in a deep breath as I struggle to find my words.

"We can't do this," I manage, already putty in his hands.

Ivan gets up and captures my mouth in a devouring kiss, while Max's hands explore my body, registering each curve with his curious, probing fingertips.

"We've been telling ourselves the same thing but to no avail," Ivan purrs in my ear, then nibbles on the lobe until I whimper helplessly in their arms.

I take a deep breath and tilt my head back while Max kisses me deeply.

He kneads my breasts through my sweater, massaging my flesh until I melt in Artur's arms. It quickly gets to a point where my temperature spikes and I lose control.

"Take me," I whisper.

"You don't have to ask twice," Artur replies.

"We'll regret it in the morning," I say.

"Morning is still far away," Ivan points out. But he's already out of his jacket and loosening his tie. I hear Artur's clothes falling to the floor, one item at a time, while I watch Max take off his shirt.

"It doesn't mean we're back together," I feel the need to reiterate.

Ivan hooks his fingers through the waist of my pants and pulls them down. "It doesn't mean anything unless we decide to give it meaning."

A moment later, I'm naked and wanting, trembling with desire as my men gather around me. Their hard bodies respond to my touch, cocks thick and twitching and ready to dismantle me down to my very core.

"Come here," Max beckons me toward the armchair, then has me sit down. "Spread your legs for me, baby."

I gladly oblige as Ivan and Artur watch with dark delight. Max eats my pussy, his tongue sliding between my wet folds, flicking my swollen clit faster and faster. My hips tilt up and down, responding to his laps, while whimpers escape from my throat. He suckles on my tender nub, causing an eruption to blow through me before sliding his fingers inside of me.

By the time I register what's happening, the world's entire axis has shifted under me. I'm trembling, crying out in sweet ecstasy as Max finger-fucks me out of my mind. I grip Ivan and Artur's cocks and take turns pleasing each of them with my mouth.

My breasts bounce gleefully with every thrust, prompting Max to wrap his lips around each nipple to tease, lick and suckle, just the way I like it. My core tightens, pressure quick to gather again. I lose my mind and body at once, and when Ivan and Artur fill me with their cocks I realize this never should've ended in the first place.

I come again, shaking and screaming, unraveling in every which way, forgetting that there's a whole world out there that's dying to see us part ways. To destroy us.

"I've missed you so much," Max leans down and whispers in my ear.

"Me, too. I... I..."

"It's okay," he says.

Artur gives me a lazy, sweet smile. "We'll figure something out."

"But we're better off staying apart for now," Ivan adds.

It's a bitter moment, despite its sweetness. As we all come down from the clouds, basking in the afterglow of what is likely only the first of many lovemaking sessions tonight, reality creeps up to remind us that we are still at war.

That the odds are still stacked up against us.

22

LYRIC

One thing that has worked in Max, Ivan, and Artur's advantage is that they've managed to shake every federal tail they've had. They're never in the same place for too long, and the city of Chicago is basically their oyster. They have friends and Russian family allies who will happily cover for them. Different apartments and penthouses, various cars and offices where they can conduct their business from—none under their names.

It got to this point because the FBI has been ramping up its harassment tactics, courtesy of Director Smith and the local field office.

Smith is hell bent on taking the Bratva down unless they stay in the same system that has worked so well for him and his horde of crooked cronies. But my men persevere, and the more they resist, the more their partners are inclined to believe that maybe there's something else in store for the Bratva aside from the same old, same old.

On my end, I have a reckoning to deal with.

I must prove my algorithm right. The scenario it gave me was chilling to the very bone, but if I am to use any of its findings against my father—and therefore against Bowman and Smith, as well—I need more concrete evidence. Based on the guys' own intel regarding my father and Shelby, I decide that I have to take a step forward and put my friendship with Shelby to the test.

Despite my earlier warning, she doesn't know what she's getting herself into, that much is clear. Dad is a wolf in sheep's clothing, and while I hate myself for thinking so, Shelby is better off seeing for herself who he truly is.

"It's been a while," she says as we sit down for coffee at one of our usual cafes uptown. "You look good, Lyric. You're glowing."

"Pretty sure that's just sweat," I say, laughing lightly.

"No, I mean it. You look wonderful," Shelby says. "Though I'm not sure what's changed." She pauses, her tone taking a temperature dive. "I heard about the argument you had with your father about the Sokolov's."

"You heard?"

"Yeah, he tells me pretty much everything. I've become his confidante lately."

She says it with a hint of pride, and I need to take a deep breath before I'm about to gently rain on her parade. I give her a soft smile.

"He trusts you then."

"He does," she replies with a confident nod. "I mean, it's hard to trust anybody in politics these days, so I'm glad he feels like he can trust me."

I nod slowly. "Look, Shelby, my father's got it all wrong regarding the Sokolov's."

"Does he though?" She narrows her eyes, carefully analyzing my expression.

"What do you mean?"

"Well obviously, I never told him anything about your involvement with them, Lyric, but even so, he can tell that it's not the right path for you, especially under these complicated circumstances."

"Are you talking about how the FBI are constantly harassing them for no good reason?" I shouldn't get so defensive, but I can't help myself. "Let's face it, Shelby, they're just using them as scapegoats at this point. They have nothing on them."

"Yet."

I give her a confused frown. "Yet?"

"Your father says it's only a matter of time before the Feds start digging up the right corpses. And when they do, you don't want to be anywhere near them, Lyric."

These are delicate waters I'm treading. One wrong move, and I could end up turning Shelby against me. She has already gotten way too close for comfort where my father is concerned. The last thing I want to do is push her all the way into his arms.

I look at her, listening intently as she voices her feelings regarding my relationship with the Sokolov's, though part of me wishes I could just smack the sense back into her head.

"I love you like a sister," she says, "and you know that. I'm all for you finding true love, no matter how weird or taboo it may seem to the rest of the world, because I believe in your ability to discern right from wrong. Which is why I'm here, talking to you about all this. Your dad has no clue how deep your dealings with the Sokolov's goes, and I would never tell him. But Lyric, it's time to get serious. The Chicago Bratva is going down, sooner or later. I don't want to see you get hurt."

I offer another mellow nod, just so she'll feel heard. "Thank you, Shelby. It means the world to me that you care so much about me. I care about you, too, and don't you ever doubt it for a second. Which is why I need you to listen to what I have to say as well, okay? Can you do that? Can I talk straight like you just did?"

"Of course," she smiles softly. "I wouldn't have it any other way."

Brace yourself, Shelby. Because you might end up hating me by the time I'm done with you, I think to myself.

"So, here's the thing. I know my father better than most people. Better than you, believe it or not," I say.

"I believe it."

"I've seen his rise up the political totem pole. I've seen how far he's willing to go, how dirty he's willing to get in order to win," I continue, watching as Shelby's expression gradually shifts from openness to wariness. "Matthew Phelps preaches fairness and righteousness, but he doesn't practice it. You have no idea the kind of bribes he paid to even get on the city council ballot. The backdoor deals he made along the way. The favors he owes to some pretty shady people, that I know of. I can't imagine what I don't know about. I can give you names, dates, places, just so you understand that I'm not making any of this up."

"I have no reason to distrust you."

"I know he can be charming and he can really knock your socks off. And it's easy to believe him, because his record appears spotless from the outside," I continue. "I completely understand. But do you remember all those times that I aired my grievances with you about his political exploits?"

"I do. I just—"

"You believed me then, and you know, deep down, that you still believe me now," I say. "You fell into his sweet honey trap, I get it. I would've too, if I planned on devoting my life to making the world a better place. You want to believe him, and you see all these good things that he does. Charity, social justice, calling members of Congress out to show more consideration toward his constituents, but even you know that they're all just photo ops while he continues meeting with unsavory monsters behind closed doors. You must've seen it for yourself by now."

Shelby lets a heavy, shuddering sigh roll from her chest. "I understand that politics is a dirty game, Lyric. I also understand that if you want to do some good in this world, you have to make deals with unsavory monsters as you call them, in order to get your agenda at a table where it has the best chance to be turned into reality."

"What you don't understand is that my father's agenda is a pure work of fiction," I tell her, discreetly pushing a USB drive across the table between us. "My algorithm can prove it. I can link every decision he's ever made to a consequence that directly benefitted him or his cronies while it ultimately screwed over the very people he claims to serve. Every tax cut, every incentive, every bill and regulation he passed through the city council all leads back to him, his and his friends' business interests. And there's no one he's tighter with than Jack fucking Bowman, who benefitted the most."

"That's bullshit," Shelby snaps, but I insist and force her hand to close around the USB drive despite her initial resistance. "They've only known each other for a couple of years, ever since the Bureau decided to pay closer attention to the Chicago Bratva."

"No, you're wrong about that. It's all there. Proof that they go way back and that they have been working together on a variety of projects for decades."

"No."

"Yes. Believe me, or don't. Everything I'm telling you is backed by evidence. If you don't have eyes to see, you'll say it's all purely circumstantial. But I know you, Shelby, I know you won't let yourself be blinded by your own emotions. You're a brilliant woman, and I love you to bits. I trust you'll do the right thing with what I just gave you."

A frown casts a deep shadow between her brows as she gives me a doubtful look. "And what is the right thing, Lyric?"

"You'll know. If there's one thing I'm sure of, it's that you will know."

I think she already does, but she isn't ready to accept that the reality she has built for herself in my father's company isn't real. It hurts, and I can see the pain dulling her gaze. She shakes her head but tucks the drive into her pocket before tossing a few bills on the table. "I've heard enough. Be careful, Lyric. I need to get back to work. Your father has a massive fundraiser to host tonight."

"Shelby, I—"

"No, I've heard enough!" she snaps. "You tell me that I already know this and that. Well, let me tell you something you already know but aren't ready to admit yet. Your father may be flawed, but he is fundamentally a good man. He may be a politician, but he really is working for the people. He's determined to change this corrupt system. What really pisses you off is the fact that he and I have gotten closer. Too close for your taste, and that's insanely hypocritical of you. You get to hook up and screw three older dudes at once, but I can't experience something real and sweet with just one older man because he happens to be your father."

"What?"

"Let's call it what it is," she says, then walks away.

I'm left staring at her, watching her stomp out of the café. Minutes pass, and I begin to doubt myself and the motivation behind what I just did. I'll admit, I'm not exactly a fan of Shelby and my father getting together. But that's not my issue.

My problem is that his downfall will likely hurt Shelby.

* * *

I STARE at the Sokolov mansion from behind the wheel of my rental car. It would've been too risky to drive here in my own vehicle but I don't believe I was followed. They haven't been answering my calls or text messages. I tried calling their office more than once, but their secretary didn't know what to tell me. To say that I'm a tad concerned would be a massive understatement, given the circumstances.

I'm supposed to give them my algorithm results—a USB copy like the one that Shelby got. I gave it to her first as a courtesy. What if she...

"No, she wouldn't," I mumble to myself.

We may have our skirmishes and disagreements, but Shelby would never betray me. There's something else going on here and I need to figure out what it is, so I cautiously drive around the block a couple of times before pulling into the alleyway behind the house.

It's odd, I soon realize, that there isn't any security detail around.

They were supposed to have at least a couple of guys posted outside, visible for any surveying Feds to see. But it's eerily quiet as nighttime falls over the city with its dark blue blanket of stars and half-moon hanging lazily in the eastern sky.

I don't like this.

My instincts tell me to turn back. I should go home and wait for Max, Ivan, or Artur to text me or call me. The Bureau is watching this place, though I'm confident they haven't spotted me yet. I stare at the back gate for a while, struggling with my own indecision, fingers lingering on the wheel while the engine hums idly.

A knock on my car window startles me. "Oh, shit!" I yelp, then exhale sharply as I recognize the police uniform. "Sorry!" I roll the window down and give the patrol officer a shy smile.

"You've been sitting out here for a while," he says. "Do you need help?"

The name on his tag says O'Donnell. My stomach churns. I feel like a kid who got caught casing the candy store, even though I had no intention of committing any crime.

"Hi, Officer O'Donnell. No, I'm fine. Sorry, I was just stopping to text a friend of mine," I laugh nervously. "You don't want me texting and driving, do you?"

"A friend of yours?"

"Yes, sir."

He gives me a stone-cold look and I don't know what to make of it. "Would your friend be any of the Sokolov's? Because they aren't home."

"Oh." I pause for a moment, trying to figure out what's going on. "No, sir, I don't know the Sokolov's. I'm just texting my best friend, Shelby. She's doing a fundraiser with her boss tonight," I tell him, trying to sound as calm and as compliant as possible. "Like I said, I didn't want to text and drive."

"You really shouldn't lie to a police officer, Miss Phelps," he says, and my blood runs cold.

He knows who I am.

I gasp as I see his hand shoot out, something metallic and shiny in it.

I try to get away but he sticks me in the neck.

Heat instantly spreads through my skin. My head lolls and my body suddenly abandons me. I fall over the steering wheel, numb and quickly fading out of this world. My mind is racing in every which way, but I can't do anything about it.

Fuck.

I never should've rolled the window down.

* * *

My eyes peel open. It's dark and cold. The dampness makes my skin feel clammy all over as I struggle to pull myself into an upright position. My limbs are soft like jelly, my heart starting to race as I become more and more aware of my surroundings and I remember what happened.

The cop. O'Donnell.

A sense of urgency takes over, and I'm desperate to move and get off this stale, dirty couch. I wonder how long I've been out for. My body feels so weak.

"Ugh," I moan, my mouth tasting like dry cotton.

A door opens, yellow light from the hallway cutting through the darkness of the room. I look up to see who's coming. I don't immediately recognize his stocky frame, but as soon as he speaks, shivers run down my spine.

"Oh good, you're awake," Director Smith says.

"What the hell did you do to me?" I croak, dread taking over and stiffening my joints, my eyes darting all over the place.

The light coming in through the open door allows me to see my surroundings. I spot a window with iron bars on it. A dusty dresser next to it. An old coffee table with a bottle of water for me to drink, an armchair.

I think I'm going to be sick.

"Relax, you're going to be fine. O'Donnell may have been a tad overzealous with his choice of tranquilizer, but you won't be feeling much in terms of side effects. The nausea will take a while to wear off though," Smith says.

I suddenly worry that whatever he injected me with might have hurt my baby. But I can't let Smith know I'm pregnant. It would give him even more leverage.

"You kidnapped me?" I manage, giving Smith the nastiest look I can muster. "Have you lost your goddamn mind?"

"I'm making sure you stay put and out of our way," he says then leaves a takeout bag on the coffee table. I can't see what's inside, but I can smell the fried chicken and the fries from where I'm sitting. "It was the only sensible thing I could do, given that we're about to rain fire and hell on those Sokolov pricks."

I look around again. "What did that cop inject me with?"

"I already told you it was a tranquilizer, probably valium or something similar. Relax."

"Yeah, well, I'm a tad bit too relaxed under the circumstances. Director Smith, you kidnapped me. Do you have any idea what will happen when this gets out?" I say, fury finally awakening the rest of my dormant senses. My agitated heart keeps pounding and I feel like I'm becoming more alert with each deep breath that I take. "This is unconscionable!"

"Unconscionable, huh. I suppose it is." He's mocking me. There's a smirk on his face. He's downright amused.

"Not to mention illegal!"

Smith chuckles dryly. "Honey, we're so past illegal at this point that you're lucky I decided not to kill you and just be done with it. We're in the big leagues, Miss Phelps. There's no room for you on the playing field; I'm only doing this as a courtesy to your father. Don't test me."

"I don't understand."

"It took us a while, but we finally got everybody we needed on board to take the Sokolov's down, once and for all," he says. "There are major movements taking place as we speak, and once we find those rat bastards, it'll be all over for them."

"You have nothing on them!"

"I don't need to have anything on them. I just needed enough votes from the other families to make sure that I could go ahead with my contingency plan before I take them out."

Fear tightens its clutch on my throat, the grip so strong it nearly crushes my windpipe as I struggle to breathe. Waves of hot and cold wash over me, my vision blurry as this new reality begins to sink in. They caught me unprepared. They kidnapped and drugged me. And now, they're keeping me hostage. To what end, I don't yet know.

What I do know is that they're making a different kind of move against the Sokolov's. Against my men, my lovers. A violent kind of move. And the other families are now involved. This popped up as one of the least likely scenarios in my algorithm's trial runs, though I could never figure out who would bow before the Feds and who would stay loyal to the Bratva. I didn't have enough inside information.

"Where are they?" I ask Smith. "Max, Ivan, Artur. Where are they?"

"If I knew, I'd personally have already put a bullet in each of their skulls," Smith grumbles, then nods at the paper bag. "You should eat something. It'll help the tranquilizer effects wear off sooner."

"You really are as bad as they said you were," I mumble, unable to look away from this man. "You walk around, flashing that badge and pretending to be a man of justice, yet here you are—"

"Here I am, about to get richer once the Sokolov's get fitted with their brand-new cement shoes," Smith replies. "It's a wild world out there, Miss Phelps. A wild and unforgiving world. For every drug dealer we take out, three more rise up to take their spot. For every mobster we indict, three more rise up to torment the same neighborhoods we worked so hard to clean up. I've been at it for years. Bowman, too, before me. We've seen it all, and we've seen enough. We can't stop people from doing wrong, but we can at least make a pretty penny off of it. We can make sure our kids and grand-kids will never have to deal with these assholes."

"I'm sorry, is this the 'if you can't beat 'em, join 'em' bullshit speech? I can't believe you fell for it, Director Smith. You should be ashamed of yourself."

"Ashamed of what? All the zeroes in my bank account, once the Sokolov's are out of the race and the Bratva is back to doing what it does best? All those fuckers had to do was continue their daddy's legacy. It would've been easier and cheaper, not to mention more profitable for everyone involved. But no, they had to be righteous pricks. Thinking they were better than the rest of us."

"They are better. You're proving that right now."

Smith gives me a hard glare. "And look where that got them. Their own people have turned against them. You're stuck here until we bury them. Like I said, you're lucky I have too much respect for your father, otherwise, I'd—"

"Kill me. Yeah, you made that perfectly clear."

"The option is still on the table, should you try something stupid," he says. "Your old man won't need to know the details. I can make it look like an accident. I've done it before. Be smart for once, Miss Phelps, and just sit tight. Eat something and stay hydrated while we hunt those bastards down and end this circus, once and for all."

He laughs and walks out, having the decency at least to turn the light on. I hear the lock as the door shuts behind him. A single, dooming click. Every possible emotion is blowing through me right now, and it's not long before I feel a panic attack coming over me.

I take several deep calming breaths as I start analyzing my situation, choosing to focus on the solution rather than the problem.

All I can do is be careful. Not only for my sake, but also for my baby's.

Dammit, I should've stayed home.

23

MAX

We're lucky we still have friends in low places.

Rumors reached our ears and we smelled the rats. We figured it might come to this, so we prepared for the worst. They almost got us, though. Someone figured out that we had the penthouse as a safe haven. Ivan kept casing the block, almost obsessively. To his disappointment, his suspicions turned out to be true.

They came in the middle of night.

They wore black leather jackets, gloves, and balaclavas, silencers on their semi-automatic pistols. They thought they would catch us unprepared, but we were waiting quietly in the dark. They didn't stand a chance. One by one, the assassins fell, and then it was our turn.

Ivan smashes Rudy's knee with a baseball bat while Artur goes through his phone. I can barely hear myself think from all the screaming and wailing. We're in a dumpy basement with only one functioning neon light, the sound of water dripping down the old, rusty pipes.

"Cry all you want," I say, my arms crossed as I sit in a chair in front of Rudy. "No one's going to hear you down here."

The sound of his kneecap crumbling turns my stomach. We don't like resorting to such measures but they gave us no choice. Rudy sobs, his face red as he struggles to cope with the pain, while my brother stands back for a moment, bat defiantly resting on his shoulder.

"I told you," Rudy manages in between sobs, "I don't know."

"And I told you that I don't believe you," I reply. "Come on, Rudy. We go way back. I've known you since you were trying on your mother's lipstick and red pumps. Remember? Your dad came home and found you like that, then dragged you across the block to show everyone."

"Max, I swear to God, I don't know what happened."

"I'll tell you what happened," Artur cuts in. "Somebody sent hitmen after us. The other families wouldn't do that unless it was sanctioned by a vote. And we all know who stands to benefit the most from our premature departure."

Rudy gives him a troubled look. "The local Feds? Seriously?"

"Rudy, your father made a deal. It's obvious. The Irish would never turn against us, not without some kind of incentive."

"How do you know it was our guys?"

Ivan takes out his phone, showing him photos of the shamrock tattoos on our dead hitmen's necks.

"Oh, God," Rudy mumbles, drool trickling from the corner of his bruised mouth. He got quite the beating even before my brother decided to kick things up a notch. "It doesn't make sense."

"It makes perfect sense if your father decided to stick to the old ways despite our advocacy and our efforts to steer everybody in a better, safer, and equally profitable direction," I retort. "I'm going to ask you one last time, Rudy, though I hate having to repeat myself. Who did your father meet with this morning?"

"This morning?"

Artur rolls his eyes. "Come on man, even the busboys at Dalton's pizzeria knew about the big boss meetup this morning. You're going to take over for your father one day. You can't tell me you didn't know anything about it."

"Oh, he knows," Ivan mutters. "His knee is going numb, though, so he's probably thinking he can withstand more of what I'm about to deliver."

Rudy gives him a terrified look. "Wait, what?"

CRACK!

The bat meets his other knee with the same sickening sound, followed by more howls and wails. I roll my eyes, lacking any sympathy for those who actively chose to betray us. I have no mercy for traitors and spineless sacks of shit, especially when their treachery threatens not just our lives, but the lives of countless others who have nothing to do with our business.

"Who was at the meeting?" I ask, keeping my tone low and calm.

"Oh, God." Rudy coughs and gags, dangerously close to puking his guts out. Artur splashes some cold water over his face, then slaps him around a couple of times, just to keep him alert and talking. "Dad was there. I asked him what it was about, he said... he said it wasn't for me to know yet. That he'd tell me when it's over."

"When it's over," Ivan repeats after him, looking at me.

"Who else?" I reply.

"They got the Chinese and the Japanese on board. Shin and Mizuma," Rudy says. "Pretty sure the Mexicans had a delegate. One of yours too."

"One of ours?" Artur raises his eyebrows in surprise. "Who'd they send to represent the Bratva?"

Rudy shakes his head slowly. "I don't know."

"I hate that answer," Ivan says.

"The old… the old man, I think. I heard my dad talking to him over the phone. Oh, God, I forgot his fucking name."

Ivan readies his bat. "What should I swing on next?"

"Larionov. For fuck's sake. Old man Larionov!" Rudy cries out.

Artur curses under his breath. "Why doesn't that surprise me?"

Old man Larionov is making a power move, making backdoor deals with the families we've known to be resistant to our shift in the organization.

"Were the Feds involved?" I ask Rudy.

He nods once. "Bowman. He called the meeting through about a dozen proxies."

"Where did the meeting take place?"

"Houston Grill. The VIP lounge. They closed it off for the rest of the day."

Ivan gives me another look. "Houston Grill. Matthew Phelps's joint."

We knew from our own investigation that Phelps had a stake in several diners and restaurants across the city—all of which should've resulted in a major conflict of interest for many of his city council votes. But without any proof on paper and only rumors to rely on, knowing this information felt useless.

Not anymore.

Phelps, the high and mighty politician running for state senate, facilitated a meeting between mafia bosses. A meeting in which a decision was made. A decision to have me, my brother, and my best friend killed because we were spoiling a carefully crafted ecosystem of trafficking directly coordinated by the Feds' Chicago field office.

"Larionov decided to be stupid then," Artur sighs. "I'd hoped he'd be more reasonable."

"When have you ever known that dumb fucker to be reasonable?" Ivan grumbles.

My phone pings. One look at the screen and my stomach sinks. Every other noise, including Rudy's panting and wretched sobs, is drowned out by the sudden drumming in my ears. My heart is thudding as I stare at the image I just received via text from an unknown sender.

"Guys," I mutter, beckoning Ivan and Artur to come closer.

The three of us are faced with our worst nightmare, now come true. Lyric, sitting on a dirty old sofa, looking pale, terrified, and in visible discomfort. The image is accompanied by a simple but effective message.

"45th and Lennox. Midnight. You know what to do," I read the words aloud.

Ivan roars with unbridled fury and takes the bat to Rudy's knees again.

"Ivan, stop!" Artur pulls him away, making sure the bat hits the floor while Rudy pretty much soils himself in sheer horror. "Stop, man. We need a clear head about us."

"What happened?" Rudy asks, his eyes wide and glassy.

I give him a sour look. "Consequences of your father's dumb actions."

"They have her," Ivan snarls. "What the fuck do we do?"

Ice fills my veins as I abandon my emotions. My love for Lyric gets tucked away, wrapped in layers of cold, merciless darkness as I get up and shift my focus back to Ivan and Artur.

"We get her back," I tell them. "The smart way."

"The smart way," Artur repeats, doubt saturating his tone.

"We've got a couple more hours," I say. "And one more stop to make before 45th and Lennox."

The Larionov villa is well guarded, especially at night, but the old man's bouncers are slow and lazy, and no match for us. Besides, we're remarkably motivated by Lyric's abduction to the point where we go through each security detail like a red-hot knife would go through a stick of butter. One by one, they fall as we work our way to the top floor.

The clock is ticking, and I have no intention of losing this war.

We find Larionov in his private study, sharing a bottle of grappa with his daughter.

"How sweet," I quip as I burst through the double doors, leaving two more bodies behind. Ivan and Artur are quick to flank the chairs by the window where Larionov and Polina are seated. "Good. You're both here. It'll make everything go a lot easier."

Polina stills, glass in hand, panic imprinted upon her pretty face. Larionov grunts and makes a move for his ankle piece, but Ivan fires a warning shot that hits the chair leg. Wood splinters fly out. Polina screams. Larionov curses and raises his hands in a quick, defensive gesture.

"We need to talk," I say, surprised by my own calmness. "What did they promise you?"

"What are you referring to?" the old man asks, not even bothering to hide the deception anymore. It is blatantly disrespectful.

"I don't think you want to do things this way," I warn.

Artur and Ivan have their guns trained on them both. Polina seems confused and outraged, her gaze bouncing between us in growing agitation. "Max, what are you doing?"

"You know damn well what I'm doing, Polina. You brought this upon yourselves," I say. "The minute you betrayed us, you knew this would be coming."

Larionov scoffs, shaking his head in disgust. "You were supposed to be dead already."

"Sorry, your guys just weren't fast enough," Artur chuckles. "Oh, by the way, there's something you should know," he pauses, taking his sweet time to enjoy the consternation on their faces, the looks of guilt and shame, anger and helplessness, as the realization of their fate becomes inevitable. "It wasn't just Max who had a run at your daughter."

"Artur!" Polina shouts.

"The three of us had her," he says. "Day in and day out, for quite a long time. Polina was perfectly happy with us sharing her while she waltzed around your house, pretending to be your precious, innocent angel."

Larionov gasps. "How dare you say such things?"

"It's the truth and you should hear it before you leave this world behind," Artur replies. "Your daughter had all of us at once, and she loved every minute of it. It's why she's been pestering you to get Max to marry her. She's desperate to be in our bed again."

"You piece of—" Larionov moves to get up, but Ivan empties the rest of his clip in the old man's chest first. Polina screams. Artur tells her to shut up, forcing her into a sudden, shocked silence.

I wish I had a smidge of sympathy left for her but I don't.

A minute passes in heavy, loaded silence, as Larionov breathes his last muted breath while staring at me. I wonder what his final thoughts were. Artur wanted him to suffer. He wanted the shock factor to destroy him before death took him. I cannot imagine a more torturous way to die, knowing such things about your daughter, a daughter you had so highly revered.

I have a mind of doing the same to Phelps, if we all survive what comes next.

"You have two choices right now," I calmly tell Polina. "And not a lot of time to decide."

"Fuck you," she hisses, bringing her knees up to her chest. She hugs them tightly, desperate to give herself some kind of comfort while she's forced to sit there and stare at her father's lifeless body.

"Cry all you want," I tell her. "But these are the facts. You're screwed on every possible level. I know Bowman called a meeting with every mob head that would listen. I know your father was there and voted for our assassination. Rest assured, every single person who voted yes this morning will not live to see tomorrow."

"My father—"

"Your father betrayed us. He broke the code that he and his father before him were so proud to have enforced. You don't turn on your own people, Polina," I cut her off. "Now, I know that Bowman has Lyric."

"Lyric?"

Artur gives her a hard look. "I have zero tolerance left for you right now."

"Okay, so?" Polina croaks, wincing just a little.

"You either tell us what you know about where she is, what they plan to do with her, every single fucking thing, no matter how insignificant it might seem to you, or you die. Tell us and you have my word that I will let you live."

Polina narrows her eyes at me, her fury palpable. "And what's my other choice?"

"Say nothing and I will make you wish I would simply put a bullet through your head," I reply. "I will kill you slowly, until you beg me to end it. And trust me, if we don't get Lyric back alive, I will make it hurt like nothing you've ever known."

"You love her," she mumbles. "You actually love that prissy bitch."

"That's not your concern," I say.

Ivan gives me a dark look. "You're being too nice, brother."

"I'm giving her one last chance," I say, then turn my sights on Polina again. "So, what'll it be, Polina? Where do we stand?"

24

ARTUR

Polina quivers in her chair, fury and despair warring in her eyes.

"Your father voted to have us killed," I say, checking the clip in my gun, making sure that it's full. "He walked into that meeting this morning, supposedly representing the Bratva. The organization that *we* are in charge of."

"You didn't have to kill him," she says, her voice low, uneven.

Max scoffs, staring at the old man's body. "Don't lie to yourself. A crime like his could only be punished by death. He tried to make us out as pariahs just so he could get his grubby hands on the throne. Let this be a lesson to you, Polina. You reap what you sow."

"He was my father!"

I give a lazy shrug. "Now, I believe Max here asked you a question. What are you going to do next? Are you going to give us what we want, or will you be begging us to kill you?"

She gives me a hard look. "You'd really torture me?"

"What makes you think you're so fucking special?" Ivan snarls. "You bugged our office. You put Lyric in danger. You conspired against us. By all existing logic, I'm well within my rights to do whatever the hell I want to you."

"Smith and Bowman took Lyric, and we need to get her back alive," I say.

"I didn't have anything to do with that!"

"Even if you didn't, I know daddy dearest over there couldn't keep his trap shut whenever he thought he had the upper hand. This is the last time I'm going to ask you for your help, or I swear to God, you will wish you were never born."

"What address did they give you?" she asks after a long and heavy silence.

"45th and Lennox," Max says.

"She's not going to be there," Polina replies. "It's probably just a setup to get the three of you in one go. They'll most likely return her to her father once it's done."

"What did they say during the meeting?" I ask.

She narrows her icy blue eyes at me. I can see the loathing and contempt, but I don't care. I only care about getting Lyric away from Smith and Bowman. "Bowman said he'll keep her out of harm's way to ensure he'll have Phelps's support after it's over. They go way back, apparently."

"Yeah, we heard," Max says.

"He's going to take her to the FBI field office," Polina says. "From what I understood, once they caught her, she'd be held somewhere nearby until she's made compliant, and then they would bring her over to Smith's turf."

"It makes sense," I sigh deeply, "and it's fucking impenetrable."

"That's what Bowman was relying on," Polina says. "My father asked him this morning how he could keep her there, legally speaking. Not every agent is on his and Smith's payroll. It's more of a shadow organization operating from the same building as the fucking Feds."

"It's how they made it work so well over the years—hiding in plain sight and behind legitimate FBI badges. We don't even know how many of them are dirty," Max mutters.

Ivan raises an eyebrow. "I'd rather assume they're all dirty."

"Assuming that would get us killed faster than us showing up at 45th and Lennox," I tell him. "It's precisely what Bowman wants. It'll make quite the show for the media, for sure. 'Bratva bosses storm the FBI's Chicago field office, leaving nothing but carnage behind.' No, we can't play it like that."

"You need a different approach," Polina says. "They're expecting you at that address. Right now, the three of you have a minor advantage, knowing where they're keeping your bitch."

"I will hit a woman," I throw a nasty glower her way. "Don't fucking test me."

Polina rolls her eyes and it seems to me like she is finally ready to accept her fate. She's moving fast through those stages of grief. Her instinct to survive has prevailed tonight.

"You'll probably need a diversion at 45th and Lennox," Polina sighs. "Something to keep Bowman's hitmen busy while you deal with the field office. He and Smith are likely going to be there."

Max comes closer, giving me a worried look. "We need a plan. We can't just walk into that fucking building."

"I know. We don't have that many options, though. None that make me feel confident about our chances of survival anyway," I say to him.

"If we do this," Ivan cuts in, "we take them all down. Bowman, Smith, Phelps. We end it all tonight. Bring the whole Bratva in. For too long, they've tried to push us into a corner for their own gain. It has to stop. If we don't deliver the definitive blow, we'll lose the trust and respect of the other families. It's why they voted against us this morning. We need to earn their trust back."

"And what better way than to lay siege on the fucking FBI's Chicago field office?" I chuckle, well aware that what Ivan says makes a ton of sense.

As much as we hate to admit it, he's right. This morning's vote was an alarm signal for us as leaders of the Bratva. We lost the confidence of some of our allies and partners. The other families think they've got the juice to take us down.

If we're to succeed, if we're to steer the Bratva in a different direction and earn their trust back, we need to do so decisively and mercilessly.

"I guess we're going to war tonight," I mumble, shaking my head slowly.

Max puts a hand on my shoulder. "We won't be alone."

"I'm on it," Ivan says as he takes out his phone and starts making calls.

This is more than a rescue operation. It's more than revenge. Definitely more than mere defense. We're rallying our fighters from all over the city to help us. But at the same time, we need a subtler, more intelligent approach from a different angle. Matthew Phelps needs to go down tonight as well.

One way or another, we have to end it all before midnight.

2 5

LYRIC

My stomach churns as I sit in a holding cell at the FBI field office. At least it smells better than the room I woke up in.

"Here's some water," an agent offers as he comes through the door holding a chilled bottle.

"Thanks," I reply, watching as he sets it on the floor in front of me. "So, are you working with Smith on this? Are you aware that I'm a kidnapping victim?"

The guy gives me a cold grin. "You have no idea how powerful we are, Miss Phelps. But you're going to find out tonight. Just be thankful that your father is who he is, otherwise, they would've already fished you out of the river by now."

"Unbelievable," I murmur, shaking my head in dismay as the agent chuckles and leaves me alone again.

It's quiet down here. Quiet, cold, and incredibly lonely. I'm sore all over and scared for my life, for my baby's life.

Regardless of Smith's intentions, declared or otherwise, I can't bring myself to trust that bastard—certainly not with my life and well-being. Not with the life that's growing inside of me.

Oh, God, how do I get myself out of this mess?

"I'm entitled to a phone call, aren't I?" I shout, hoping that someone might hear me.

I'm worried sick. What if they get to them? What if they already have? What if tonight, the guys go down in flames, while trying to save me? I try to come up with a plan, much like I always do, but there isn't a viable solution in sight.

The door opens and my heart skips a beat. "Finally," I sigh. "I need to make a phone call. I have the right to a phone call!"

My enthusiasm dwindles quickly when Jack Bowman kneels before me. That same confident smirk as before splattered across his face. It makes me sick to my stomach, but given my predicament, I must be extremely careful in how I deal with this man.

"What are you doing here?" I ask.

"I wanted to make sure you're alright and well taken care of," Bowman says. "We're not monsters, Lyric. We're just trying to protect everything that we've worked so hard to build."

"And you call yourself my father's friend," I hiss. "Having me drugged and kidnapped."

"That was exaggerated, I know, and I do apologize," he says with a subtle, polite bow of his head. "I'll make sure that the man responsible is punished accordingly. But you'll be safe here. It'll soon be over and you can go back to your life."

I shake my head slowly. "What the hell are you planning to do?"

"Right some wrongs," he casually replies. "Letting the Sokolov's take over after their father passed away was a grave mistake. Matthew did warn me about them. Smith wasn't too sure either. But I hoped they'd take a page out of the old man's book. I sent my people to talk to them about the organization, about how the system worked between us. It should've made sense that all they needed to do was follow the same rules and traditions. If they had, everybody would've been happy."

"Right. Every once in a while, the Bureau would announce a successful sting or RICO operation. The mafia bosses would get rid of their undesirables that way, and you were able to keep your corruption machine well-oiled and running at full capacity."

"You make it sound so crass, but yes, in a nutshell. Lyric, we're doing important business here. We're working with colossal amounts of money. Domestic and foreign interests aplenty. We have political and financial influence across the entire state, not just the city, and once your father gets his senate seat, we'll strengthen our position. We won't even need the local mafia families then."

"So, forget the men and women who risk their lives as policemen and federal agents. Forget those who put themselves on the line so that criminals are punished for their crimes."

"Who said that?"

"You, the criminal standing right in front of me. The criminal that's getting away with a lot, might I add. How is any of this fair?"

Bowman crosses his arms, carefully pondering his answer as he measures me from head to toe. "Personally, I'm more interested in figuring out how you turned out the way you did, Lyric. The apple couldn't have fallen farther from the tree. What happened?"

"My eyes were opened at a young age," I reply. If this man wants to get to know me better, I might as well give him a piece of my mind. Maybe it'll sway him away from his intended path. "I saw my father for who he really was. His words didn't match his actions, and it shattered my trust in him. He lies for a living. He pretends to be someone he stopped being a long time ago. I decided I didn't want to be anything like him."

"My, my, aren't you a righteous little thing."

"Just because you decided to throw away all of your principles so you could get richer, doesn't mean that there's something wrong with the rest of us. People still hurt other people. We still need to punish criminals. Corruption is eating away at an already defective system, causing even more pain to innocent people. You're out there stomping and crushing skulls to fatten your bank accounts, while countless folks rot in a line for food stamps."

Bowman chuckles softly. "Don't tell me you want freedom and money for everyone."

"No, that would be unrealistic. I want equality and fair chances for everyone. You fellas keep tipping the scales in your favor while you're also audacious enough to get in front of the cameras and claim you're fighting for the little guy. How many charities are you currently in charge of?"

"About six, I think. And they're all doing amazing things for the people and for the planet's ecosystem, might I add." He sounds irritatingly proud about this.

"And what, you think that washes your sins away? The money you steal? The lives you destroy? Don't be delusional, Mr. Bowman. It never ends well."

"It's going pretty well for me right now," he retorts. "I've got you in my grip, calm and under control. I'll have to buy your father a yacht or perhaps a Tuscan villa to apologize for this whole circus, but it will have been worth it. I've got the Sokolov's right where I want them. The mob families are falling back in line. Life is good, Lyric."

"I'll bet."

"It could be good for you, too, if you just accept your fate. You'll be a single mother, but you will at least have spared your father the shame of his daughter cavorting with known criminals. Years from now, you're going to look back on this moment and understand that I'm doing you a favor."

I can't help but roll my eyes at him. "Yeah, I'm beside myself with gratitude." But then his words hit me, the alarm bells going off in my head. "Wait, single mother?"

"I have eyes everywhere. Money in every pocket in exchange for information. It's how I built my empire. It's how I win my battles. Information is key, sweetheart, and knowing everything about you was instrumental in my decision-making process."

My stomach drops. I feel cold, then hot, then cold again as I stare at him in sheer disbelief. I am more vulnerable than ever and he knows it. Bowman knew it from the moment he walked in here. I have been playing checkers against this man's 3D chess, and I practically got my ass handed to me.

"I can't believe this."

"Oh, believe it, Lyric. There's nothing that money can't buy except immortality. Everything else, my dear, is always for sale. One just needs the right price."

With that, Bowman turns around and leaves.

"How long are you going to keep me here?" I shout at him.

"Just a few more hours and then I'll call your daddy to come pick you up. That is, of course, if everything goes according to plan," he replies, though he's out of sight now.

I hear the door opening once more.

"And if it doesn't go according to plan?" I ask with a trembling voice.

The door shuts loudly behind him. I guess that was my answer.

I'm left in the silence and semi-darkness of my holding cell, alone with my frazzled thoughts as the parameters of my situation seem to have drastically changed. The mere fact that Bowman knows about my pregnancy adds more danger to the Sokolovs. He's bound to use it against them if he has to.

26

IVAN

Once I remove the hood from her head, Shelby freezes like a deer caught in the headlights of an oncoming eighteen-wheeler. Her eyes are wide and filled with tears, locks of her hair stuck to her sweaty forehead. She's still in her plush green pajamas, the same ones she was wearing when we barged in and snatched her out of her home.

"Where am I?" she asks, shaking like a leaf as she looks around.

"You're safe," I tell her.

"What does that mean? I was safe at home on my sofa!"

"Relax, I have no intention of harming you. I just want to talk."

We're in the back room of The Violin, my late cousin's jazz bar. It is closed for the evening, not another soul in sight.

"We were never properly introduced," I say, taking my seat in front of her chair. Her hands and ankles are bound with zip ties, but I consider it a temporary measure. I didn't even tighten them as much as I normally would. "I'm Ivan Sokolov."

Again, she stills, horror and fear engulfing her.

"Oh God. What do you want with me?"

"I promise we're not going to hurt you, Shelby. We need your help."

She scoffs, her brow furrowed with skepticism. "And you couldn't just ask me? You had to do all this?"

"Be honest. Had I simply come up to you and introduced myself, would you have been willing to help or would you have gone running for the hills?" I pause to observe her awkward silence as she averts her gaze for a second. "Yeah, that's what I thought. Listen, Shelby, you need to understand something. You're protecting the wrong people."

"Oh, no, don't think for a second that you can manipulate me like you manipulated Lyric."

"Lyric loves us, and we love her," I reply. "Nobody manipulated anybody. What happened between us just happened, Shelby. Love is love. Surely, you can understand that better than most, given all the water that you've been carrying for Matthew Phelps, of all people."

"That's not a fair comparison, I—"

"Jack Bowman kidnapped Lyric. He's holding her hostage until my brother and me and our friend surrender," I cut her off.

Shelby's jaw practically hits the floor. "Wait... what?"

"Here," I say, showing her the image and text message that Max received. "This was sent to us a few hours ago. And we know for a fact that the address is where we're going to die, unless we get ahead of this and play it smart. Shelby, Matthew Phelps is not a decent man. He, much like Bowman and Smith, is a criminal, and likely a murderer by proxy."

"I don't want to hear it!"

"It's the truth and you know it. I see it written all over your face. You know what kind of person he is. And you're conflicted because Lyric is such a good and kind human being. It probably made sense to you that her father, despite his political panache and sharp debate skills, would also be a good and kind human being. I get it, I really do. But Lyric herself gathered plenty of information proving otherwise. And I know she wanted to talk to you about it."

"She did. Earlier today," Shelby lets a sigh roll from her chest. "Oh, God, I saw her. She was worried about you guys, about me, about how it would all turn out."

I nod slowly. "Bowman is using her as leverage right now. To get to us."

"Does Matthew know? I need to tell him!"

"He can't do anything about it. Bowman and Smith outnumber and outpower him right now. He is useless. But you, Shelby, you can help us."

"How?"

"I'm betting that you know which closet it is that Matthew keeps his skeletons. I need proof that he's a part of this conspiracy. That proof will put Bowman and Smith in the same pot. I need evidence to show the guys at Quantico before I accuse their entire Chicago field office of egregious acts, decades-long corruption, bribery, racketeering, and God knows what else. I need proof Shelby, so that I can get to Bowman and Smith before they do something awful and irreversible."

She narrows her eyes at me. "They want the three of you in jail for life. How is that awful?"

"What part of 'they kidnapped Lyric' didn't you understand?"

Shelby stops, briefly glancing at her bare feet.

"How did it get to this?" Shelby asks herself, tears streaming down her cheeks. "It doesn't make any sense. It's out of control. Matthew would never—"

"Don't think for a second that he will ever go against Bowman or Smith," I say. "They will never be punished for taking Lyric away, even if it's just for a few hours. They're depriving her of her freedom, Shelby. You can't let them do that. You have to pick a side—Lyric or her father. What will it be?"

"This is insane."

"You've known Lyric for years. You're best friends. Or you were best friends. As far as she's concerned, you still are, Shelby. What about you?"

"She has always been like a sister to me. I would never even think about hurting her or letting anyone else hurt her. I just can't believe her father would do something like this."

"You have to believe it. Look back on every interaction you've ever had with Matthew," I insist. "Look back, try to remember. How many times has Matthew said or done something that gave you pause. That made you worry or doubt him, if only for a second?"

Shelby gives me a pained look. "Too many times. I just chalked it up to politics."

"But it wasn't just politics, was it?"

"What can I do? I need Lyric to be okay."

"So do we. We also need all the ammo we can get against Matthew and his buddies. You're close to him, Shelby. Close enough to help us."

She shudders for a second when I slowly take out a small pocketknife and show it to her. She soon realizes what I intend to do with it, reaching her hands out so I can cut the cable ties off.

"Matthew will never forgive me," she mumbles as I get rid of her ankle restraints next. "But he's responsible for all of this. I can't stay blind forever."

"You're a good friend."

"He keeps a small, secret vault in his campaign office. It's filled with a variety of files—cash, flash drives, minidisks, that kind of stuff. He calls it his blackmail stash. I thought it was a joke at first until the time he met with one of his city council opponents, supposedly to talk. He took out one of the flash drives, put it into the guy's laptop, and played a few clips for him. By the end of the meeting, Matthew had the votes he needed to get a specific regulation to go through. His opponent resigned the next day. They found him dead about a week later from an overdose."

"Were you present for that meeting?"

"Yes, but I couldn't see the screen. No audio either, I think the video was on mute. Or maybe it was CCTV footage with no sound, I don't know."

"Do you remember the context of the conversation?"

CLAIMED BY THE BRATVA BROTHERS

She nods once. "I tried to talk to him about it after the guy left. Matthew said that it was the cost of fighting for the good people of Chicago and that he had no regrets. Getting his hands dirty in order for city legislation to pass felt like the right thing to do."

"And when he heard about the guy offing himself? What did he say?"

"Nothing. He didn't want to talk about it. But he was laughing, almost jovial. Accepting congratulations for other projects. Excited to do his fundraiser later that evening. Jesus, I've been ignoring a lot of stuff. The more I think about it—"

"The more you realize how awfully wrong you were about this man. I get it."

Shelby looks at me, shame burning red in her eyes. "I can show you the vault. I caught a glimpse of his access code."

"You need to be the one who hands the contents of that vault over to us. Legally, you'll stand a better chance against any retaliation from Matthew or his lawyers if you do," I warn her. "This will get ugly. But I promise, we'll get you the best counsel available. We'll protect you."

"I don't think I care about any of that right now but thank you. I just want it all to stop. I want Lyric back, Ivan, and if this helps you make that happen, I'm willing to do whatever you need."

This will tip the scales so hard, and so fast that Bowman, Smith, and Phelps won't even see it coming. I just hope we can get to Lyric before it's too late, and that once it's all over, we've all survived. Otherwise, I am ready to go down swinging if that's what it takes to protect the people I love.

With Shelby's intel, we'll be able to do the one thing we weren't sure we could do.

Our affairs in order, Max, Artur, and I prepare ourselves for the single, most challenging battle of our lives. The battle that will either cost us our lives in this war against this crooked faction of the Feds or win it. Everything is at stake. Everything can vanish into a puff of nothingness if we're not careful.

Or it could lead to that fabled happy ending that we never imagined we'd ever see, let alone have within our reach. It's almost there. I can almost touch it. I can almost taste its sweetness.

"Let's see how many of them come to our aid," Max says as we get out of the car.

We've been parked across the street from the FBI's Chicago field office for almost ten minutes. Watching. Waiting. From the outside looking in, it seems like a pretty standard institution. I wonder how many of the people who work there are aware of the dirty operations that take place behind some of its closed doors. I also wonder what they will do when the truth inevitably smacks them across the face.

"I'm not going to hold my breath considering this morning's vote," I mutter.

Truth be told, I am hopeful, but hope is a fickle and dangerous thing. It can feed you delusions and have you blinded to outcomes that would otherwise be considered inevitable. This is a wholly different kind of war that we're fighting.

"Word of Larionov's demise has already gotten out," Artur says. "I am curious as to how many will understand that it had to be done."

"Frankly, we're going to have our hands full either way," Max replies. "The Chinese and the Japanese were the first to raise their hands in that meeting. We'll need to have a sit-down with those fuckers."

"Provided we survive tonight," Artur scoffs.

"I don't know about you, but I plan on surviving."

"We have plenty to live for, don't we?" he says.

"We made it this far," Max chimes in. "We're almost at the finish line. If we pull through, the other families will have no choice but to accept our terms."

"It's insane either way," I say. "It's going to be one hell of a mess to clean up no matter the outcome."

"Then we'd best make sure it's the kind of outcome we're going to enjoy cleaning up after," Max replies with a deep frown. "I'm tired of this bullshit. And I'll bet you Lyric is tired, too."

Silence falls heavily over our shoulders whenever her name comes up. She's in there, scared and alone, at the mercy and whims of veritable monsters. The woman we love, the woman we intend to live the rest of our lives with—she's trapped, being used as bait to draw us out.

Max's phone pings. "Here we go," he mutters. "Our crew's about to converge on 45th and Lennox. Perfect timing."

"Good. Let's roll," I order, getting out of the car first.

Artur and Max follow, and the three of us cross the street with calm movements, our chins up. The closer we get to the building, however, the greater the dread clutching my heart.

Its grip tightens as we go up the front steps. Agents stare us down.

"Who are you and what are you doing here? It's midnight. The field office is closed to the public," one of them says.

"Let Director Smith know that the Sokolov's are here to surrender," Max replies.

The agents exchange stunned glances before one of them takes out his gun and points it at us. "Don't move."

"I said, we're here to surrender."

"Just don't move!"

"Alright, alright. Calm down," I grumble and slowly put my hands up.

Artur and Max do the same, their eyes scanning every inch around us, every movement. There's plenty of lighting in this area, mainly because of the federal buildings that line the street, along with the three major banks farther down the road. Cameras everywhere, and uniformed officers frequently out on patrol. Therefore, our faces will be clearly visible on multiple instances of CCTV footage. Time stamped and everything.

The first agent steps to the side and reaches out to a colleague inside the building via his radio. My ears twitch as I listen in. "Cole, I've got the Sokolov's here asking for the Director. Were we expecting them?"

The reply that comes through is muffled, but my guy seems to understand the words perfectly as he nods once.

"I see. Okay. We'll wait," he says, then puts the radio away and comes back to us with narrowed, suspicious eyes. "Are you carrying any weapons?"

"No, sir," Max replies. "You can search us."

He takes out a metal wand detector and runs it up and down each of us. It beeps in all the usual places: the belt buckle, the change in my pocket, my Rolex, the metal screws in my left shin. I lift my shirt and roll my pant cuffs up for him to see that I am, in fact, clean. After running the wand over us, they proceed to pat us down too, prompting Artur to chuckle.

"You fellas are a tad overzealous," he says.

"You're the fucking Bratva. Do we look stupid?" one of them replies and takes a step back, somewhat irritated that he hasn't found a single concealed weapon on any of us.

Artur shoots him a cold grin. "Don't ask questions you don't want the answer to."

"You're dead anyway," the first agent says, a sneer on his face.

Director Smith comes out, practically bursting through the double doors. He's accompanied by six heavily armed tactical agents, clad in black and Kevlar, their semi-automatic weapons pointed at our heads.

"Gentlemen. I didn't expect to see you here," Smith says.

I know he's being sincere. I can see it all over his face, he can't seem to hide it. He definitely did not see us coming, which is good. The element of surprise will work in our favor, hopefully. It doesn't stop my blood from rushing, however as I stare each of the agents down, tension stretching through my muscles until I feel as though I'm dangerously close to snapping.

"It wouldn't be the first time you underestimated us, Director Smith. But you've crossed a line," Max says, "and we need to talk."

"Oh, is that how you think this is going to go?" Smith laughs. "Sure. Let's talk." He looks at one of his agents. "Cuff them. Take their phones. They're going into holding downstairs."

"You do whatever you want," Max interjects. "But we need to see Lyric first."

Smith's lips stretch into a devious grin. "You know, when I first heard the rumors about the three of you, I thought, eh, people have fetishes, urges, whatever. But an actual relationship? You, fellas, are something else. It's almost a shame to see you go."

"I don't know what you're talking about," Max replies.

"Okay. I see how you want to play this," Smith chuckles, nodding back at the double doors. "Chop, chop."

We're cuffed and brutishly pushed through several doors before we're crammed into an elevator. Once we reach the basement, the entire atmosphere shifts into something dark, unsettling, and downright suffocating. The six agents escorting us split into two groups: three ahead, three behind. Smith leads the way, annoyingly chatty.

"I honestly didn't think you guys would make it here," he says. "Who'd you send over to that address we gave you?"

"It doesn't really matter now, does it?" Max replies.

Smith laughs. "Cannon fodder either way. You're right." He takes us through another massive steel door and the holding cell level opens up before us. I hear Lyric's rushed footsteps before I see her. "Here. As promised," Smith adds.

We reach Lyric's cell and she freezes with her fingers wrapped around the bars. "Oh, no," she mumbles, horror draining the blood from her face. "No, you can't be here."

"But we are," I say, giving her a faint smile.

"Are you okay?" Max asks while Artur scans her carefully from head to toe. She seems fine at first glance, but none of us is taking the emotional toll into account. Given the circumstances, I'm just grateful to see her awake and alert. "Did they hurt you?"

"They—"

"We had a bit of a snafu with the officer in charge of retrieving her," Smith cuts her off. "But she's good now. She's safe. As long as you three don't try anything stupid."

"You guys shouldn't have come here," Lyric says, a sense of urgency making her voice tremble. "They're going to kill you."

We know.

I can't really say that aloud, though. I can't give Smith that kind of satisfaction. But we walked in here knowing precisely what to expect, thanking the gods for every second that we still have on this earth. The longer Smith drags it out, the better for us.

We were banking on him to be his usual self-flattering, self-indulging, narcissistic, gloating piece of shit. So far, he hasn't disappointed us.

"Lyric, you're a smart girl. It's time for you to accept that there are things in this life that you simply cannot change," Smith says with a wry smile.

A few more seconds.

It's all we need.

27

LYRIC

My heart hurts. My throat burns.

I can't bear to see them down here, looking so helpless in those cuffs. The six agents surrounding them are trained and equipped to kill. How could they just walk into this? What were they thinking?

Instinctively, I place both hands on my belly, trying so hard to keep my composure while Smith revels in this so-called victory.

"Gentlemen, it's time we settle this," he says to the guys, while the armed agents take a few steps back to clear the corridor in between holding cells. With the "enemy" cuffed, they have nothing to worry about anyway. It makes me sick to my stomach. The door opens again, and in comes Bowman with a giant smile drawn upon his face. "Ah, the man of the hour," Smith chuckles as he greets his boss.

"I'm so glad I made it," Bowman replies. "How are our guests faring?"

"You two make quite the team," Artur mutters. "One just a little more psycho than the other."

"We're entrepreneurs, and intrepid ones at that," Bowman shoots back, eyeing each of them closely. "You three have been a handful for far too long. But tell me, what gives? We were supposed to meet you elsewhere. Didn't Smith give you—"

"I gave them the address," Smith rolls his eyes. It's the first sign that he is growing tired of Bowman. "They knew where to go."

"And yet here we are," Bowman says, nodding slowly. "I see. So, the three of you decided to surprise us?"

Max smiles. "Let's just say we decided to bring the circus to your doorstep. We've had our fun and now it's time to end this."

"You're in no position to play coy with me," Bowman replies, slightly irritated. "You've cost me a lot of time, and a lot of money. And your audacity to fucking kidnap me and hold me hostage hasn't been forgotten."

"Had we known you were the one in charge, I would've personally blown your brains out," Ivan says. "You're a lucky SOB."

"You win some, you lose some." Bowman laughs. "But let me tell you something—there's no bigger losers here tonight than the three of you. How does it feel?"

Artur raises an eyebrow. "I genuinely don't have the patience for your self-indulging bullshit."

"How does it feel knowing that all of your work was for nothing?"

"Not really for nothing. Larionov's dead," Ivan chimes in.

Bowman gives him a hard look. He wasn't prepared for that. A muscle twitches in his square jaw, but that's all the emotion he's willing to show over the news. "Your organization will move forward without you. The families are all on my side."

"It's funny," Max chuckles softly. "You've been covertly working with the underworld for so long and yet to this day, you still don't seem to understand that you can't trust anybody. Not really."

"Bold words for the Bratva's leadership," Smith replies. "Given your predicament."

"Tell me, Max, how does it feel knowing you're going to leave this world behind," Bowman adds, taking his gun out, "without ever meeting your child?"

My knees cave. I can barely hold on to the steel bars, the blood draining from my body with each passing second of heavy and confused silence. My breath falters. "No," I whisper. "Shut up."

"What did you say?" Max asks, never taking his eyes off Bowman.

But Artur and Ivan are watching me. Quiet. Motionless. Terror grips me tightly by the throat as I try to push through, to keep my chin up.

"Your precious Lyric here is with child," Bowman says, adopting a dramatic tone. "You didn't know? She didn't tell you? Which one of you is the father? Oh, that's right. It could be any one of you."

"Oh, God," I mumble, my face burning as I look down. This is not how I wanted them to find out. This is not how I wanted any of it to happen.

Max looks at me. "Lyric?"

"I was going to tell you," I manage, shaking like a leaf.

"Are you telling me you kidnapped a pregnant woman?" he asks Bowman. "That you've been holding a pregnant woman hostage to get to us?"

"Whatever it takes," Bowman replies with a shrug. "But tell me. Be honest. How does it feel to lose so much in less than twenty-four hours' time?"

"You're delusional," Max says. "Did you really think we'd come down here just so you can kill us?"

Smith laughs lightly. "We're prepared for anything, Mr. Sokolov. Granted, we thought we'd handle you at a different address, but this works just as well."

"Does it? How many cameras show us coming up to the building and peacefully surrendering?" Max asks.

"Doesn't matter. Footage can be scrubbed," Smith says.

It's Ivan's turn to laugh. "Have you heard from your strike team over at 45th and Lennox yet?"

Bowman and Smith both give him a troubled glare. I see it in their eyes. The doubt. The sudden concern. I can almost hear their thoughts, the self-assuredness dwindling and fizzling away as a different scenario begins to take shape in their minds.

It's relatively easy to fuck with a powerful man's head if you know which buttons to push. It didn't take a psychologist to figure these two out, and Ivan knew exactly where to hit them. Drunk on their own Kool-Aid, having gone unchecked for too long.

"Well?" Ivan asks, grinning. All I can do is hold my breath and watch the nightmare unfold, bracing myself for any potential outcome—though I don't know how I'll cope if the worst happens. "Any word?"

"What the fuck are you talking about?" Smith grumbles and takes out his phone.

"We were supposed to be there at precisely midnight, right?" Ivan asks. "What time is it now?"

Bowman gives Smith a curious look. "It's ten minutes past. Did they check in?"

"No," the director replies and starts calling his crew. A few rings in, and it begins to dawn on the guy that there's nobody left at 45th and Lennox to pick up. "You son of a bitch," he growls at Ivan. "What did you do?"

"What did I do? Nothing," Ivan retorts. "We've been here the whole time. What did our cousins do? Well, that's something else entirely, but it was probably exceptionally bloody and brutal. The Ivanovich boys, they're wildcards. But I'm sure you already know that."

Max exhales sharply. "I understand that power and success can warp your reality to the point where you feel invincible, Mr. Bowman. But life and the families that control Chicago are nowhere near as predictable as you think they are. That little vote you held this morning? Consider it scratched. We're not going down that easily."

"Wanna bet?" Bowman hisses and removes the safety on his gun. "On your knees. We're done here."

"Oh, you might want to rethink that," Max says.

Mayhem erupts from somewhere upstairs. Loud bangs and boots thudding along the upper floors. Glass breaking. Men shouting. Smith glances over his shoulder, his brow furrowed with concern. "What the fuck is happening?"

"Go check," Bowman snarls.

"With me," Smith tells the armed agents. He heads for the door, but the men give each other clearly hesitant looks. I'm sure they understand what's going on upstairs and they don't want to be on the receiving end. "What are you doing?" Smith asks when none of them move.

"You said it would be a clean operation," one of the agents replies.

Max shoots them a cool grin. "That's Quantico upstairs. The cavalry has arrived, and trust me, they're not here for us."

"What?" another agent croaks, shocked enough to take his mask off as he gives Smith the ugliest look. "What the fuck did you do?"

Smith points an angry finger at him. "Follow my lead. Let's go upstairs and see what's going on. Now."

"Fuck that. You go," the agent insists.

"Come on," a third guy gives him a nudge.

There's some mild protest, but nothing that Smith's barking orders can't handle. These are lower-level agents. Tactical gearheads who follow orders no matter what. And dirty as hell.

Reluctantly, the team of agents follows Smith through the door, leaving Bowman with the four of us. But Bowman seems unsettled and ready to blow. Fury mars his features, causing a vein to thicken and throb along his temple as he looks at the men.

"What the fuck is this?" he asks, his voice barely a whisper.

"Your reckoning, you piece of shit," Ivan answers.

"We called Quantico and delivered all the proof they needed to come down here and clean house," Max adds. "Your bestie Matthew foolishly kept a treasure trove of incriminating evidence against you and your entire crew. And all of that precious material is now in the hands of the Deputy Director of the FBI, who sounded pretty pissed when I reached out to him about all this."

"What evidence?" Bowman asks, unable to keep a clear focus.

"You name it, he's got it. Paper trails. Photographs. Video. Court and bank documents. Statements. Photocopies of each of your ledgers," Max replies. "Your pride is going to be your undoing, Mr. Bowman. You don't go after the heads of the Bratva and expect us to just quiver and bow down."

Bowman exhales deeply, then raises his gun and points it at me. "Then I start with Lyric first."

2 8

LYRIC

I'm paralyzed with fear, staring right into the muzzle of Bowman's weapon. I can almost feel its cold steel pressed into my forehead, even though there are still several inches between us. Thick air that reeks of death and violence.

"You don't want to do this," Max warns him.

But he, Ivan, and Artur still have their hands cuffed behind their backs. Bowman is keeping them at a reasonable distance. Ivan tries to step toward him, but Bowman fires a warning shot at the ground close to his boots.

I scream and burst into tears, shaking as I move away from the bars.

"Bowman, stop!" Max shouts, his shoulders broad and heavy as he gives him a murderous look. "It's over. For you, for Smith. It's over. Don't do anything to make it worse."

"You forget, I'm still the one holding the gun." Bowman points it at Artur next. "And I swear the second bullet I fire will go right into her pretty little head if you don't stay where you are."

"Please," I mumble, "please, Mr. Bowman... Jack... stop this. I'm pregnant, my baby doesn't deserve to die. Please."

"I decide who lives and who dies tonight. And I've had about enough of you."

He sets his sights on me again.

Time slows down to a halt.

I hold my breath.

I can see his finger squeezing the trigger. I'm frozen, unable to breathe, unable to even think.

My heart stops for what feels like an eternity.

Suddenly, I see movement out of the corner of my eye. Ivan, as big as a mountain, lunges at him. Bowman is too crazed and determined to kill me that he doesn't see Ivan until it's too late. Ivan rams into him with the full weight of his massive body. I hear Bowman's lungs deflate as he's knocked down and Ivan lands on top of him.

"Fuck." Artur drops to the floor.

POP. POP. POP.

Gunshots erupt somewhere just beyond the door, getting louder and louder, as Artur struggles, twisting and turning himself until he manages to get his cuffed hands to the front.

Ivan and Bowman are wrestling on the floor. Bowman gets the upper hand and pulls himself to his feet.

He delivers a kick to Ivan's ribs that steals his breath for a minute before Artur tackles him back to the ground.

Max comes in and kicks Bowman in the face. I hear his jaw crackling from the sheer force of the blow.

Everything happens so fast. They're all scrambling for control. Bowman is desperate to get to the gun before any of my guys can. Artur almost reaches it, but in the scuffle and confusion, the gun gets kicked closer to me, sliding just outside the bars.

I don't hesitate.

I rush and drop to my knees, sticking my hand out between the bars to grab it.

Bowman has Max in a headlock. I can see my love's face draining of color, his eyes losing focus. I point the gun at Bowman. "Stop it!" I scream.

"Look at you," he chuckles, then lets Max go. "What are you going to do with that? Shoot me?"

"Don't move!" I reply, both hands shaking as I struggle to keep the gun aimed at him. I'm not sure I'm able to sell this but it's worth a shot. Anything to buy us some time, just until the real Feds get down here. "Do not fucking move."

Ivan groans as he tries to sit up.

Bowman chuckles again and pulls another gun, a smaller piece, from an ankle holster.

"Don't!" I warn him.

But I cannot reason with this man. He's well past any kind of redemption. He isn't interested in salvation. He just wants to take as many of us down with him as he can. His all-or-nothing mentality is out of control.

"Bowman, stop!" Max coughs and wheezes, still recovering from that gruesome headlock.

"Don't do this," Artur says, the handgun now pointed at him.

"I'll do whatever the fuck I want," Bowman snarls as he curls his finger over the trigger.

BANG.

I fire the gun.

The bullet pierces Bowman's torso. Blood seeps through his suit and shirt. Everything turns red as he gives me a stunned, wide-eyed look. His lips part, ever so slowly. "You little bitch," he whispers.

I watch as he falls to his knees, dropping the gun.

Artur kicks it away and takes a step back as Bowman falls flat on his face.

"Oh, God," I whimper, realizing what I just did.

"It's okay," Max says to me. "Lyric, look at me. Look at me."

I look at him, rivers of tears streaming down my cheeks. "Max…"

"It's okay," he says it again.

We're alive.

I killed a man. But we survived. I killed him so that we would survive. My brain is wrapped in a cold and heavy fog. I'm unable to process anything. Max keeps talking to me. I can hear him, but I'm not sure I understand. Artur and Ivan are on their knees, waiting.

They're all looking at me.

Scared. Worried. Relieved. A million emotions flash through their eyes at once. Everything moves in slow motion as the door bursts open. The corridor is suddenly flooded by over a dozen FBI agents and SWAT operatives.

I drop the gun.

I barely register reality.

But it's over.

29

LYRIC

"Be careful, she's pregnant," Max tells one of the EMTs.

We're outside the field office now. I'm sitting in the back of an ambulance, with a full view of a mass arrest in progress. There are about six emergency crews present, along with two coroner vans and a slew of black SUVs. Quantico descended upon this place with its full and unforgiving force. Max sits next to me, getting his bruises and cuts treated by another paramedic.

Artur and Ivan are just a few steps to our left, giving their statements directly to the Deputy Director of the FBI, who is flanked by two supervisory agents and two internal affairs supervisors. This entire situation is a giant stain on the Bureau, and I have no idea how they'll manage to clean it all up.

"Pulse is good," the EMT tells me. "Blood pressure's a little high, but that's likely from the shock. You're going to be okay, but I'd still like to take you to the hospital for a full checkup, just to make sure."

"Okay."

"How's it looking?" Max asks him.

My cheeks burn as I feel his gaze searing a hole into my very soul. He knows I'm pregnant now, and I reckon he's got questions, concerns, things he wants to say to me. Artur and Ivan too. They keep stealing glances my way, but there is so much going on, all of it at once, that we can barely focus, let alone process anything.

"It's a goddamn mess," the EMT says. "I haven't gone in yet but I heard it through the radio. Lots of casualties."

"Where's Director Smith?" Max calls out to the Deputy Director.

"In custody. They're bringing him out now," he replies, then continues to take Ivan's statement.

I give Max a curious look. "How did you know I'd be here? How'd you get Quantico involved?"

He chuckles softly, then winces when the paramedic applies disinfectant to a small gash above his eyebrow. "Fucking hell."

"Sorry, man."

"It's alright," he sighs and looks at me. "I told you we were doing things by the book. That meant taking Bowman and Smith out the legit way, too. Your friend Shelby was instrumental in all of this. She really came through for us."

"She did?" I can't help but smile, thankful to know that Shelby picked the right side.

Commotion erupts among the police officers and federal agents present outside the field office building as Director

Smith is brought out in cuffs, roughly handled by his own colleagues. They look angry while Smith keeps staring into the ground, his lip bruised and his left eye gradually reddening and swelling. I guess they smacked him around a bit before they put the cuffs on.

"There he is, that piece of shit," one man says.

"We were lucky they got here in time," Max says, then gives me a subtle nudge with his shoulder. "And you did the right thing."

"I killed a man," I reply, a knot still tightening in the back of my throat. "I know I had no choice. I know. But it doesn't change the facts."

"You're going to have to process all of this one day at a time. You'll have to forgive yourself, baby," he says, keeping his voice down while our attending paramedics go over to other injured agents to check and make sure they're good to go. It got surprisingly messy in there. I'd have thought that the crooked Feds would surrender upon seeing their colleagues, but one too many of them chose to go down swinging, unable to cope with the shame of having been exposed. "Lyric," Max pulls me back into the present. "You're going to be okay, I promise."

"I'm already okay," I tell him. "We're alive. It's all that matters."

"There will be congressional hearings," the Deputy Director tells Artur and Ivan once he's done with their statements. "I hope the three of you will attend."

"Only if you keep your end of the bargain," Max politely cuts in.

"I gave you my word. Full immunity," the Deputy Director begrudgingly replies. That means about a dozen active investigations will be coming to an abrupt end, but given the shitstorm that they'll be dealing with, I think they're better off not bothering with the Bratva for a while.

Ivan comes over and plants a kiss on my forehead. "How are you feeling?"

"Better now," I say, giving him a weak smile.

"They're going to run some tests at the hospital," Max tells him. "Just to be sure."

"Good," Artur says.

"It's been quite the ride," I say, once Max and the guys are done bringing me up to speed with how we got to this point in the first place.

But they were true to their word. They swore they'd turn the Bratva's businesses legit, and they used an iron fist to get the job done.

"We still have a long way to go," Max says. "But from what I can tell, the other families are on board. For real this time."

"And the Larionov's?" I ask.

Max shakes his head. "They have no choice."

"We'll be having some conversations with the Chinese and the Japanese and anyone else who was at that meeting with Bowman," Artur adds. "It's going to get worse before it gets better. We expect some retaliation as a consequence of our decisions but we'll deal with it as it comes."

The coroner comes out while his assistants push Bowman's gurney through the open doors. The mere sight of that black bag fills me with dread and a peculiar sickness of the soul. I'm responsible for that, and like Max said, it's going to take a while for me to deal with it.

"Lyric!" Shelby cries out while two officers try to hold her back from breaching their line. But she manages to slip past them. She runs right at me, while Artur motions for the cops to leave her be. "Oh, Lyric, I'm so sorry!" she says as she throws her arms around me. "I was worried sick about you."

"It's fine, Shel. I'm okay, I promise," I reply, softening in her embrace.

The strange comfort she gives me is something I didn't even know I needed until now. Her warmth, her familiar face, her unending kindness—it all prevailed against my father's wretched charms.

"I heard what happened," Shelby says, her eyes searching my face. "Are you hurt?"

"More like sore," I sigh deeply. "And still shaking."

She glances down at my trembling hands, a pained flash dancing in her gaze. "That's the adrenaline wearing off, babe. You'll be okay."

"Let's hope so."

"And Bowman?"

I shake my head slowly. "He didn't make it."

"What happened?"

"I don't want to talk about it," I mumble, and Shelby is quick to catch on. Besides, the worried looks on Max, Ivan, and Artur's faces speak volumes. Just enough to give her a rough sketch of what happened. "What matters most is that it's over."

"More or less, yeah," Shelby replies. "Your father won't fare well."

"I guess not."

I don't enjoy the thought of what's to come. My father will pay for his share in these egregious crimes. It's been a long time coming. But it's one thing to suspect him of being dirty and corrupt, it's a whole other thing to have concrete evidence about it. It's downright heartbreaking. My worst nightmares coming true, one after the other, in the span of a single day. I'll need a year's worth of sleep to recover from this madness.

"I'm sorry, Shelby," I tell my best friend. "I'm sorry you found yourself in this situation. I'm sorry you had to choose between me and my dad."

"Don't even go there," she says. "The choice was obvious. I learned a lot from you over the years. I'm the one who's sorry. For what it's worth, I lost myself and I forgot about us. I was so focused on your father and his attention, affection, theatrics, whatever you want to call it. I was so drawn into him that I wasn't being a good friend to you."

"I'm sorry you had to find out the hard way that he only cares about himself."

"Well, let's see him care about himself in prison, 'cause that's where he's headed," she grumbles, but I can sense the hurt in her voice. He broke her heart, and she will need time to mend it. However, I'm glad she's free of him. "I already told your guys that they can count on me to testify against him.

They're all going down, Shelby. Matthew Phelps can kiss his political career goodbye."

Artur lets out a dry chuckle. "You do realize that you'll be like active uranium in the political world, right Shelby? No senator or congressman will want to work with you after you bury Phelps."

"That's okay. I'm getting my master's in political science. It doesn't mean I have to pursue a political career," she replies with a casual shrug. "I will have plenty of other opportunities."

"Analysts make a ton of money through TV appearances," Max suggests.

Shelby thinks about it for a second, then glances back at the swelling mass of reporters clamoring beyond the police line. "You know what? You're absolutely right. If you'll excuse me, I should go introduce myself." She kisses me on the cheek and casually walks away, eager to take the media head on.

"I'm gob smacked," I laugh lightly. "I've never seen anyone landing so gracefully on their feet. Shelby is amazing."

"That, she most certainly is," Max says. "But we still need to talk about the proverbial elephant in the room." He moves closer and wraps his arm around my shoulders, pulling me in. "You're pregnant?"

"I... yeah," I sigh. "I was working up the courage to tell you. I just wasn't sure when it would've been the right time. You were dealing with all of this."

"So we're going to be dads," Artur concludes, amusement twinkling in his grey eyes.

"If you want to be," I mumble.

Ivan frowns. "What do you mean, if we want to? Of course we want to be dads. We almost got ourselves killed to get you back, Lyric."

"I never would've forgiven myself if anything happened to you."

"And I couldn't possibly live with myself if we didn't take this thing between us to the next level," Max says. "Through thick and thin, Lyric. We're stuck together, you hear me? You, me, Ivan, Artur, the little one here," he adds, gently cupping my lower belly. "We're stuck together."

"It's not the worst thing that's ever happened to me," I quip, smiling as a golden kind of warmth fills my heart and spills into my chest, my muscles gradually relaxing against Max's hard, strong body.

Artur chuckles, carefully looking around to make sure that nobody can hear. "I wonder which one of us did it."

"Honestly, it doesn't matter to me."

"It doesn't matter to us either," Ivan says. "Unless it's for medical reasons, I'm fine with never knowing which of us is the biological father."

Max kisses my temple. I wish I could just lose myself in their arms right here, without a care in the world. But there are too many people around us. Too much law enforcement. Too much press. Too many eyes watching. We must be careful. We may have prevailed against Bowman and Smith, we may have survived one hellish nightmare, but we can't risk getting ourselves embroiled in another scandal that could yield unwanted consequences.

"I love you," I tell my men out of the sweetest, nocturnal blue.

"We love you too, Lyric," Max promptly replies. "More than you can imagine."

Artur smiles. "More than we ever imagined we could."

30

LYRIC

Watching my father testify against Smith on video is quite something. I should be practicing my dissertation, but the video just came out on social media, and I couldn't resist. It's been a month since Bowman died. Smith and my father were arrested, along with other prominent federal agents, police officers, lawyers, judges, and congressional staff members, not to mention dozens of associates, businessmen and others involved in what can only be described as one of the biggest and most influential networks in Chicago's history.

I've given my share of interviews to the FBI and the police, though I managed to steer clear of the press altogether. Max and the guys have had one of their top lawyers by my side through it all, covering my back against any potential charges.

From what I hear, Smith's attorneys have been slinging mud in each direction in an attempt to get their client out of trouble, but it sounds like his best option is to make a deal.

"I had no knowledge of Mr. Bowman and Director Smith's plans to kidnap and hold my daughter hostage," my father tells the judge on camera. "Had I been aware, I would've called the police myself."

"Yeah, right," I grumble, knowing full well that he would've hesitated and sought ways to cover his own ass first.

I will need a lot of time to get over it all. Until then, however, I resort to mumbling and cursing under my breath, not able to bear even hearing his name mentioned in conversation while I focus on my future, my career, and my babies.

I was shocked when the doctor told me I was having twins after the incident at the field office, but the guys and I couldn't be more thrilled.

"Miss Phelps, the board is ready for you," the dean's assistant says, poking her head through the door. "They're waiting."

"Thank you," I reply with a smile and put my phone away.

I take a deep breath and follow her into the main chamber—a large circular hall with massive marble pillars and wall-mounted portraits of the city's most revered scientists. The University of Chicago was my home for four long years, and it could be my home again if my dissertation is accepted and published.

I greet the board members with a courteous nod and give my flash drive to the assistant, who loads it into the projector-connected laptop.

"Good morning, Miss Phelps. It's a pleasure to see you again," Dean Johnson says.

"Likewise, Dean. It's an honor to be here," I reply, working hard to control my breathing as I look at each of the board members and try to figure out which one of them will be rejecting my project. One of them always does. Never in the history of UC has a dissertation passed without some kind of academic dissent. "But just to be clear, I will not be discussing my predictive algorithm for this thesis."

Johnson gives me a startled look. "Hold on. I thought that was your focus. You've been very adamant about it even before you earned your Bachelor's. What gives, Miss Phelps?"

"I was actually excited to hear about it," Professor Gallan chimes in, her brow slightly furrowed.

"I know and I do apologize. While my work continues with the algorithm, it still has a number of considerable kinks to iron out before it's ready," I reply. "I promise that when it is, you'll be the first to hear about it."

The board members exchange curious and confused glances.

I've decided that I cannot have my predictive algorithm anywhere near the public domain. It can be a dangerous tool in the wrong hands. I've seen what bad men are willing to do for power—my father, Bowman, Smith. I shudder to even imagine what someone like them would do with my algorithm at their fingertips.

The world isn't ready for this, and I'm not ready to risk it. It wasn't an easy decision.

"For what it's worth," I say as the projector comes on, the first page of my slideshow filling up the main presentation screen behind me, "I can assure you my dissertation subject will incite your interest."

Johnson stares at the title for a while, then bursts into laughter.

"Turning the Mafia Legit: An in-depth how-to for organized crime to redesign their business model," he reads aloud. "Miss Phelps, I admit, I'm already curious."

"It took a lot of work to put this together in such a short period of time, but I am satisfied with the results of this study. The business model itself can be extrapolated and applied to other fields, as well. It follows a specific formula with numerous ramifications."

"Please, do go ahead then."

And so it begins.

The next stage of my life, of my career, as I steer myself in a slightly different direction. Nothing has ever gone according to plan for me, yet somehow I managed to flow like water, to adjust and adapt and make the most of every situation. Through it all, nothing has been more beautiful and more rewarding than my relationship with Max, Ivan, and Artur.

No matter what the board decides today, I'm walking out of here as a happy and already accomplished woman, with only the sky as my limit.

I power through the dissertation one slide at a time. It's a good subject with practical applications, studied and observed over the span of a few months. I have solid data to back up my claims, and the board grows increasingly fascinated as I progress with my conclusions.

My confidence grows as I notice their expressions softening as I near the end, especially Dean Johnson's. His opinion matters the most— it's his vote that will get me my PhD.

"Therefore, the model I presented follows a real-life application," I say in closing.

"I think I recognize the real-life application," Johnson chuckles softly. "Is it the Sokolov Corporation? Or am I wrong?"

"You're not wrong," I reply with a smile.

He nods slowly. "I must admit, I've been following their story closely since the whole FBI debacle. What a mess that was."

"Indeed, it was."

I still have nightmares about it, but I sleep wrapped in the arms of three incredible men. Men whose dark sides are always ready to crush those who intend to do us harm. It doesn't get any better than this for me, and I don't want it to.

I live in two different worlds and I love it. I have an odd sense of peace now. It didn't end well for most of the people involved—my father included—but I survived and found happiness. Justice prevailed.

"I'm sorry you had to go through all that," says Professor Raskolnikov, a macro-economy specialist and Russian defector.

"It shouldn't have any bearing on my performance here today," I reply with a soft smile. "I refuse to let any of that define me as a doctor and a scholar in my field, Professor."

"Nor will it, despite the interesting choice of subject for your thesis," Raskolnikov says. "I do, however, appreciate your dissertation, more than you might ever understand. You basically took the very concept of oligarchy and demolished it."

"While simultaneously crushing capitalism as well," Johnson adds. "Well done, Miss Phelps." He pauses and looks at his colleagues. "What do you say, ladies and gentlemen? Has

Miss Phelps raised herself to the standards of a doctorate, today? Is she ready to advance her academic career and perhaps even join our research team?"

The minute that follows feels like the longest in my life.

I hold my breath, my body quivering. I'm getting closer to my due date. I'll be a mother soon. The thought both terrifies and exhilarates me at the same time. Everything is happening at once, and not a day goes by that I don't thank the stars for putting me in the company of Max, Ivan, and Artur.

Whatever the board decides, I know I'll be happy.

THE SOKOLOV MANSION is peaceful now. The tabloids have dubbed it the "Fort Knox of Chicago" and for good reason. It is constantly guarded by an elite team of security experts, all former military and SEAL operatives. Rough men with hard, sharp eyes and inscrutable instincts.

The FBI has stepped away from most of its investigations into the Bratva while they clean house—and boy, do they have a mess on their hands. It has allowed us to breathe again and relax.

I pull into the driveway and get out of my car. Olya, one of the guards, greets me and offers to park it in the garage. More than once, he has noticed me struggling and has made it his personal task.

"Don't worry about it, Miss Phelps. You're a genius in other aspects of life. Any monkey can park a car, but not anyone can do what you do with numbers," Olya chuckles as he gets behind the wheel, noticing my blushed cheeks.

"You're too kind," I giggle and go inside.

"There she is!" Max exclaims as he comes out of the kitchen to greet me. "How'd it go?"

Ivan and Artur join us in the hallway, all three greeting me with broad, sparkling smiles and big, round eyes. It melts my heart to see them like this. There's nothing I love more than to come home to them. Nothing.

I hold up my degree, which I stopped to have professionally framed on the way back. "Got it."

"Congratulations, baby!" Max exclaims and lovingly wraps his arms around my generous waist. "I knew you'd get it."

Artur snatches the degree away and squints at it. "Turning the Mafia Legit. I can't believe you went ahead with that title. I suggested it as a joke."

"It's a catchy joke and it worked," I laugh.

Ivan rests a hand on the small of my back and smothers me with quick, soft kisses. "I'm proud of you, Lyric. So damn proud."

"Thank you, babe," I mumble and kiss him back.

"Hold on, I want some of that," Artur chuckles as he sets the degree aside and rushes in, capturing my mouth in a long, ardent kiss. "I've missed you."

"I've only been gone a few hours."

"I always miss you when you're gone," he says. "No matter how long or short of a time."

Max runs his fingers through my long hair, pulling my head back gently so he can plant wet kisses along the side of my neck. "Oh, wow," I gasp as Ivan's fingers get to work on unbuttoning my shirt. At the same time, I hear Artur's belt unbuckling.

"We've been waiting for you," Max whispers and licks my lower lip.

Artur comes up behind me, heating my core with his strong, athletic frame. "You're dangerously addictive, Lyric, I thought you knew that."

"I don't mind hearing it again now and then."

"It's true, we do miss you when you're gone," Ivan says. My shirt drops to the floor and he gets to work on my pants next. Before long, I'm naked and wanting, wedged between my equally naked and wanting men. Liquid arousal trickles down my inner thighs. "It makes having you all to ourselves all the more special."

Max lets his fingers slide between my wet folds. I crumble under his touch, moaning harshly as he stimulates my clit in a slick frenzy. He is ruthless in his conquest, while Ivan fondles my breasts and takes his sweet time nipping, sucking, and licking my nipples until they're perked and dark pink.

"Your breasts are spectacular these days," Artur groans, moving to the side so he can better watch what Ivan is doing to me. "Motherhood is already looking so good on you, baby."

"Oh, God, I need you inside me," I cry out, nearing the edge of madness as he strokes me harder and faster. My pussy clenches, the pressure building up. We've been a tad more careful with how far we push things during this final lap of my pregnancy, but we haven't been able to keep our hands off each other. I grab him and Ivan by their cocks, squeezing and stroking them at the same time, letting my hands revel in the hard feel of their manhood as Artur shifts back behind me. "I need you, now."

Artur gently places a hand on my back, between my shoulder blades, prompting me to bend slightly forward. Max flicks my clit one last time and I come hard, gushing and whimpering in sheer ecstasy just as Artur fills me to the brim. He can feel me twitching, pulsating as I wrap myself around his massive cock.

"Oh, yes," I groan as I let him stretch me, slowly at first, while Max and Ivan grin like devils, gently inviting me to service them with my mouth, not just my hands.

I smile back, my vision hazy with drunken love, as I take turns sucking them off.

Artur goes deeper and harder. "Fucking hell, you're still going," he groans, realizing that I'm still riding one hell of an orgasm with him inside of me. It only makes him fuck me harder. I love the sound of skin slapping skin, and the way he smacks my ass only adds to a new wave of pressure gathering in my core.

I look up at Max, my lips stretched, my mouth full of him, and give him a playful wink. It makes his cock twitch as he bites into his lower lip, tucking a lock of hair behind my ear. Soon enough, I've got them both on the tip of my tongue. I lick them, suckling their heads and tasting the salty precum as they grow bigger and harder in my hands.

Artur picks up the pace.

"Yes baby!" I groan as I feel another climax coming.

I surrender to the rhythm, welcoming him harder and faster, parting my legs and bending a bit more forward so that I can feel him even deeper. I listen to the sound of his ragged breath as he claims me, his hand slipping around my hip so he can tease my clit until I come again.

Ivan grunts harshly, locking both hands on my head as he briefly takes over from his brother. "Open wide, Lyric."

"Mmm…" I unhinge my jaw as he slides down my throat.

So many inches. Tears spring from my eyes as he fucks me deeper, as well, while Artur has complete dominance over my pussy. I'm close to exploding when I feel Ivan's seed shooting down my throat. I swallow every drop, moaning as I feel him coming, over and over, pumping me full of him while Artur spills himself inside of me.

I moan, rippling from the center to the very edges of the universe as I fall over into the sweetest darkness. Max rushes to reclaim his position, and I take him in my mouth once again.

Artur slaps my ass as I clench and squeeze his cock dry.

I hold Max with both hands and suck hard on the tip, massaging the shaft until I feel him explode.

"We didn't even make it to the bedroom this time," Artur chuckles and drops a kiss on my shoulder as we gradually come down from a deeply intense afterglow.

My hair falls over my face, sweat sticking it to my forehead and cheeks. Max gingerly helps me back into a standing position, then escorts me upstairs. Ivan and Artur follow.

"I love this look on you," Artur says.

"Naked and glowing?" I giggle softly. "Pregnant? All of the above?"

"All of the above," he replies.

It sparks an instant fire inside as I realize how perfect this entire moment is. We don't even reach the bedroom, only the top of the stairs, when I stop, turn around and look into their eyes.

"Have I told you all that I love you today?" I ask.

"You're telling us now," Max replies.

"I'll tell you every day, if you'll let me."

"I wouldn't have it any other way," Ivan mutters and bites into my shoulder.

And just like that, we're on again. Engines rumbling, bodies crashing into one another, souls dissolving and reaching for the upper heavens.

It's been a crazy ride and then some, but we made it. We survived violence and chaos of the worst kind. Treachery, death, manipulation. There were so many forces against us yet we prevailed.

The road ahead will not be easy but it will be different.

The ride will be smoother because we'll be together. We're building a future. A family of our own. A weird slice of heaven that is ours and ours alone. It cannot get any better than this.

EPILOGUE I
LYRIC

"They're perfect," Ivan says, looking down at our sleeping twins.

"I still can't believe there's two of them," Max adds, a somewhat bewildered smile on his face.

"Double the trouble," I jokingly warn him, then wince from the pain in my lower belly. The painkillers will wear off soon, but it was worth it. I'll have a quick and seamless recovery, the doctors and nurses assured me. "If we keep this up, gentlemen…"

"We'll increase the population of Chicago in no time," Artur quips.

My men slowly approach the bed and take turns holding their newborn sons. I love seeing them like this. I admire their features as they soften, as they practically melt and fawn over the boys, filling my heart with nothing but joy and endless love.

I'm exhausted and still somewhat groggy from the anesthesia, but I'm also hungry and ready to take this new challenge on.

The guys take turns shuffling the babies between them before placing them in their bassinets next to my bed.

Max smiles and comes to my side, eager to kiss me, lovingly caressing my face. "You were incredible, Lyric. You've truly blessed us."

"And I cannot love you more," Ivan adds and kisses me. Deeply. Sweetly. Pouring his heart and soul through his lips and flooding my heart with his.

I welcome their love. Artur's delicate pecks on the cheek. His honeylike whispers. Max's gentle caresses. I welcome everything they're so eager to give me while our sons sleep soundly in their little beds, warm and comfortable swaddled in their blankets.

"I never thought I'd find myself here," I say, melting in Max's embrace.

"Neither did I but I welcome every second," he replies.

"We have kids now," Ivan says, laughing as he slowly shakes his head. "I didn't think we'd ever see this day, to be honest."

Artur gives him a smile. "Given what we've been through, it's a miracle, isn't it?"

"Lyric is our miracle," Max declares. "Our boys are just the first of many bonuses."

"We never settled on names," Artur reminds us. What are we naming them?"

EPILOGUE II
LYRIC

"They're perfect," Ivan says, looking down at our sleeping twins.

"I still can't believe there's two of them," Max adds, a somewhat bewildered smile on his face.

"Double the trouble," I jokingly warn him, then wince from the pain in my lower belly. The painkillers will wear off soon, but it was worth it. I'll have a quick and seamless recovery, the doctors and nurses assured me. "If we keep this up, gentlemen…"

"We'll increase the population of Chicago in no time," Artur quips.

My men slowly approach the bed and take turns holding their newborn sons. I love seeing them like this. I admire their features as they soften, as they practically melt and fawn over the boys, filling my heart with nothing but joy and endless love.

I'm exhausted and still somewhat groggy from the anesthesia, but I'm also hungry and ready to take this new challenge on.

The guys take turns shuffling the babies between them before placing them in their bassinets next to my bed.

Max smiles and comes to my side, eager to kiss me, lovingly caressing my face. "You were incredible, Lyric. You've truly blessed us."

"And I cannot love you more," Ivan adds and kisses me. Deeply. Sweetly. Pouring his heart and soul through his lips and flooding my heart with his.

I welcome their love. Artur's delicate pecks on the cheek. His honeylike whispers. Max's gentle caresses. I welcome everything they're so eager to give me while our sons sleep soundly in their little beds, warm and comfortable swaddled in their blankets.

"I never thought I'd find myself here," I say, melting in Max's embrace.

"Neither did I but I welcome every second," he replies.

"We have kids now," Ivan says, laughing as he slowly shakes his head. "I didn't think we'd ever see this day, to be honest."

Artur gives him a smile. "Given what we've been through, it's a miracle, isn't it?"

"Lyric is our miracle," Max declares. "Our boys are just the first of many bonuses."

"We never settled on names," Artur reminds us. What are we naming them?"

Extended Epilogue: Lyric

My father stares at me in sheer disbelief.

"Lyric, why didn't you tell me?" he asks from behind a thick, bulletproof glass pane. The orange prison jumpsuit makes him look pale and sickly. Then again, he's been here for almost a year now. Matthew Phelps is but a shadow of the man he used to be, and judging by the healing bruises on his face, his inmates don't like him much. "You have twins?"

"Sasha and Alexander. Twin boys," I reply, calmly seated in my chair.

He reaches out, touching the glass with a look of longing in his eyes. "I'm happy for you."

"They're Sokolov sons. I'm not sure how happy that makes *you*," I mutter.

"It doesn't really matter anymore," he says with a heavy sigh. "I'm spending another nine years in this place. It's all water under the bridge. I've made my peace."

"Have you, really?"

I don't believe him. I know from our lawyers that he has been trying to appeal his sentence. Former Director Smith sang like a bird once he was confronted with the prospect of twenty years in general population. As a member of law enforcement, he wouldn't have survived his first year.

So he sang and then some. About Bowman, about my father, about other state and city officials who worked closely with his group. Heads rolled. Prison sentences were meted out aplenty. My father didn't stand a chance, though he did try to make a deal with the Attorney General.

But he had nothing of value to give them.

The information that Shelby provided rendered him ripe for the picking. The jury was swift, the judge was unforgiving. Lucky for him, the magnitude of his crimes only got him a decade in prison. It's better than nothing, our lawyers reiterated.

"What do you mean?" my father asks, looking innocently confused.

"Did you really think you could get away with trying to smear my name?" I reply, smiling and remaining calm, just like Max taught me. "Did you think the editor of Chicago's biggest tabloid wouldn't reach out to the Sokolov Corporation when you first approached him with your salacious gossip about me? Are you for real, Dad?"

He leans back, growing increasingly uncomfortable. I hit a nerve. "I don't know what you're talking about."

"Calls from prison are recorded," I say. "And given Max's connections, rest assured I heard every word you said to that editor. Luckily, he knew better than to attempt a name-trashing campaign against the heads of the Bratva. He told us everything."

"Lyric…"

"Even in prison as you pay for your crimes, you're still trying to hurt me."

"You put me in here!" he snaps.

"No, you put yourself in here. Fucking own it, you coward," I shoot back, pointing an angry finger at him. "You were supposed to be my father. Instead, you got involved with the worst kind of people. You managed to get Shelby under your spell by manipulating her, almost turning her against me while you did Bowman's bidding. Everything that happened, it happened because of you and nobody else."

He shakes his head, downright denying responsibility. "It wasn't like that."

"There's proof, Dad. So much proof, in fact, that the jury took less than an hour to deliberate, remember?" I say. "You let Bowman and Smith do whatever they wanted. To be honest, I still think you knew what they were going to do with me."

"No, Lyric, I swear to you, I had no idea!"

"Either way, it doesn't matter anymore. I'm safe now. The FBI is still busy doing its spring cleaning, getting rid of their rotten apples. The city council, too. Everybody's got a hell of a reckoning to deal with, but it's looking better and better. The world is a safer place with Bowman dead, with you and Smith behind bars. And it's breaking my heart to have to say such things."

My father nods slowly, but not because he agrees with me. He just wants this to be over with. I'm not sure what I'd hoped would happen when I came to see him. A year has passed since he was found guilty. A year, during which time my Sokolov-funded think tank has brought the algorithm to a whole new level of excellence, while the guys and I have been raising our sons and building a wonderful life together.

"How old are the boys now?" my father asks after a long, uncomfortable silence.

"They're going to turn two next month," I say, cradling my belly underneath the counter. There's a third one on the way, but I haven't told the guys about it yet. The doctor just confirmed it this morning. "They're strong and healthy. Happy and safe."

"When am I going to get to meet them?"

I chuckle dryly. "You will never come anywhere near my family."

"You're being cruel," he says. "They should know their grandfather."

"After you tried to feed me to the wolves? Fat chance. You had plenty of opportunities to be a father to your daughter, Dad. You're not getting another. This is your life now."

He's on edge, restless in his seat. But he can't bring himself to walk away from me either. Max thinks he's like this because, deep down, he does love me. I'm his daughter. His only child. But he loves his career and his ego a whole lot more. It's an ongoing personality clash unfolding within him. It doesn't make me feel any better, but it does make some sense of his sometimes-contradictory behavior.

"So the Bratva is still running the show, huh?" he asks.

"They've gone mostly legit. The businesses that stayed under were passed over to family and friends who chose to keep a more traditional trajectory," I reply, still remembering that meeting behind closed ebony doors between the biggest Brava families. "The Sokolov Corporation took most of the holdings and refurbished them into legal sectors. What's left behind is no longer their concern, but they retain their influence and notoriety. People know not to mess with them, and the city is safer because of their business decisions."

"I find that hard to believe," my father mutters, looking away for a second.

"Oh, I almost forgot to mention—my algorithm is coming along nicely. I'll be the only one using it though."

He gives me a startled look. "What do you mean?"

"Well, as a researcher at UC, I now have free reign over the research department. I also have the Sokolov think tank behind me. Limitless resources to test countless scenarios, including the political field. Oh, the possibilities."

I can see the life draining from my father's face. "You can't be serious."

"I am serious. See, Dad? Everything worked out for the best. Well, not for you. But it's what happens when you get drunk on your own power. You lose sight of your own mortality," I say.

"You seem to be enjoying this a little too much."

I lean forward and give him a hard look. "I had a gun pointed at my head, Dad. Your best friend was holding it, and he was ready to kill me, convinced that you'd forgive him. That you would choose to believe him. It was in that very moment that I understood we're not really family. By blood, yeah. But family isn't blood anymore. It's in the bonds we build. All you ever wanted to do was use me. Or my algorithm. Or my best friend. You never wanted me as your daughter. Not really. You never even bothered to really get to know me.

"And what hurt me the most, Dad, is that even after you were sentenced, after you were supposed to see the evil of your ways, you decided to double down and try to screw me over some more by giving a Chicago tabloid dirt about me and my supposed relationship with the Sokolov men."

"Lyric, I didn't—"

"I have you on tape, Dad," I cut him off and get up, swallowing back my own tears. I will not let him see me cry. "This is the last time we meet."

"Lyric, hold on, I want to see them!" he calls out, standing up in sheer despair.

"Who?" I give him an over-the-shoulder glance.

"Sasha. Alexander. My grandchildren."

I shake my head. "I will not have my sons exposed to criminals such as yourself."

And with those hard-hitting words, I leave. His incessant pounding on the glass, his strings of words bouncing between begging me and insulting me become mere mumblings that echo on the heels of my red pumps as I walk out of the prison building and get in the passenger seat of Max's SUV.

 "Are you okay?" Max asks after a long minute of watching me breathe deeply, in and out, while I process that entire conversation and the sour taste it left in my mouth.

"I am now," I say, looking at him.

Artur reaches out from the backseat and gently massages my shoulders. "You're going to be better than okay. You know that right?"

"I know," I reply, enjoying the feel of his lips on my cheek. "Where are the boys?"

"Ivan is picking them up," Max says. "We're going to that Christmas Wonderland thing."

"Oh, right," I reply, feeling better already. "Gift shopping."

Max leans in, his eyes searching my face. "Lyric, we're going to do great."

"I know we are. We've been knocking it out of the park so far," I laugh lightly.

"No, I mean with a third kid. We're going to do great. Alexander and Sasha will make amazing big brothers."

I stare at him, my brain feeling suddenly frozen. A system reset is underway, during which time I'm unable to say a word while Artur snorts a chuckle and takes out a copy of the ultrasound I had earlier this morning.

"Oh," I mumble, breaking into a cold sweat. "I was wondering where I'd left that."

"On the side table in the foyer," Artur replies. "It didn't take a genius to figure you out before that though."

"You've been moody, on edge," Max adds. "At first, we thought it was about this visit with your dad. But then we saw the baby snapshot and a few other tiny hints sort of added to it."

"Tiny hints?"

Max and Artur exchange amused glances, then look at me with nothing but love and lust sparkling in their eyes before shifting their focus down to my slightly swollen, increasingly tender breasts. I follow their gaze and realize precisely what they mean.

They can tell that my girls have gotten bigger. "Okay, that tracks," I whisper.

"It's the best news you could've given us," Artur says.

"Technically speaking, I didn't give you the news."

"Either way, we're golden, baby," Max laughs and pulls me into a kiss.

I relish the feel of his lips on mine. I have found safety and love in their arms. Comfort and kindness in their company. They're fierce protectors but doting fathers. Worshipping lovers but playful friends. When I first stumbled into that hotel room and saw them, when they introduced themselves as the heads of the Bratva, I quivered. But the fear died quickly as I looked into their eyes.

I knew then just as I know now.

Our love is one of a kind.

And we're about to take it to the next level.

The End

61306040R00179